The Donner Party:

Fateful Journey

Enjoy!
Frankye Craig

Frankye Craig

The Donner Party:
Fateful Journey

Published by Frankye Craig,
Reno, Nevada
www.donnerpartyhistory.com
©2008, Frankye Craig
ISBN-13: 978-0-9794904-1-5

Cover Illustration: Frankye Craig
Design and Production: Frankye Craig
1st Printing: June 2008

Forward

Those who recognize the name Donner will think of cannibalism. That was an occurrence during the entrapment, it is a historical fact. But why dwell on that when the story itself has so much more to offer?

This retelling of the saga takes the basic facts from various accounts of that time for the historical framework, but to make the story whole and to allow the reader to understand the characters, some fiction is used. The fictional characters, besides the Narrator, are the three mountain men: Tobias Smithson; Zebediah Hayes and Mr. New. All the other names, places and people are real, and the experiences are from the emigrant trail of 1846.

All of the letters and diary entries were actually written by the people of those times. For the most part, I have not changed their spelling or punctuation, except in a few instances for clarity. They are as they were written so many years ago.

I greatly credit the researchers and writers, both contemporary and past, who have done the research that has brought to light information not only on the Donner Party, but on the history and people of the great migration of 1846.

You will find maps and a full listing of all the members of the Donner Party in the back of the book.

Frankye Craig

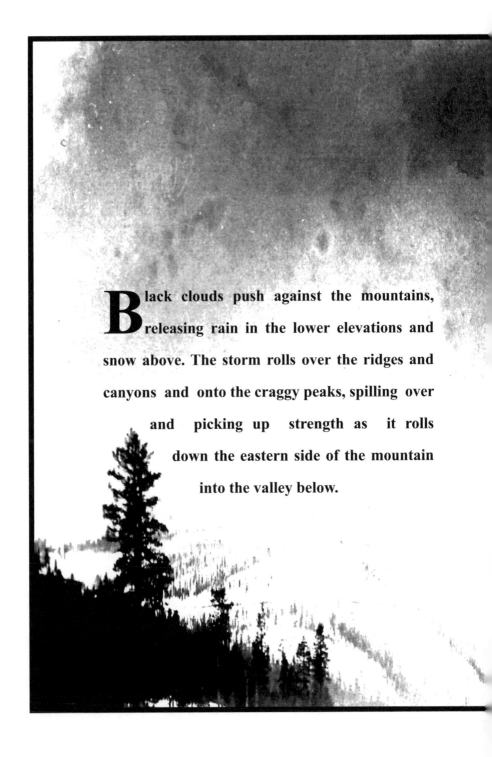

Black clouds push against the mountains, releasing rain in the lower elevations and snow above. The storm rolls over the ridges and canyons and onto the craggy peaks, spilling over and picking up strength as it rolls down the eastern side of the mountain into the valley below.

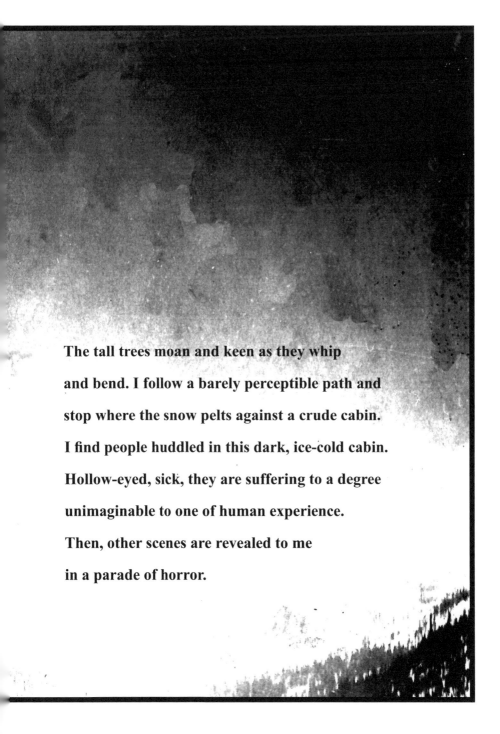

The tall trees moan and keen as they whip
and bend. I follow a barely perceptible path and
stop where the snow pelts against a crude cabin.
I find people huddled in this dark, ice-cold cabin.
Hollow-eyed, sick, they are suffering to a degree
unimaginable to one of human experience.
Then, other scenes are revealed to me
in a parade of horror.

April-May, 1846
Gathering Up On The Missouri

At that time I was a field of energy dwelling in a dimension that was not of the earth but somewhere that was nowhere. That instant of interest swept me into a vortex surrounding the scenes, and I was drawn in, unable to separate myself. I lost the ability to relate to other dimensions in space and time and found myself in a condition of being in but not of the earthly space. So it was that once again I experienced the earthly domain.

I found myself caught up in an excitement that had been building and had now become a reality. It was the spring of 1846, and thousands of people and hundreds of wagons were poised to cross the border between the furthermost outposts of civilization and the beginnings of the wilderness. They were headed for the new lands of the Pacific Coast—Oregon and California. In my earthly life I had planned to make the journey to California, so it was with much interest that I observed the beginnings of a great emigration near the village of Independence, in the Missouri Territory.

Steamboats crowded the river at Westport, unloading wagons, freight and people. A mass of all kinds of equipment, animals, and humanity surged along the roads and streets, sinking deep into the mire of red-brown Missouri clay.

Wagons had been rolling in for weeks. People swarmed through the streets in all manner of dress: dandies from the East, buckskin clad mountaineers, blanket wrapped Indians, apron covered storekeepers, homespun clad emigrants, and the men of the mountains, the fur trappers and traders. The glory years for the mountaineers had ended a few years back, not by the Indians, but by circumstances of a free economy. The price of beaver fur didn't earn a man a living in the mountains anymore, besides, the beaver had been trapped out.

I'd been floating around, so to speak, trying to get myself grounded, when I decided to visit Nolan's Tavern, one of the establishments that I'd frequented many times in the old days. A group of the mountain boys, clad in buckskins well-polished and blackened by grease, were hunkered down on their heels in a corner shooting the breeze. I was shocked to see Tobias Smithson there, with one foot on a chair, holding forth.

He was a lot older-looking than I remembered, although it had been just a few earth years since I'd seen him last. He was tall and rangy, his face deeply weathered, his long braid of hair and scraggly beard now iron-gray. He looked out at the group with deep-set blue eyes, his always cynical mouth a little thinner. He'd been a mentor to me, just a kid when I went to the mountains. He was telling one of his stories.

"… an' the old chief, see, he comes to me, says he wants to talk, an' he asks me, are there no squaws in the land of the long knives?"

The men in the circle laughed, understanding. Between them, they'd left a passel of half-Indian children in the high mountain country. Tobias took his leg off the chair.

"I got to git, my comp'ny's likely comin' up now."

Toby picked up a Hawken rifle, hooked his pack over his shoulder and headed for the door.

"Hey Tobias … Toby …" I called. Tobias stopped walking and stood for a moment but paid me no mind. I still hadn't got used to the fact that I was not a physical being. He walked up the street, his feet sinking into the deep mud, the ensuing string of curses familiar, a certain music to my ears.

I followed him to the edge of town, to a little rise on the side of the road. Here, where the green grass was thick, he cleaned some of the mud off his feet, took out his makings and got his pipe going. He squatted down, waiting. An hour or so passed when the sound of moving wagons and livestock floated to us on the breeze.

Toby stood and observed their coming. At the head of the caravan rode a man on a blooded horse. He had an arrogant way about him, sitting his fine horse as if he were a lord looking over his domain. Toby shouted a greeting, ambling down the rise to the road. The man leaned from his horse and shook Toby's hand.

"You're Tobias Smithson?"

"Yessir."

"I'm James Frazier Reed, from Springfield, Illinois. Maxey wrote me that you'd meet us."

James turned his mount, called to a young girl on an equally fine horse, and rode back to the approaching wagons. Toby stood in the road, waiting for the wagons to come up.

Reed's wagons were the first in the caravan. The wagons, and their trappings, marked him as a wealthy man. One wagon was different than the rest. It was larger—wider, actually—as it had been built out over the wheels lengthwise, with a door on the side, similar to a stagecoach. There were nine wagons in the caravan:

Reed's, and those of two brothers, George and Jacob Donner. Reed introduced Toby to the two brothers.

"George, Jacob, this is Tobias Smithson. You remember I told you I'd corresponded with a friend in Independence? He sent Tobias to meet us, help us get whatever we need and inform us about the companies that are forming up."

"We need all the help we can get," said George, shaking Toby's hand. I immediately felt a liking for George. He was a good-looking man for his advanced years; tall—well over six feet—well-built, dark hair streaked with just a touch of gray. A slight stoop made Jacob appear shorter than his older brother. Jacob was thin and knobby, and his colors showed that he was not in good health. His wife, Elizabeth, seemed a kindly woman, a touch nervous-like and a little wore down, which was understandable with all the kids hanging on her. She was tall and thin, wearing an apron of linen over a plaid homespun dress.

It was Tamsen, George's wife, that took my notice. A small woman, with dark, braided up hair and blue eyes that turned down at the corners. She was wearing clothes that bespoke the look of a Quaker, but far more fine and costly. Her sunbonnet was of a gray woven material that matched her dress. She had a quality about her that I was drawn to. It came to me that she was a New Englander, from Newburyport, Massachusetts. That strengthened the bond that eventually came between us—at least on my part, for I grew up in New England.

The company had three teams of oxen on each wagon and it looked like they had plenty of equipment and extra teams. Tobias looked in the wagons to see what they were bringing and was disgusted at all the trappings. In Reed's big wagon were coach seats with storage compartments underneath; two beds; a stove and other goods and paraphernalia.

"Pshaw!" Toby mumbled to himself. "Damn greenhorns,

takin' all this stuff. I doubt they'll listen to reason."

Reed had a large entourage which included his wife, Margaret; Margaret's mother, Mrs. Keyes; and four children. There were three teamsters: Milford Elliot, Walter Herron, and James Smith, and two family servants, Eliza Williams and her half-brother, Baylis. Baylis had white skin and hair and pink eyes. A little startling to the observer at first, but everyone paid the strangeness no mind.

With George Donner was his before mentioned spouse, Tamsen; George's two daughters, Elitha and Leanna—pretty girls in that in-between child and grown-up stage that makes them so silly and fickle in the company of young men—and three little daughters of Tamsen and George; Frances, Georgeanna, and Eliza, all under six years of age.

With Jacob Donner; his wife Elizabeth and her two sons by a previous marriage, Solomon and William Hook; and five smaller children from ages three to nine, skittering around like startled bugs. On the journey with the Donners were four young men: Noah James, Samuel Shoemaker, Hiram Miller and John Denton. They would exchange their labor for their way to California.

I assessed the capabilities of the men in the group. Reed, now, he was a leader, but the wrong kind of a leader to my way of thinking. He was a handsome man of middle age, rather short and stocky, but strong and energetic. What he lacked in stature he made up with an implied superiority and arrogance. He'd been in the furniture manufacturing business before pulling up stakes.

It was rumored that he'd been badly hurt in the depression that was gripping the country and had left Springfield with some bills still unpaid. He'd had little experience in journeying across a wilderness that should have been frightening to anyone had they investigated the nature of it, but his confidence knew no bounds.

George seemed a capable man. It came to me that he

knew something of picking up and moving—he was born in North Carolina, and had moved four, five times from Kentucky, to Indiana, Illinois, to Texas, back to Illinois—it seemed George had a powerful tickle-foot. Some would wonder why a man in his 60's, well fixed, with grown children and grandchildren living close-by, would sell the farm and move 2,000 miles to the Mexican Territory.

It was a frightening thing to contemplate, this journey to California. They would travel across mostly unknown wilderness, through the lands of wild and savage Indians. After leaving the Missouri Territory there would be rare vestige of civilization for hundreds and hundreds of miles, and that would only be crude fur trading forts peopled by a few white men who were half-savage themselves.

Some might say George was too old to be starting out on a journey such as this, but never mind, he was sprightly for his years. Having a wife considerably younger might have tended to keep him out of the rocking chair.

The hired hands all seemed to be stalwart and capable of the hard work they would be expected to take on with energy enough after a day of hard driving for the evening merriment around the campfires.

It was the women of the emigration that would have the brunt of it—breaking out the camp and cooking gear; leaning over a fire in the ground in wind, dust, rain, and sleet; taking care of the children, usually one on the breast and one in the hopper, the rest tearing around and getting into all kinds of mischief. Sometimes they'd stay up all night with a sick child, sometimes a sick husband, father or mother.

Then they would pack up the gear again and walk all day beside the wagon, sometimes even driving the team. It looked to me like these women could take it—that is, except Reed's wife,

Margaret. She spent most of her time in the wagon, her servant girl, Eliza, doing the chores, while Eliza's half-brother Baylis—the afflicted one—did the work of fetching wood, building fires, and setting up and breaking down camp.

Tobias told them of the best places to purchase supplies and obtain livestock, taking them around to Weston's blacksmith shop to talk about repairs on the wagons. Weston was backed up with orders, so they used a blacksmith that was set up under a tree near where they camped.

When they were satisfied that everything was in order, and they'd read all the newspapers that had information on the emigration, they decided to go on to Indian Creek where many of the emigrants were gathering to form up into companies. At the prospect of leaving Independence, some wrote letters back home. Tamsen hastened to finish a letter to her sister back in New England.

May 11, 1846

My dear sister, I commenced writing to you some months ago, but the letter was laid aside to be finished the next day & was never touched. A nice sheet of pink letter paper was taken out & has got so much soiled that it cannot be written upon & now in the midst of preparation for starting across the mountains I am seated on the grass in the midst of the tent to say a few words to my dearest only sister. One would suppose that I loved her but little or I should have not neglected her so long, but I have heard from you by Mr. Greenleaf & every month have intended to write.

My three daughters are round me, one at my side trying to sew, Georgeanna fixing herself up in an old India rubber cap & Eliza Poor knocking on my paper asking me ever so many questions. They often talk to me of Aunty Poor. I can give you no idea of the hurry of this place at this time. It is supposed there be 7000 wagons start from this place, this season. We go to California, to the bay of Francisco. It is a four months trip. We have three wagons furnished with food & clothing etc, drawn by three yoke of oxen each. We take cows along & milk them & have some butter though not as much as we would like. I am willing to go & have no doubt it will be an advantage to our children & to us.

I came here last evening & start tomorrow morning on the long journey. Wm's family was well when I left Springfield a month ago. He will write to you soon as he finds another home. He says he has received no answers to his two last letters, is about to start to Wisconsin as he considers Illinois unhealthy.

Farewell my sister, you shall hear from me as soon as I have an opportunity. Love to Mr. Poor, the children & all friends.

Farewell,

T.E. Donner.

At Indian Creek we found a huge encampment of emigrants. The chaos was too much for Toby who camped a distance off under a tree. The men filled their time talking about the business of the journey and assessing each other's equipment and animals. One of the men who came around camp didn't think much of Reed's big family wagon.

"That's a fine wagon there, Mr. Reed, but it concerns me that you don't have a jointed pole on such a heavy wagon. In rough country it's bound to break."

I'd noticed that Reed never took kindly to criticism. James

looked at the man disdainfully. "This wagon was custom built to stand bad conditions. I daresay there's no better anywhere on this road now or in the future."

"I agree you've a good wagon, but I'm a carriage maker by trade, so I've some experience. I'd hate to see you get in a tight spot and have trouble. It's likely it could be changed out here."

James's tone was curt and he scowled darkly before he turned away. "I appreciate your concern, Mr. Eddy, but I don't believe I'll have any problems."

"It's our Palace Car," Virginia, Reed's step-daughter, said to an acquaintance that was admiring the wagon. "My father had it 'specially made so that Grandma will be comfortable. She's very old and sick with consumption."

"Well, why on earth didn't you leave her behind in her home? That's bound to be more comfortable than a jolting wagon," exclaimed the other girl.

"She wouldn't be left. Mama is her only daughter, and besides, my uncle, Caden Keyes, will probably meet us on the road. Grandma won't die until she sees him again. He's been in the new lands almost two years now. He promised to come back this year."

"A good many sons never come back," muttered Toby, to nobody in particular.

Toby was ambling around and suddenly he stopped, his attention on a grizzled buckskin clad fellow that I recognized to be Zebediah Hayes. Zeb was leaning against a wagon expounding to a group of people. Toby sauntered around to the rear of the crowd, his posture careless, his eyes sardonic.

Zeb put his foot on a stump and leaned forward, spitting into the grass at his feet, just missing the boots of a listener.

"Most a' my life I been in the moun'tins trappin' an' huntin' beaver," he said. "I've fought Injuns dozens of times, still got an arrow or two whar they got me. I lost my outfit two, three times from bein' attacked by the varmints. The Blackfeet are the worst, by damn, I hate the Blackfeet. An' the Crows are bad too."

He was telling it right about the Blackfeet. One of them ended my natural life. My people left me for dead—Toby was one of them—cut out on me. Took me two days to die. Just another mountain man that drew the wrong card.

Zeb stood up and opened his shirt, showing some terrible looking scars. The boys in the crowd gasped in awe. Zeb wiped his mouth with his sleeve, squatted down and began stabbing the ground with his hunting knife.

"The beaver business, it don' shine no more. It's through, gone. Now the thing is Oregon and California. That's whar the opportunities be. The fur-men are lookin' for new prospects, some're guidin' greenhorns—like y'all—out to the new lands. Ol' Bill Sublette an' Black Harris, they're doin' it. I'm headin' west myself." Zeb jerked his thumb towards the wagon behind him. "I'm guidin' this here wagon party out to the Oregon Territory."

"Do you know much of California?"

Zeb put one foot on a stump, crossing his arms over his upraised leg. He used his tongue to gather up his chaw and spit it out. "I think it be a good land. Thar's no winter an' anythin' kin grow all year round."

Taking a plug of tobacco out of a pocket he bit off a chunk, his jaws working it as he squinted up his eyes and considered the question. "Thar ain't many people, mostly Mexicans. Thar's no more'n five or six hun'ert whites in the whole damned country. The Mexicans don't like work, they spend thar time doin' fandangos an' such like. The men wear outfits all fancied up with embroid'ry an' silver an' thar saddles 'er the same way, they are. But as horsemen, they shine, let me tell you. Yes, it be a good land and thar's land a'plenty fer the takin'. An' I believe that soon she'll be United States territory."

"How's the best way to get there? To California?"

"I'm of a mind that the Oregon Territory is the best place, but if'n yer needle's set on California, I allow it's the next best. Now, how to get thar?" Zeb squeezed his eyes into slits and slowly scratched his beard while he contemplated his answer.

Zeb pointed towards the west. "Ye foller this here Santa Fe trace to the Kansas River. It's a good-sized river, ye'll have to ferry a'crost this time a'year." He paused to spit. For Zeb, because of missing teeth, spitting was not a neat affair and as a result his beard and the front of his buckskin shirt had a dirty brown stain down the middle.

"Then yer gonna head north to the Platte River an' foller it west to the Shining Mountains. Then ye go along the Sweetwater to Bridger's Tradin' Post. 'Course, you could take Sublette's cut-off just shy of Bridger's if'n ye wanted to an' didn't need supplies. It'll take ye to Fort Hall a little shorter. From both it's north to Fort Hall an' then west, then south to Ogden's River. Foller on 'til the river ends in a sink. Keep on west 'til ye gits to high mountains, higher than anythin' ye seen so far. After the last mount'ins ye'll find the holdin's of John Sutter. New Helvetia, he calls it. I've heard he's mighty fine to Americans."

"Who's he?"

"He's some kind o' furriner. He owns most 'a the valley o' the Sacramento terr'tory, got hisself a land grant cozyin' up to the Mexican gov'nor, Alvarado. He's got Injun slaves, e'en made some into soldiers, fancy uniforms an' such like. He's got a fort an' does ranchin' an' farmin'. He has a sight of mills, e'en a tannery. I heered tell he has nigh on to six hun'ert workin' fer him, mostly Injuns. He's wantin' more Americans in the country."

Zeb cleaned one of his fingernails with his knife and then stuck the knife back in his belt. As the crowd began to move away,

Zeb called out. "Mind ye now, ye don't want ter git to the high mountains late in the season, 'cause the passes close with snow. Ye could be trapped fer the winter."

That encounter with Zebediah took me back to the days— to the years—of my odyssey in the human form in the mountains. It was a life wild and perilous, but free. We learned to be Indians, but we were better than the Indian. We mastered the wilderness with only a horse, maybe a pack mule, a few traps, a bag of possibles, and a rifle. We traded furs for the necessities of tobacco and powder, and if there were any left over, we spent them all on the excesses of the annual rendezvous. Then we would turn and go back into the mountains, to wade through icy streams and dare to face the dangers that were too much for lesser men. It was we who blazed the trails and opened up the wilderness.

I was drawn to these people, the Donners and Reeds. Somehow I knew they were part of those scenes that had been revealed to me, so I determined that I would go along with them on the journey to California, to learn the meaning of what I'd seen.

That night at the campfire they talked about moving out the next day. Solomon, Elizabeth's boy, squatted down next to Toby and began stabbing the ground with a huge knife, moving a chaw awkwardly around in his mouth. "Mr. Smithson, you goin' back to the mountains?" he asked, sucking some wayward tobacco juice back into his mouth.

Toby looked at Solomon; a skinny kid with big ears sticking out of a shock of yellow hair. He noted the brand new buckskin shirt, the way-too-big knife. Toby leaned forward and spit into the fire. "I reckon I might, just to see what's goin' on."

"Do you think I might could go with you?"

"What for?"

"I'm thinkin' of learnin' to be a mountain man, like you."

"Huh. You're twenty, thirty years too late." Toby's eyes

became distant, sad. "This was man's country once, the rivers full'a beaver, buffler everywhere you looked." He gazed around the group. "No crowdin' a damn greenhorns comin' in, everythin' purty an' new, no tracks of man exceptin' Indians ..."

Toby sighed, looked down, brushed some dirt around with the toe of his moccasin. "No, son, best you stay with yer mam, there ain't a life no more in the mountains."

Solomon thought it over. "Huh. Then why you thinkin' 'bout goin' back?"

"I don't know ... visitin'. I got a couple young'uns I ain't seen in years. I'm kinda wonderin' how they's doin'.'"

Solomon was disappointed, he'd been imagining himself as a mountain man. *Oh, well, California's gonna be excitin'. Geez, four months to get there, seems like we been on the road that long already,* he thought to himself. Then he remembered a conversation he'd had with Zeb and he got up to sit next to his uncle.

"Hey, Uncle George, I asked Zeb 'bout a way to get to the big Salt Lake without havin' to go by Fort Hall an' he said he'd never heard of a way to go with wagons. An' he should know, bein' a famous mountain man an' all."

"Wagh!" croaked Toby. "He ain't no famous mountain man, just a fort hanger-on, all he is." He spit another stream of tobacco into the fire. Solomon was obviously in awe of Toby's ability to spit that far with accuracy. He tried and failed, the squirt of tobacco juice splattering on his legs and feet.

"Didn't Hastings write in his book there was a road? An' didn't Frémont come through that way?" asked Jacob. Not to be outdone, he spit into the fire, just a little less skilled than Toby, he leaned forward before letting go.

"I haven't read anything of Frémont's journey," said James, "I've only heard of it. But we do have Hastings' book. Virginia, would you please go to the wagon and get my valise?"

When Virginia returned, James took the Hastings book out and thumbed through it until he found the page he wanted.

"I can find only one reference. It says the most direct route for the California emigrants would be to leave the Oregon road about two hundred miles east from Fort Hall and thence bear west and southwest to the Salt Lake and continue down to the Bay of Francisco. Hastings speaks well of the route." James looked around the group. "He says all streams are easily forded, buffalo herds are plentiful beyond the Rocky Mountains and the California Indians are inoffensive."

"I never heard of this here Hastings feller, but he don't know his ass from his elbow!" exclaimed Toby. "There ain't no buffler on t'other side of the Rocky Mountains! They been hunted out fer years now."

Toby accidentally knocked his hat off with an arm movement and the wind flipped it into the fire, making a sudden shower of sparks. Toby got up, twitched the hat out of the fire with a stick and brushed off the ashes, frowning at the group.

"Ain't you heard about Jed Smith's an' Walker's troubles with them California Injuns? Walker killed a bunch a Diggers like so many piss-ants, an' now they're stirred up." Muttering to himself, Toby stalked away, hitching up his pants, blasts of flatulence following him. "Damn stupid greenhorns …"

George looked after Toby thoughtfully. "Well, we'll find out more as we go along. Might be good to have Toby along to guide us." George looked at James. "Did you talk to him?"

"We don't need him. I can do the scouting and hunting."

"Yeah, Mr. Reed, but what about Injuns?" asked Solomon. "Toby's fought Injuns fer years and he says—"

James gave Solomon a withering glance. "I don't think you can put much stock in what that old has-been says. I've been told the Kansa Indians are peaceable and there's no reason the other tribes will be hostile. They'll mostly just try to pilfer whatever they can. I'm more concerned about the Mormons."

"I'm keepin' my pistols to hand," said John Denton. "I heard the buggers are five thousand strong and likely to kill every non-Mormon they come across."

"The Mormons just want to get away from bein' persecuted 'cause of their religion," said George. "Missouri was supposed to be their promised land an' now they're bein' driven from there. I think if you leave them alone, they'll leave you alone. I just hope they ain't goin' to California. They need to find a place to themselves."

"The word is that there's some two thousand Mormons that have crossed the Missouri but were peaceably disposed," said James. "There's another rumor that a party of Englishmen is on the trail aiming to stir up the Indians, inciting them to acts of hostility against the American emigrants."

"Why would they do that?" asked Solomon.

"It ain't settled yet if Oregon is a possession of the United States or Britain." replied George. "Some people think the British want to discourage Americans from emigratin' to the Oregon country."

"You know," said Tamsen, "it would make sense to have someone with us who knows the country and can converse with the Indians."

"Yeah, I'll talk to Toby," said George. "James, we still plan on pulling out tomorrow? If we are, we got a lot to do tonight."

James got up from the log he was sitting on. "Yes. I'm anxious to start. There's a large company under the leadership of Colonel Russell some days ahead of us. That's the company we'll want to join. George, I can't see any reason for burdening ourselves with Smithson, when we'll be with a large group."

"Yeah. Well, it won't hurt."

Toby went back to Independence to get an outfit, planning to catch up and journey along with the group as far as Ft. Bridger.

"Sure, I'll mosey along with you, unofficial like," he told George. "I ain't hankerin' to tie myself to a bunch of ignorant greenhorns though. I can get myself out of a fix—ain't sayin' I can do the same fer you."

I observed amongst the throng of emigrants all the elements that would make the pending emigration harder than it should have been—total ignorance, anxious stupidity, and above all the inability to get along with one another. I was discomfited by that because I knew the journey would be an enemy of these people.

The Weekly Reveille, St. Louis
THE CALIFORNIANS

The following letter is from a friend—one of the California boys. It was written after leaving the settlements, and gives an idea of the grand prairie picture, humanized by the string of emigrants and their rude appointments.

We have passed through the Shawnee, Pottowatamie, and are now in the Kaw nation—said to be great thieves—we are obliged to keep a strong guard out to protect our animals. I will place you at Independence, the last of civilization; the town full of mules and oxen, for sale. Here comes a long, low, raking, black wagon, that might be taken for Whitney's locomotive, a stove pipe projecting some two feet above the top, under way, and the smoke rolling out ... now we will leave for Indian Creek, say thirty miles; the election comes off—great excitement ... speeches are made; a fuss kicked up; part leave the ground with the yells of the Indians; Gov. Boggs and Col. Russell candidates for the high honor; Russell elected by a large majority; committee go out to draw up laws. Col. R. "treats" at his marquee; a few slightly inebriated.

The wagons lurched forward, the white tops swaying as the wheels rolled over deep ruts in the road. Mists were still clinging to the hollows and streams. It was a moment of tearing away, but there was also expectation and the thrill of embarking on a new experience. As the wagons strung out on the road, a rainbow formed in the west, a beautiful and perfect arch.

"Look, it's glorious! It's like a magnificent gate to the Kingdom of the West," exclaimed Tamsen.

But behind the rainbow came a black curtain of clouds, and suddenly cold air swirled around us, everything becoming gray, the atmosphere crackling and humming.

George was looking at the sky. "It looks likely to storm any moment. We'd better get under cover. Tamsen, what's wrong?"

Tamsen had cried out, gathering the girls in her arms.

"Oh, George, there's something frightening me. This is surely a mistake. We shouldn't go."

"It's just a rain storm. It ain't like you to get upset. C'mon, let's get the girls in the wagon."

The storm soon passed over. Everyone climbed out of the wagons and the train began to move again. In mid-afternoon the skies cleared and the sun shone warm and bright. We made camp and the wet bedding and clothing was taken out and spread around to dry. George was concerned about Tamsen.

"Honey, are you still upset?"

"George, I'm quite all right. I just had … I don't know … a case of the jitters, I guess."

"It's not like you to have jitters."

"It's a feeling, oh, like a foreboding. Oh, George, we were safe at home, and comfortable, and had everything. Now, all we have is in these three wagons and we don't know what will happen or can happen."

"We've got everything we need to get us to California in fine shape. We've got the best animals, the best equipment, plenty of food, money, an' all the books an' supplies for your girl's school—"

"That you wanted to leave behind."

"I put it all in, didn't I? An' that damned rockin' chair that we have to take out ever' time we stop the wagons, and God knows what all you put in when I wasn't lookin'."

"George, please don't use curse words."

• • •

As we proceeded, the wagons constantly bogged down in the mire and had to be pulled out by double and triple teams and cursing men. One storm came right at breakfast time, putting out all the cooking fires.

"Oh, God!" said Elizabeth, "Our bread's not gonna cook,

it ain't been on the fire long enough. It's gonna be cold mush an' cold coffee again. I'm sick of all the rain, the wind, the wagons full'a wet clothes an' beddin', everythin' gettin' moldy an' the mud stickin' to my feet in a ball where I cain't hardly walk. The men're crazy to put us through this!"

"Elizabeth, it will all get better an' it could be worse. We ain't had sickness, or any accidents—"

"George, don't you mean to say we haven't had?"

That's one thing I noticed about Tamsen. She was always correcting the grammar of George and the children, and the hired men too. And she hated swear words.

Toby commented on it right off. "It's just downright irritatin'. There's nothin' like good cussin' to take the edge off things, an' proper grammar, there ain't no call for it in these parts."

The rain continued relentlessly. Everyone huddled under the fly-tent, a canvas stretched overhead. Tamsen bent over, peering under the wagon.

"I think I have some kindling left. It might be enough for coffee, but our meal is going to be a cold one again."

Several in the company began gathering when they smelled the coffee. The rain was a steady fine mist, the air so wet it made everyone cough. It ran steadily off the canvas, wetting the backs of the men trying to crowd underneath.

George squeezed the water from his mustache with the knuckle of his forefinger. "I wonder if we shouldn't lay by until things dry out. It's too hard on the animals."

"We need to do some repairs anyway," said James. "I think I will ride ahead and visit with other groups to get a feel for the group we might want to join."

We'd been traveling and camping mostly by ourselves but the aim was to join up with a larger group as soon as possible.

James was intent on the Russell group that was a week or so ahead of us. As he got up to leave, he spoke to Tamsen.

"Mrs. Donner, would you visit with my wife? She's not feeling well. Her mother is having a lot of problems these last few days and Margaret is taking it hard. Perhaps in your medicines you have some laudanum or something that will help her sleep?"

I'd been drawn to the Reed wagon earlier by the vibrations that bothered my equilibrium. Margaret was crying and moaning, laying propped up in bed, her family and servants all a'twitter trying to help her.

"James, I'm going mad with this headache. Please, ask Tamsen if she has laudanum. Why didn't you bring more? You know it's the only thing that relieves me."

"I'm sorry, Margaret. Are you sure there's no more?"

"James! Please. There is no more."

Tamsen slogged in the rain and mud to the Reed wagons. Eliza and Baylis were sitting on stools under the fly-tent.

"Poor Miz Reed," said Eliza. "She's not feelin' good."

"Yes, I'll try to help her, Eliza."

Margaret raised up on one elbow to see who was entering the wagon and then fell back on her pillows. "Oh, Tamsen, this is the worst headache I've ever had."

"I have a tea for you that might help, but first I want to treat your mother."

I could tell by the colors surrounding Mrs. Keyes that she had only a short time in the earthly world. Tamsen knew it too, but wanted to make the old woman more comfortable in her last days. She gently brushed back the thin gray hair from Mrs. Keyes' forehead.

"I've brought you some medicines, Mrs. Keyes. They'll relieve the coughing and help you sleep. "

Patty brought a cup and spoon and Tamsen held Mrs.

Keyes up a little so she could take the medicines. It was hard for her to swallow without a coughing fit. "I don't think … anything can help … but thank you, Tamsen."

"It should make you more comfortable."

Tamsen turned away from Mrs. Keyes and knelt on the bench seat next to Margaret's bed.

"I've brought some medicines. Margaret, can you sit up and drink this tea?"

"The laudanum helps, but I've used it all. I thought you would bring me some." Margaret looked with distaste at the cup Tamsen was holding. "What is it, anyway?"

"It's a tea made from skullcap and valerian. It will ease the headache, relax you and help you sleep."

"You don't have any laudanum?"

"Laudanum is not good for a healthy person. It makes you feel better for only a short time and then you feel worse than before, requiring even more laudanum. Try the tea."

Margaret's face crumpled and she began to cry.

"Margaret, there is a quart of tea in this jar, drink a cup every hour until it is gone. It would be best if you could warm it a little."

Tamsen left the wagon, Margaret still crying.

The next night we camped in a curve of the Wakarusa River. James came back with news that the Russell people were waiting at Soldier Creek for us and some other people.

Toby came in to camp leading a mule, walking stiff and uneven from the saddle. He told us that several people were on the road behind him; three of Daniel Boone's grandsons, the former governor of Missouri, Lillburn Boggs; and Mr. and Mrs. Thornton. They expected to catch up later in the evening.

Toby took George aside. "You know about Boggs? He was the gov'ner of Missouri. He put out an extermination order to get rid of all the Mormons in the territory. One'a their leaders tried to kill him, shot him in his house. You look to be careful takin' up with Boggs. The Mormons hate him, an' they might be trackin' him down. They might think we're in on his doin's."

"Huh. You really think—?"

"It don't hurt nothin' to be careful, Donner."

The Thorntons were from Quincy, Illinois. They said they were making the journey for the more healthful atmosphere of the Pacific lands. Boggs was an affable man, in spite of his reputation as a killer of Mormons.

That night terrific storms struck with almost continuous thunder and displays of lightning. The tents took off to parts unknown, the wagon covers flapping themselves into tatters in the violent winds and heavy rain.

We passed what was called "Lone Elm", a solitary tree serving as a marker on the prairie. It was here we encountered a group of hunters returning to the settlements with furs. They gave us some dried buffalo meat and told the group that they had no idea what they would suffer before reaching California.

"Pshaw. What do those fellers know? They ain't never been to California," scoffed Solomon.

Toby looked at Solomon in exasperation. "What do you know, knuckle-head? Them men knows what's ahead. Flat country with no wood, deserts as dry as a red-brick kiln, alky water that'll sicken and break down yer animals, no game to speak of—that you greenhorns could catch, anyways. An' we're gettin' into Injun country, never know what the savages will be up to. Tomorrow their supernaturals might tell 'em to kill all the whites that's crossin' into their terr'tory."

The next afternoon we came across a group of returning Santa Fe traders driving a herd of very poor-looking mules. They'd obtained the mules in Chihuahua, Mexico, to sell in Missouri.

They palavered with the men for a time, then whipped the grazing mules back into a herd and moved out. Jacob stood watching as the group departed.

"You believe what that man said? That his journey's been a hard one, but ours would be much harder an' would shorten our lives by ten years? That's the second time we heard such like—it's gettin' to affect my attitude."

George chuckled. "You think it's been that hard? Seems like we been on a continual picnic."

Jacob sighed. "I don't figure I have ten years no-how, so I guess it don't matter."

The wagons diverged from the Santa Fe Trace, following the wagon road to the right, which became the Oregon Trail. In the afternoon a creek was crossed and camp was made in a grove of large timber. In the evening we were visited by a group of Potawattomie Indians. They held out small pieces of silver, grunting "whiskey, whiskey".

Tamsen was horrified. "How disgusting! Now this depravity of the white man has been pressed upon these poor savages. The Indian has as little resistance to its effects as he has had to the diseases that have marched right along with our so-called civilization."

"Yer right about that, ma'am," said Toby, "but you can no more stop the degradin' of the Injun than you can stop the wind from blowin' or the river from runnin'. These here Injuns have been influenced by their doin's with the white man for generations. There's thousands an' thousands in tribes that are still wild an' they're goin' to have the same fate. When the white man sets his sights on claimin' the whole damn country he'll keep on 'til he does it."

The second group of Indians we encountered consisted of two men and two squaws with their children. They were a sorry looking lot. Tamsen and Elizabeth gave them some bread and meat. Then we were accosted daily by single families or groups of Indians, begging for hand-outs.

"I don't see no call to encouraging these savages," griped Toby. "There'll be no end to their pestering if you gives in an' gives 'em stuff. Just pay no mind and keep movin'!"

The rain finally ceased as our march continued, the landscape becoming a high rolling prairie. The wagon caravan wound slowly over hill and hollow and only the mutter of the wind and the creaking of the wagons, occasionally interspersed with a snippet of conversation or the "gee-haw" and "whoa-haw" of a teamster, disturbed the quietness of the land.

James had been out ahead scouting the road. That evening the men conferred about crossing the Kansas River.

"I feel we should cross on the Indian ferries. A dollar a wagon is a small price to pay for the time we'll lose going out of our way," James told the group.

"How far is it to a crossing we can manage without flatboats?" asked Mr. Thornton.

"I scouted it out," said James. "It's at least six miles. That'll add half a day or more."

"I am offended to pay that much," said Mr. Thornton.

"Yes, it seems high," said George, "but we want to catch up with the Russell group, and no telling how long they'll wait. I say let's cross on the ferries. Mr. Thornton, we understand your feelin's. If you want to go on to a better place, that's up to you."

Mr. Thornton ended up agreeing to use the ferry and the wagons were put on two at a time. The livestock were driven into the river to swim over. They balked, eyes rolling wildly, heads jerking around as they tried to scrabble back up on the river bank. But finally some were driven in and they had to start swimming or drown. The rest followed. It took most of the day.

We came up with the Russell party in two more days, camping away from the main crowd. Toby was unhappy with the prospect of camping with so many people and wagons.

"I don't cotton to being in such a crowd. Forage will be hard to find an' the dust'll be downright intolerable. We don't need to be in this large a'group."

I followed Toby as he surveyed the camps. It was a tumult of moving wagons, livestock, dogs, and people. Toby visited around, catching up on the latest news. When we returned to camp it was already past supper and the men were having their evening ease, smoking and talking. George tossed the stick he'd been chewing on into the fire and stood up.

"I heard there's thirteen wagons gonna split off tomorrow. They're led by a man named Gordon. Maybe we should join up with them."

"They already have the number of wagons they want," said James. "I prefer the leadership of Mr. Russell."

"Yeah, an' we already been voted in. I guess we should stay with Russell," said George. "Jacob, what's your feelin'? Will you go along with that?"

"I reckon. There'll be more men to stand watch when we get into the Injun country, we'll get more sleep. An' speakin' of sleep, I didn't get a wink last night with the damned dogs barkin' all the time."

Tamsen frowned at Jacob but didn't say anything about the curse word. The night had been a particularly bad one with a group of wagons coming in next to us with what seemed a hundred dogs. The barking ranged from high-pitched yelps to deep baying, and was answered, of course, by all the dogs in our group.

"Dog meat's good eatin'," said Toby. "I remember the time when I was with Fitzpatrick headin' through South Pass for the Popo Agie ..." Another one of Toby's stories.

"Yeah," said George, pointing to a white and black floppy-eared dog that was lying peacefully by the wagon. "That one's goin' to end up bad if he doesn't stop messin' with the oxen."

"Too old. Half-grown pups is best fer eatin'," said Toby.

The dog was constantly causing trouble with the ox, Bully. He had a perverse attachment to teasing the ox, nipping at his heels, neck and ears when the ox was yoked to the wagon. Bully would try to retaliate, but restrained by the yoke he would only cause a disruption in the progress of the team. Noah would whack him with his whip to get him settled again. The ox tried to keep an eye on the dog who would retreat, grinning from ear to ear, waiting for the next opportunity to repeat the torment.

One day after the noon stop when Bully was being led to the yoke, he spied his tormenter lying asleep on a pile of hay, limp in relaxation, lips twitching as a dream flitted through his head. With a massive bellow, Bully lunged for the dog, flipping him in the air with his horns several times before the dog managed to crawl under the wagon, more dead than alive.

"It serves him right," said Tamsen, "but I feel sorry for him, he's hurt so terribly. One leg is broken and I'm sure he has cracked ribs too."

Tamsen put a splint on the dog's leg and put him in a sling under the wagon, where he lay for days, yipping with every jolt. Bully would snort in derision whenever he was led past the wagon. The dog recovered but stayed well away from the oxen when the wagons rolled, crawling into his sling when they were free from the yokes.

The next day was the Sabbath and the company stayed in camp. Everybody attended services which were led by Reverend Dunleavy. I went too, thinking that maybe I needed to get some credits in my present state of in-between-ness, but I was just as antsy as the little girls. They were looking enviously at the kids who were sneaking away and dashing off to play. Tamsen kept them glued to their seats with a finger to her lips and a narrowing of her eyes.

After the last blast of righteousness and a plea for God to watch over this company of sinners, the service ended and the congregation fled for more enjoyable pastimes. We walked back to our camp, the girls skipping happily ahead.

"Seems like all that preacher can talk about," said George, "is fire and brimstone. I don't see how a lovin' God could ever be mean enough to create a place like hell. There's enough hell on earth without there bein' any call for it in the hereafter."

"Amen," said Toby.

Several families brought food and joined us at our wagons. I was amazed at the amount and variety of dishes that the women could put together out of a very spare pantry. The men stuffed themselves and then broke out the smokes, retiring to a men-only conclave in the shade of the wagons.

One of the men, Mr. Bryant, impressed me. He was a news-paperman from Louisville, Kentucky. He planned to write a book about the journey. Every evening he would take out his journal and record the day's events, the aspect of the country, and the flora and fauna. He was a man of intelligence and education. He was think-ing what I was thinking.

"It's nice to observe the Sabbath, but we're moving much too slowly," he told the group. "It seems that many people are desirous of shortening each day's march and when once encamped are reluctant to move. I'm fearful that winter will find us in the mountains of California, or that we will run short of provisions."

The group looked up at the approach of a tall man, thick in body and florid of features, wearing a Panama hat. He had a cigar in one hand and a flask in the other. James greeted him.

"Colonel Russell, I want you to meet the rest of my party.

This is my friend and neighbor, George Donner, and his brother, Jacob Donner. You already know Mr. Bryant, and Mr. Boggs— have you met Mr. Thornton?"

"Yes, I believe I have. I am mighty pleased to make the acquaintance of such fine upstanding citizens. Y'all from Springfield?" George nodded. "Do y'all know that esteemed gentleman, Abraham Lincoln?"

"We know him, sir," replied George, "but have not had the pleasure of speaking with him lately. He's been on a galloping horse these past few years."

"Yes, yes. Well, I want to address the fine group of people you have here."

Russell climbed up on a wagon tongue and somebody banged on a metal pan with a spoon until most of the group gathered around.

"Good afternoon, welcome to the Russell Company." Russell made a short bow, almost falling off the wagon pole. He quickly regained his composure, although his cigar had flipped into some dry grass. Mr. Bryant quickly moved his foot over it before it could start a fire.

"Thank you, ladies, for adding your delightful presence to this epic journey. I hope y'all," Russell waved his arms to include everyone, "realize that y'all are part of Manifest Destiny, a part of history. Do not think of history as somethin' remote that concerns only kings, queens, an' generals. It concerns *you*."

He gestured expansively toward the west. "You and your families march across the pages of history. Remember, the farmer that plows a furrow is of more importance than the leader of an army. The army can destroy, the furrow can feed."

Russell's audience applauded politely and he stepped down, wiping his brow with a handkerchief. "Mr. Bryant, Mr. Donner, y'all have been invited to serve on our board of governors. I would consider it an honor if you would accept."

"Yes, I'll serve," said Mr. Bryant, and George was fool enough to say yes too.

"I enjoyed your speech, Colonel," said Mr. Bryant. "It's true, the movements of history are sums of private accident and private will. I believe we are entering upon momentous times."

Mr. Bryant wrote long entries in his journal most every day. This day he noted his impressions of the wagon company.

> *The camp this evening presents a most cheerful appearance. The prairie, miles around us, is enlivened with groups of cattle, numbering six or seven hundred, feeding upon the fresh green grass. The numerous white tents and wagon covers before which the campfires are blazing brightly, represent a rustic village; and men, women, and children are talking, playing, and singing around them with all the glee of light and careless hearts. While I am writing, a party at the lower end of the camp is engaged in singing hymns and sacred songs.*

The company crossed a stream known as Vermilion Creek. The eastern bank was very steep and the crossing difficult. The country between the Vermilion and the Big Blue River would have neither wood nor water. Water casks were filled and the slings under the wagons filled with firewood.

As camp was made, a violent storm struck with deafening crashes of thunder, fantastic meteoric displays of lightning and a torrential downpour that wet everything. The wind was so strong the wagons were in danger of overturning. Toward sunset the storm ceased as suddenly as it began. A bright streak of clear red sky appeared above the western edge of the prairie, the horizontal rays of the setting sun streaming through the clouds.

The next morning ropes were strung up in the wagons and wet bedding and clothing were hung on the lines in an effort to dry things out rather than stop for the day. The wagons wound their way through a fertile valley, on the one side a chain of mound shaped hills, and on the other by a creek.

We'd been followed by several of the Indians and one gave Mr. Bryant a root which his man Brownell prepared. The root was pronounced as good as the Irish potato.

"Yer man, Brownell, reminds me of the man my sister married," Toby told Mr. Bryant. "Never could figure why she teamed up with that skunk, less'n she had to."

Our route continued over a rolling and rather broken country. From this we continued to ascend over elevated ridges, until we reached the bluffs that overlooked the Big Blue River. Descending from these bluffs we found the river much swollen from the recent rain, and not fordable.

May 31, 1846
The Big Blue River

The company was delayed for three days at the Big Blue. Here the journey ended for Mrs. Keyes. The Englishman, John Denton, cut a stone and services for Mrs. Keyes were conducted by the Reverend Cornwall. While they waited for the water to recede and rafts to be built, some of the party explored a little, finding a beautiful glen with a cold, pure, flowing spring. Mr. Bryant christened the site "Alcove Springs".

It took a day to get across and the march continued. Groups would split off and regroup again with others, so that we were introduced to new people and reunited with old friends every few days or weeks.

Sickness visited young and old, healthy and frail. The cold and rain awakened ague and other maladies, and epidemics of diarrhea raged through the camps. Almost everyone in the company was experiencing violent stomach cramps and trots.

Tamsen tried to get everyone to drink a tea she'd made of

chamomile as a remedy. Toby was the only one that didn't seem to be affected by the water, his years in the mountains seemingly giving him a system that could withstand anything.

The following morning came dark, gloomy and rainy, with a howling wind piercing the people through soaked clothing to their very bones. We were delayed starting off because one of the drivers was wretchedly sick from the effects of a drunken spree the night before. He was put in one of the wagons where he lay moaning. Toby looked in at the pitiful teamster puking all over the supplies in the wagon.

"Pshaw," said Toby to the sick teamster, "that little bit of liquor you had would make me no never mind."

Tamsen was snappish. "When is the supply going to run out? I'm getting so peeved about it. At least, George, you could control it in our camp."

"Yeah, I'll lay the law down."

Then, more aggravation. One of the oxen, the best one, had become tangled up in the rope by which he was tied and was thrown to the ground with great force. After struggling some time, he rolled his eyes, showing all the symptoms of death by a broken neck, or some other fatal injury. The rope was cut, but he was motionless and apparently breathless.

The herd was searched and another ox brought up to be yoked when the downed ox very calmly and deliberately rose upon his legs and began to feed as composedly as if nothing had occurred. He'd thought himself dying and acted accordingly.

"It's always somethin' that keeps us from gettin' started early," complained George.

When camp was made that evening, Tamsen refused to use the water George brought to her.

"George, I believe it's the terrible water that is giving us this physicking. Every camp has water that has been fouled by the livestock and is full of salts and minerals. We just have to find better water even if we have to travel to get it."

"Tamsen, there ain't any to be had. I sent Noah and Samuel out an' there wasn't any for miles in any direction."

"I just will not use this filthy water. At least have the men go upstream away from this mob of people. I can make out with a bucket or two."

"You ain't got no choice. The water's been used so much it's nothin' but a mud puddle now."

George went off grumbling and Tamsen was left staring at the pail of water he'd brought earlier. Shaking her head, she went to the wagon and pulled out a sack of cornmeal and the butter churn, calling Elitha to help.

"Look, Elitha, pour the water—it's settled out some, be careful and only take it out down to the mud—pour it into the churn ever so slowly. I'm going to sprinkle in some of this cornmeal."

"Why're you using the churn to stir up johnny-cake?"

"I'm not. The cornmeal will soak up some of the dirt and salts in this horrible water. It's a shame to waste the cornmeal, but there's nothing else to do. We'll let it settle out. It will at least make coffee. Thank God, our cows are still giving milk."

A woman carrying a baby and a bucket approached.

"Ma'am, would y'all have any water to spare?" she asked Tamsen. "My men an' girls are out tryin' to scare up some water an' they ain't back yet. My grandbabies are a'dyin' of thirst." Setting the baby and the bucket down on the ground, she brushed strands of wet hair away from her flushed face.

"No, I'm sorry, my husband brought me just this one bucket of water and it is not fit for use. I'm trying to clean it up a little." Tamsen looked down at the baby. "I have some milk if that would help."

"Ma'am, I'd be so grateful. We don't have any stock but

the teams. Haven't had any milk for the babies—most of the milk cows in the company have dried up. We was gettin' some from Miz Harlan."

Tamsen moved to the back of the wagon and took out a pail of milk. She poured some into a jar, placing it in the woman's bucket.

"I'm Mrs. George Donner." Tamsen motioned to Elitha. "And my step-daughter, Elitha."

"I'm pleased to meet y'all. I'm Levinah Murphy, an' this is my daughter's baby, Catherine. Harriet has two little ones—this one's only a year an' Naomi's just two. They're a handful. I'm so worn out by this journey—bein' a widow woman an' all. I wish that I'd stayed back to home, but there ain't no turnin' back now. I do have my two son-in-laws. God knows, I couldn't have come without them."

Tamsen looked at Mrs. Murphy more closely. She did indeed look tired but she still showed the vestiges of having been attractive, her long dark hair framing a pretty face. She was slender and several inches taller than Tamsen, who just barely reached five feet.

"Where was your home? My ear tells me you might be from one of the southern states," said Tamsen.

"You're right. I was born in South Carolina. But after I married Mr. Murphy, we moved to a farm in Tennessee. That's where we started this journey from, Tennessee."

I'd been idling around, half listening to the women talking, when my attention narrowed on a woman who was ambling by. She was a fleshy woman, unkempt looking, with light-colored hair. Her mouth had a funny expectant smile but her facial expression was flat and dull.

"Oh, that woman needs to be run out of camp," exclaimed Mrs. Murphy. "She's caused no end of trouble. She's travelin' with the Harlans—I know who she is 'cause that's where we were gettin' our milk. Miz Harlan is fit to be tied with her doin's."

Tamsen looked around and found the object of Mrs. Murphy's gossip. "Oh, whatever is the problem?" Elitha had been edging away but now moved closer so she could catch what was being said.

"It's—" Mrs. Murphy took Tamsen's arm, turning away from Elitha, who moved even closer. "Her name's Lucinda. She's causing problems with some of the men. You know—wantin' to get with one and then another—she's already been married to one an' he ran off from her. She pestered one of the Harlan teamsters so much he went off to another company. An' her talk would blister an oak!"

"Hmm, that's too bad. Well, it's been so nice to talk to you, Mrs. Murphy. I think my fire is down enough to start supper. If you would just return that jar?"

"Oh, yes. I need to get busy too. I'll send someone back with it. I'm mighty thankful." She looked around for the baby, who had crawled over to one of the dogs and was pulling herself up by his ear. The dog's lip was beginning to quiver over bared teeth. "Oh, my." Mrs. Murphy grabbed one of the child's arms, but couldn't get her released from the dog with one hand. Tamsen disengaged the baby from the dog's ear, picked her up and handed her to Elitha.

"Honey, carry the baby for Mrs. Murphy, it's hard for her with the bucket too."

At the fire with us that evening was Charles Stanton, a gentleman who had come to our camp back in Independence, asking if there was someone who would carry his belongings in one of the wagons. It had been agreed, and he spent most of his time in our camp. He was a smallish man, dressed in the costume of men from the eastern states. We learned that he had been in business in

Chicago, and when the business failed, he'd caught the fever and determined that he would journey to the new lands. He helped out in camp whenever he saw something that needed to be done, then he would light up his pipe, lean against a wagon wheel and write letters to his family back home.

News was brought to the train by a Mr. Webb, editor of the *Independence Expositer,* and Mr. Hay, the great-grandson of Daniel Boone. They reported trouble on the Rio Grande between Mexico and the United States. Everyone wondered how this war would affect them upon arrival in California. Most felt that California would soon become a territory of the United States either by war or by purchase. Many of the young men were excited by the prospects of a revolution and hoped that the war would wait for them to arrive so they could participate. George was of a different opinion.

"We ain't goin' to California to create a revolution or do anythin' that would be a discredit or a dishonor to ourselves or our country. I'm fearful that ambitious men will cause a spirit of war amongst the emigrants an' those folks there who already favor comin' under the domain of the United States. I'm hopin' that it can be done in a peaceable fashion an' in good order."

Standing guard that night was an exciting affair. One of the emigrants had made an arrangement, unbeknownst to the rest, to sell whiskey to some of the Indians. They snuck into camp and were found out. After a great hullabaloo they were taken prisoner. They were on the sneak because they didn't want their chief, who had pledged no trouble in exchange for gifts, finding out about their foray. The trade fell through and the Indians were sent back to their camp to face their chief.

"Who is selling whiskey to these Indians? George, it's an absolute disgrace. Mr. Russell should punish them."

"Tamsen, Russell can't tell people what they can or can't

do. It's a free country and every man does as he sees fit."

"There ain't no law against selling whiskey," said Jacob.

Tamsen was reluctant to concede the issue. "There are rules and laws for proper order. We have governors of the company—you're one of them, George. You should do something."

"Tamsen, selling whiskey ain't—is not breaking wagon train law! It ain't right, but nothin' can be done about it!"

Tamsen looked at the group around the campfire. The men shuffled their feet and looked at the ground. "It'll run out, soon enough," mumbled Noah. "It'll jes take some time, Miz Donner."

"You men aren't very understanding. We should have pity for these poor wretched Indians."

"You shouldn't feel sorry for 'em," said George. "They should start doin' for themselves 'stead of makin' their livin' beggin' an' stealin'. They don't have the least sense of the natural wealth of the country. If they would just learn to use the hoe an' some seed they wouldn't have to scrounge the countryside searchin' for the little game there is."

"Or waitin' for emigrants to come along so they can pester for hand-outs," said Jacob.

"You're just looking at a small part of the picture. They are a neolithic culture, hunter gatherers. I'm not sure they aren't perfectly happy spending their days in the freedom of these wild spaces rather than tied to the plow. These Plains Indians are a nomadic people. Someday they will be forced into a more civilized manner of living. Their wild country will shrink away in the face of an onslaught of westering white people and they will have no choice. But it seems a shame."

"Hmmph." George didn't agree. "It's a waste of good resources to have only a handful of Indians holdin' sway over so much good land."

"I agree with you, George," bellowed Mr. Boggs. "When

country which might support so many actually supports so few, then, by thunder! the inhabitants have not made good use of the natural possibilities. It surely is justification for invasion, peaceful if possible, forcible if necessary. The Mexican territory is a case in point."

"Yes, but these Indian tribes, and the Mexicans also, have led a life they are quite happy to maintain," said Tamsen. "Why can't we, I mean the white people as a whole, be content with what we have? Why do we have to take their land from them? Every one of us crossing this land had enough where we were but we want more, and in order to get it someone else—the Indians, the Mexicans—have to move over and let us in."

"We ain't takin' their land, Tamsen."

"Are not taking, George. No, not us. But someday it will be taken by others just as it has been from the Atlantic to the Missouri. As we travel through their land we use the grass, foul the water, hunt and kill the animals. We take these things from them."

"I ain't—I'm not hankerin' to have anythin' to do with the Indians or their country. We have to cross their land. They're gettin' their price by all their beggin' and stealin'."

In one of the innumerable meetings, Mr. Boggs, a ruddy faced man with a gigantic mustache, demanded that the company eject the Murphy family. "My wife is fit to be tied, and I admit I'm nervous all the time, worrying about one of them sneaking up in the dead of night and killing my whole family."

"I believe your fears are unjustified, sir," said Mr. Bryant. "I have heard that, indeed, Mrs. Murphy is of the Mormon faith, but her son-in-laws have no connection to that Church."

"I thought the men were Mormons. Still, the woman could be spying for the Twelve, sending word about my whereabouts."

"Mr. Boggs, we can take that up before the assembly, but I'd rather not," said Mr. Russell. "I'll investigate this matter, if you'll just hold your fire. It's natural, given your history with the Mormons, to be a little worried. I understand your feelin's."

He rose from his chair and the men began leaving the meeting, Mr. Boggs still grousing about the Murphy family to his friends. We began walking back to our camp.

"George, what concerns me is the slow travel of the company," said Mr. Bryant. "Many seem to want to shorten each day's march as much as possible and once in camp are reluctant to start again. Would you back me up in a resolution aimed at getting a better discipline imposed?"

"I feel it's hopeless, but next time we have a meeting we'll see if we can get the board of governors to beat on people a little. I'm more interested in gettin' some of these cantankerous people to back off and let each other be. I never experienced so much cussedness in one place in my whole life."

• • •

The train halted for a day to catch up on repairs and take care of housekeeping chores. Water was heated but Tamsen and Elizabeth found they didn't have enough soap to wash the huge stack of laundry and had to boil ashes and grease to make more. It took half the day before the water and the soap were ready.

Toby was squatted near-by, whittling on a stick. "Yer makin' the soap reminds me of a story 'bout a family of the greenhorn emigrators—the women were makin' soap in a kettle over the fire. It'd been boilin' fer a good spell, gettin' thickened up and such when some Indian men came into camp. They looked at the kettle of stuff cookin' and signaled that they wanted to partake of the meal. They got right insulted when the women shook their heads, sayin' no, no, it warn't somethin' to eat."

"Yuk," said Leanna.

"But the Injuns just wouldn't take no fer an answer an' the biggest one steps up to the fire, dips a cup into it an' takes a swaller. He makes a sour face, but he nods an' hands the cup off to the next Injun. Same result, an' that one hands it off to the third. He was a little more discriminatin' an' he spits it out." Toby laughed. "That cured those Injuns of beggin' fer food."

"If childbirth don't get'cha in yer twenties and thirties, the hard work a' washing the clothes will surely do you in by yer forties," griped Elizabeth. "Look, my hands are already red an' blistered and I ain't even started the scrubbing yet."

"I have some glycerin to put on your hands, Betsey," said Tamsen. "I finally found it in a trunk in the supply wagon. I was afraid I hadn't put it in."

"I ain't had no kids, but the work I have to do fer Miz Reed will do me in early just the same," complained Eliza, Margaret Reed's maid. "She wants her beddin' changed ever' week, dirty or no. An' Baylis is worn out hauling the water into the wagon so she can have a bath an' then all the children too an' clean clothes most ever' day. I'm havin' to do all the cookin' fer the family an' the hired men. Virginia, she could help but she don't do nothin' but ride around all day with the mister. When I get to California, I ain't a'gonna work fer Miz Reed!"

"I told our men that I would wash their clothes if they would bathe," said Tamsen. "They look like pigs and smell worse. But George told them to wash their own clothes and bathe too. I'm relieved, it's hard enough doing ours."

"Takin' baths is unnatural, Miz Donner," said Toby. "You're likely to get all yer men sick with somethin'."

Tamsen frowned at him. "I think you could use a little soap and water yourself, Mr. Smithson."

"Our teamster, Jim Smith, he's smarter than the rest," said Betsey. "He's sparkin' that daughter of old man Brunell an' gettin' her to do his wash. The other boys are lookin' to do the same. The old man's wonderin' why his old maid daughter is all a'sudden so popular."

"What those fellas need is a squaw," said Toby. "A good squaw can keep the miseries out of life, let me tell you. I wouldn't trade three a' you white women fer one squaw."

Tamsen stopped her work, looking at Toby in exasperation. "Mr. Smithson, don't you have something else to do?"

"Miz Donner, why'n't you just go ahead an' cuss? It helps, you know, when you gets all het up an' mad like. Gets you past some a'the frustration—"

"I have never found it necessary, Mr. Smithson. Using swear words or improper grammar shows a lack of education. A person using such words does not have enough command of language to use more suitable expression."

Some of the men were displeasing Tamsen by all their careless use of swear words and horsing around with the young ladies at the campfire at night. Then they really got into hot water.

I'd joined several of the teamsters and Toby where they were squatting down alongside the wagon, talking, cleaning guns, and doing other small work that was a constant thing on the journey. I'd begun to nod off, lulled by the soft warm breeze, the rustling of the cottonwood trees and the far-off sounds of children playing along the stream when my ears perked up at some of the conversation. I opened one eye a little and saw the object of the conversation, walking along the stream. The infamous Lucinda.

"Too fat for my taste, but you know Bunzel? That big oaf that's in with Harlan? He's been throwing his leg over that mound regular like, but pretends he don't know her come day-time."

"She's chasin' after Noah here. You give in yet, Noah?"

"I'm so damn horny I'd take up with most anythin' but

not that one. I heard she almost kilt ol' Zins, almost squashed and smothered him an' he deflated like a stuck rubber mattress. He only lasted part of a night."

They all laughed uproariously.

"Well, pretty soon it don't matter what it is, it starts lookin' good after dark."

"When we get into the real Injun country a man might find a willin' squaw. I heard tell these Injun women like it."

Toby had the voice of experience. "All you need to do is give 'em a few beads or ribbons an' they spread wide an' their men make the arrangements."

Just then Tamsen stuck her head out from under the wagon cover and started yelling at them. The men looked up in surprise and consternation.

"What trash! If you men even *think* of dallying with any woman in our camp or any Indian woman, your employment will be immediately terminated! Do you understand me? You should be ashamed of yourselves."

"No ma'am, no ma'am. We was just talkin', didn't mean nothin' by it."

"I did not mean to eavesdrop, but I could not help over-hearing. Nevertheless, I mean what I say."

"Yes'm, we sure won't—"

"You won't what?" asked George, who had just walked up. The men all scattered like quail, disappearing into the camp. When Tamsen explained what had happened, George was not very happy.

"Tamsen, that's nothin' a lady should have gotten involved with. You should have pretended you never heard. Now the men'll be all embarrassed an' not actin' natural. It was just men talk."

"Don't give me that nonsense, George. I will not have our men involved in such dirtiness. Think about our girls."

"It's life, it's human nature. It's a side of men—look, what they do on their own an' out of camp is their own business."

"George, if I hear one snippet about any of our men the guilty party will be banned from our camp."

"Don't you think you're over reactin' a little?"

"I am not going to back down, George."

"Why did I think you would?"

[Bryant Journal]
June 2
   ... several unpleasant difficulties and altercations have occurred today, from the perverse obstinacy of some of the men, who refuse obedience to the orders of our captain. The standing committee appointed to adjust such matters have been in session the whole of this evening.

There was another terrible rainstorm that night with deafening crashes of thunder and crackling of lightning. Two of Mr. Grayson's oxen were found dead in the morning, struck by lightning.

The weather took a chill turn, the kind of raw chill that creeps through the clothes and draws up the skin. Soon masses of black clouds rolled in and it commenced to rain. The fall in temperature and the rain made the night extremely uncomfortable. It seemed the middle of winter rather than early summer. In the morning we moved from the bottom land of the Blue to a high rolling prairie. Timber was becoming scarce.

There were numerous accidents and breakdowns. One day it was Mr. Bryant's wagon, a broken axle-tree. Several hours would be needed for repairs. The train moved on, but our men and several others stopped to help, among them Mr. Eddy.

That evening, as we grouped around the fire for conversation the mosquitos were particularly bad. Tamsen lit some sage branches, swooping them around the area and then inside the wagon where the children would be put to bed, trying to smoke the swarms away from the wagons. The mosquitos hardly noticed the inconvenience.

Jacob slapped at his face. "Damned pesky varmints!"

"Did'ja know that skeeters are the most vicious of the prairie wildlife?" Toby asked. "If'n you're the kind they dote on, you might smear yer'self with mud, like the animals do."

The conversation turned to the day's events.

"Bryant got his wagon fixed up in good fashion. Smart of him to have an extra axle-tree," said Mr. Stanton.

"William Eddy is a good man to have near-by, given all the breakdowns," said Jacob. He stretched his legs out, fingering a tear in his pants. "Do you know what part of the country he hails from? He said Illinois, but he don't talk like it, I'm thinkin'."

"Said he started from Belleview, in Illinois, but I heard he's from the East somewhere. He and his wife are travelin' alone, I don't think he's got any other kin with him, jes' two little'uns."

William Foster, Mrs. Murphy's son-in-law, had come to return a plate Tamsen had carried to them earlier with some food. He brought his wife, Sarah, and their little boy, Georgie.

"Thank you kindly for the food, Mrs. Donner. It took a little getting used to, but it was good. What was it?"

"It was the hearts of prickly pears. I collected some today while we were waiting for everyone to come up. I've heard that eating the plant will help prevent scurvy. The country is changing, it's getting hard to forage wild foods. A body needs fresh foods to stay healthy."

"Pshaw! That's girly stuff," growled Toby. "All a body needs is some good buff'ler meat. I lived on buff'ler fer months, never had no sickness a'tall. You're a bunch a sissies."

"Mr. Foster," said Tamsen, "I know Mrs. Foster's family is from Tennesee, but you don't seem to have the same way of speaking. Are you from the east?"

"Yes, ma'am. I'm from Pennsylvania."

"So how was it that you met the Murphy family, living in Tennesee?"

Mr. Foster chuckled. "Well, it's kind of a funny story, I guess. You see, William Pike, Harriet's husband—"

"Mrs. Murphy's other son-in-law?"

"Yes. William and I were working on a riverboat that Mrs. Murphy and her children took out of Warsaw, Illinois, on their way to St. Louis. Well, that riverboat got grounded. Actually, it was frozen in the ice right after leaving and was stuck there for several weeks. That was an excellent opportunity to get well acquainted with my mother-in-law's charming daughters. One thing led to another and we married in the same ceremony. I think Mrs. Murphy was getting desperate to marry off Sarah, being an old maid at fifteen—"

Harriet hit William with the piece of a bush she was carrying to fan away flying pests. "She was not an old maid!" Harriet blushed. "I was only fourteen, didn't even want to get married, truth be told."

"I think her mother was looking to get some men in the family—it was hard on her raising all those kids by herself."

"I don't understand," said Tamsen, "I thought Mrs. Murphy always had lived in Tennesee."

"Mostly, ma'am, but after her husband passed away, she decided to go to Nauvoo—you know, the Mormon city? She only stayed there a year or two. They were on their way back to Tennesee, on the riverboat."

"Oh, then the family is Mormon."

"Well, she is. We aren't." He looked at Harriet. "Will and I aren't, anyway. Mrs. Murphy expects that there'll be a large community of Mormons settling in California. You know, they passed the word that they were moving out of Illinois in search of a promised land and they're scouting out California. She wasn't too happy in Tennessee, felt persecuted—wasn't that so, Harriet?"

Harriet looked at the ground and dragged her toe through the dirt. "I guess."

Harriet was the shy one of the daughters, her sister Sarah was a talker. I thought it was a good thing that both son-in-laws seemed to get along well with Mrs. Murphy. She seemed pious, but never joined in the services that were held most Sundays. I figured it was because she felt unwelcome, but there were many who didn't attend services. I wasn't a bible thumper, so to speak, but I'd always carried my bible and read it, all those long nights in the winter camps.

"We should be getting into buffalo country soon," said Reed. "I'm anxious to experience the hunt. I have heard that the Indians have horses that are trained for the buffalo hunt. But I daresay none can equal my horse, Glaucus."

The group looked at James and I knew what they were thinking. James was always bragging, not right out, but he got his point across—his field knowledge was better, his wagons were better, his guns were superior, his horse was superior—well, his horse was a fine one, but you didn't see too many blooded mounts out here in the wild lands. He would race Glaucus against other horses and Glaucus always won. But people don't take to a person who hold themselves to be superior, and most didn't take to James Reed. So he was descended from Polish nobility—that didn't cut it in the wilderness where all men were equal.

[Charles Stanton]
June 12, 1846

   Everyone is anxious to reach the Platte. We have now traveled four days up the Blue, and one day's march would take us to the great river. This day's march, therefore was resumed with alacrity.

   We had to cross a high elevated plain, the dividing ridge between the waters of the Kansas and the Platte....

   We could perceive, as we crossed the highest elevation, that the land gradually descended both ways, and far in the distance could see the little mounds or hillocks, which formed the ridge or bluffs of the noble river ... when, in ascending a high point of land, we saw, spread out before us, the valley of the noble Platte. The bluffs are from ten to fifteen miles apart, the river, of over a mile in width, flowing through the centre. The bluffs suddenly fall down from 50 to 100 feet, when there is a gradual slope to the water's edge. There is not a single stick of timber to be seen on either side of the river—it is one interminable prairie as far as the eye can extend; yet there is relief found in the numerous islands of the river being generally covered with wood.

· · ·

William H. Russell to the *Missouri Statesman*
June 13, 1846

   ... well it is a queer life we are living, all our teams are oxen, and our travel of consequence is vexatiously slow not averaging more than 16 or 17 miles a day. We get up at daylight, get breakfast as soon thereafter as practicable, always mean to start or break up the caral at 7 o'clock.

At 12 we stop and noon it, rest about an hour, and then travel until between four and 5 o'clock, P.M., when we stop for the night. I keep up a regular guard, and if I could only keep the militia from falling asleep on their post I should be secure against surprise.

My duties as commandant are troublesome beyond anything I could conceive of. I am annoyed with all manner of complaints, one will not do this, and another has done something that must be atoned for ... I sometimes get out of patience myself, and once I threw up my commission, but to my surprise after I had left the caral I was again unanimously re-elected, and a committee with Gov. Boggs as chairman raised to request a renewal of my duties. My vanity of course was flattered, and again after a general lecture resumed the yoke.

June 13, 1846
On The Platte River

The whole company was on alert for buffalo. Several times the hunters raced out of camp on the chase, but it would turn out to be a bush or horsemen or something else on the horizon and they returned disappointed. We'd been using the dung of the buffalo for fuel, as the prairie was mostly barren of trees. At first they were squeamish about using the fuel.

Toby had good advice. "Make sure it's good'n dry, you don't want a wet one, an' tip it over with a stick 'fore you pick it up—sometime's there's bugs an' such underneath."

An Indian scare made everyone nervous and galvanized Russell to double up the guard. The Pawnees had ran off over a hundred head of livestock in a company ten days ahead and a man was killed when he and another man attempted to recover the stock.

Toby raced ahead, eager for an Indian fight, but the Indians had disappeared.

"The man killed was named Trimble," Toby reported when he came back. "It was stupidity, goin' off chasin' those Injuns, just two men. If'n you show the Injuns strength, they backs off. They'll always turn tail and run if they think they have the worst of it. Best you don't go out unarmed or alone."

Day after day, week after week, the company went through the same weary routine. Breaking camp at day-break, cooking over a fire of scrub-oak, buffalo chips or sagebrush, packing up again the cooking stuff, tents and bedding and rushing to put it all away and gather up the children before the wagons would start rolling again. More than once in the confusion one of the children in the group was left behind and much excitement ensued until the missing child was found and returned to its mother. It was always thought the Indians had gotten the wayward child.

Then Miss Lucinda caused more consternation amongst some of the women in the train. One night some noise and activity was heard in the bushes by the river, and the guards thought it was Indians. They searched through the reeds and willows, guns at the ready. One of the searchers stumbled over a form on the ground and noticed a man hopping away, trying to pull up his pants. "What the hell?"

"None a'yer damned business!" Lucinda yelled, and got up, shaking pieces of brush and dirt off her skirt. She glared at the man who'd found her and stalked off.

"It's not Injuns," the man called to the others who were crunching through the dry underbrush. "It's nothin' to worry about. Just a man relieving hisself," but under his breath he grumbled, "that woman is a caution." The men retreated back to their wagons and guard posts.

Just before nooning the next day, a woman was standing in the road, shading her eyes with her hand as she waved for Noah to stop the wagon. Sweat trickled down her flushed face.

"My God, but it's hot, ain't it?"

Tamsen was a little surprised at the visit, but greeted her with good nature. "Well, good day, Mrs. Hoppe. Will you come up and join me?"

Mrs. Hoppe was a large, fleshy woman and after some effort and a helpful hand by Noah, she got into the wagon. Tamsen offered her a dipper of water but she waved it away.

"I will be so glad when we are out of this dust. I've heard that you're a healer and I wonder if you would have a treatment for my eyes."

"I do. I have two that have helped us a great deal. I'll give you some of both when we stop at nooning."

"That would be mighty nice. I'll send one of the children to fetch it when we stop. Miz Donner, this evenin' some of the ladies is gonna meet at my camp. I'd be pleased if you and the other Miz Donner would come."

"What is the purpose of the meeting?"

"Well, this is embarrassin' for me to talk about, but I'm at my wits end. You know of Lucinda?"

"Yes."

"Well, I took her into my camp 'cause Miz Harlan was wantin' to get shut of her. I thought she'd help with my children an' the cookin' and such—an' she does help some but the help I get just ain't worth the trouble. Last night Mr. Hoppe found her in the bushes with a man from the Harlan party an' he come back mad as all get out. So I'm asking some of the women to help me decide what can be done. Will you come?"

"Yes."

"Well, thank you kindly. If you'll ask your man to stop the wagon I'll get down. I want to talk to some more ladies."

When Tamsen told George where she was going that evening he got a little huffy about it.

"Tamsen, we don't need to get involved with Mrs. Hoppe's problems."

"George, I have already agreed to go."

"Godamighty! Don't agree to have anythin' to do with that Lucinda woman. I don't want her in our camp."

"Neither do I, George. Will you stop your ranting? Give me some credit for having some sense."

"The best thing is for her to be banished from the company."

"Really? What about Mr. Bunzel? Shouldn't he be banished also?"

George looked puzzled. "Why would we do that?"

Tamsen threw her dish towel into the wagon and took off her apron. "Elitha, you and Leanna look out for the little ones while I attend the meeting."

Elitha put her hands on her hips and sighed as though the burden of the world had just been put on her. "Oh, Mother, we were just going to the evening music. Why do we have to mind them? Why can't they stay with Father?"

"He has a meeting too."

Elitha flounced around a little, but then gathered up the girls and with Leanna and a group of young people started off, giggling and talking about Lucinda. Tamsen frowned at their retreating backs as she started to walk towards Jacob and Betsey's camp, then turned around and came back.

George raised his eyebrows. "Forget somethin'?"

"Yes, I meant to take Jacob some medicine. It seems to help him."

Elizabeth and Tamsen walked to Mrs. Hoppe's camp. I went along, never having attended a meeting of such upright and righteous ladies with such an interesting subject.

There were seven ladies altogether besides Mrs. Hoppe.

As they settled themselves under the fly-tent of the wagon, several boys drove livestock past the camp raising a cloud of dust that drifted over everything.

"You'd think they'd have more sense than to drive them animals where the wind carries the dust right into camp," complained Mrs. Dunbar. "They ain't got no more sense than the critters they's drivin'."

"Y'all know why we're meetin'," said Mrs. Hoppe. "Somethin's got to be done with Lucinda. I cain't tolerate her another day."

"You know, I don't understand how she came to be with you in the first place," said Mrs. Crabtree.

"Well, she started out with the Harlans—"

"Did you ask Mrs. Harlan to come to the meeting?"

"Well, I did. She said she'd had enough of Lucinda an' wasn't goin' to get involved again. Anyways, I was tellin' y'all about Lucinda. I don't know how she started with Mr. Harlan's group, but she got married to Mr. Zins. Actually, I don't think a preacher spoke over them. That lasted only a night an' he run off. Then, what got the Harlans mad was she started on one of their drivers an' he run off to get away from her. I agreed to take her, thinkin' she'd help with the children an' we didn't have any single men in our camp, but that didn't stop her from botherin' the men in other camps. There's somethin' wrong with her. She's dumb!"

"She cain't talk?" asked Mrs. Crabtree.

"No. She ain't got no brains. She's stupid. Last night she was out in the bushes, you know, with a man."

Mrs. Dunleavy waved her head scarf to get the attention of the group. She spoke in a queer little up and down voice.

"The Reverend thinks you should try praying with Lucinda. Get the Lord in her and then she'll give up her wicked ways."

"I tried that, I really did. I don't think Lucinda ever got the hang of what we was prayin' about," replied Mrs. Hoppe.

"What does Lucinda say?" squeaked Mrs. Dunleavy.

"She just keeps sayin' she wants to get married up. She says there wouldn't be no trouble if she just had a man. She likes the beddin' down."

Mrs. Dunleavy gasped and pressed her handkerchief to her mouth. A shocked silence descended and everyone stared at the ground.

"There's something not right about Lucinda," said Tamsen. "Her mind has not matured and her thinking is like that of a child. It's like she has an itch and can see no good reason why she shouldn't scratch it. I don't think she understands that her deportment offends."

"But what if she gets with child?"

"Well, let her," said Mrs. Dunbar. "Why worry ourselves. It wouldn't be born before California, anyways."

"Mrs. Hoppe," said Tamsen, "perhaps there is someone who has a wagon and would allow Lucinda to stay in it alone. She's big and strong and I'm sure she's capable of driving a team. If you would provide the necessities for her, she wouldn't need to bother you in your camp. You could close your eyes to what she does."

None of the other ladies had any other ideas to offer Mrs. Hoppe and they chatted about different things for awhile and then the ladies got up to leave.

"I'll talk to my husband," said Mrs. Campbell. "We've got three wagons and only one driver. My ten year old's been drivin' fer us. I'll see what my husband says about lettin' this Lucinda woman take one off a'ways by herself."

Mr. Campbell reluctantly agreed provided that Lucinda would take reasonable care of the goods that were in the wagon. At first it seemed to work well, but in a few days it all fell apart.

After the company had formed camp for the evening, Lucinda's wagon was nowhere to be seen. Mr. Campbell became uneasy and decided to go back on the trail to find her, but just then he saw her walking up to camp.

"What's the trouble?" he asked.

"I'm tired of fussin' with those damned ox," yelled Lucinda. "I'm goin' back with Miz Hoppe. I ain't no ox driver."

"How far back you left 'em?"

"Where we stopped fer nooning."

"Damn it. That's at least six miles. The Injuns probably got the oxen and the wagon goods too!"

Mr. Campbell and his driver jumped on their horses and pounded off in a flurry of dust, rifles across their saddles. They didn't return until late in the night. The next morning they brought the wagon up to the Hoppe camp. Mrs. Hoppe was just starting her breakfast fire. "I wouldn't let her near my camp last night. Most likely she's out in the bushes."

"I could have lost my outfit and the oxen too. By damn, I'm through tryin' to help that woman," yelled Mr. Campbell.

He motioned to his driver and they began to throw Lucinda's things out on the ground. Just about that time Lucinda came out of a thicket, yelling and screaming at the men. A crowd formed and the commotion attracted Colonel Russell.

"We cannot leave a woman by the side of the road. I do not believe we have sunk that low … yet," he intoned. "This is a company of Christians. Will one of you help this woman?"

He looked sternly at each person, his faded blue eyes rheumy and bloodshot. One by one the crowd turned away. Mr. Russell sighed deeply.

Lucinda started gathering up her things, alternately crying and cursing. Mr. Russell opened a small trunk that Mr. Campbell had thrown out of the wagon and stuffed some of Lucinda's things that were on the ground inside.

"Come with me," he said to Lucinda. He led her to the Harlan's camp.

"I ain't gonna have that woman in my camp," Mrs. Harlan yelled when she saw them approaching. "You take her on out of here."

Mr. Harlan was hitching up his oxen and tried to ignore Mr. Russell, but he stepped in front of him.

"Mr. Harlan, there is nothin' to be done but you take her in. Zins married her and that makes her a part of your company. I have the full weight of the company board behind me."

Mr. Harlan threw the gear he had in his hand down on the ground and kicked a wagon wheel. "Dammit!"

• • •

Now the rigors of the journey were beginning to take a toll. Trouble that had been simmering between two normally peaceable men boiled over into a fist fight with knives drawn. This triggered a division of the already too cumbersome company into those for Oregon and those for California. The Thorntons moved off with the Oregon contingent, causing tears in the eyes of our ladies, who were sad to see them go. This split-up didn't seem to lessen the frayed nerves and short tempers of the group, as now the travelers were prone to violent quarrels on the slightest provocation.

We were now in the country of the Pawnee Indians, a tribe known to be vicious and skilled in thievery, but the company was vigilant. Toby stayed out well ahead looking for signs of trouble.

The most pressing problem was the condition of the wagon wheels. The dry atmosphere was causing the wheels to loosen and sometimes they would roll off, causing much consternation.

Quite often there were accidents, sometimes fatal. A child would fall under the wagon wheels; someone would be trampled or kicked by livestock; a wagon would capsize crossing a stream.

Occasionally a gun would go off accidentally, and one time, on purpose, two quarrelsome men in the company engaged in an argument that resulted in the shooting of one.

"They called it an accident," said George, "but I don't reckon it was. The committee let it go. Seems like when mankind gets away from the restraints of society an' law their animal natures start showin' through."

"I did what I could for the man, I don't think he'll live," reported Mr. Bryant when he joined us at our fire.

The next day we came up to a stream that had steep banks causing a delay in the forward movement of the train. The women and children waited under a cottonwood tree, watching as the wagons skittered one by one down the side of the near bank and then slowly ascend the far bank, pulled by the oxen in front and pushed by sweating and cursing men in back.

One of the wagons began to tilt. A warning was shouted, but once started the wagon could not be stopped from falling. The helping men jumped out of the way as the wagon fell over on its side, throwing a woman and small child into the water and mud.

Our forward wagons passed as the wagon was being pulled out of the stream. George stopped to see if he could be of assistance, but signaled his wagons on. "He has a broken wagon tongue, but he's got plenty of help."

That evening, Betsey and Tamsen discussed the unfortunate family.

"I feel sorry for her," said Betsey. "Such a nice, pretty little woman. That man treats her terrible like. You can tell she's constantly in fear of excitin' his temper. And so far along with child. Something should be done about it."

"Done about what?" asked George.

"You know the man with the turned-over wagon?"

"Name's Keseberg."

"He has a violent temper and takes his anger out on his wife. He beats her," said Betsey.

"I don't know the man, but I've heard that he's downright unsociable."

"I wish that you would speak with him."

"Tamsen, I ain't interferin' in another man's affairs."

"If you saw this man approach another with the intent to batter him or shoot or knife him, what would you do?"

"That's not the same thing."

"How can you say that? It's an assault no matter how you look at it."

"Tamsen, we ain't goin' to get involved."

"I disagree with you, George," said James. "A man that is brutal to women disgusts me. I shall confront him."

That evening, James went to Mr. Keseberg's wagons. He found him returning from the stream with a pail of water. Mr. Keseberg seemed defensive even before James spoke to him.

"What you want?" he exclaimed.

"You have been observed beating your wife and it will not be tolerated."

Mr. Keseberg looked at his wife at the fire and motioned James behind the wagon. "What affair is it of yours?"

"I'm making it my affair. If such treatment happens again, I will see to it that you are expelled from the company."

"You have not the right to tell me what to do, Reed, and you cannot expel me from the company."

James's tone was short. "I advise you that you will be removed from this company if you mistreat your wife again. Good day, sir."

The German watched Reed move off, then went around the wagon to his wife who was bending over the pots on the fire. She straightened her back slowly and stiffly, looking at him with apprehension.

"I have talked to no one," she exclaimed.

He dropped the bucket in front of her, half the water sloshing over her bare feet, beading up in the thick dry dust.

"Here is your water. I am going to see to the oxen."

Mrs. Keseberg nodded, thankful that his anger hadn't been directed at her.

• • •

June 16, 1846
My dear friend:

We are now on the Platte, 200 miles from Fort Laramie. Our journey, so far, has been pleasant. The roads have been good, and food plentiful. The water for a part of the way has been indifferent—but at no time have our cattle suffered for it. Wood is now very scarce, but buffalo chips are excellent—they kindle quickly and retain heat surprisingly. We had this evening buffalo steaks broiled upon them that had the same flavor they would have had upon hickory coals.

We feel no fear of Indians. Our cattle graze quietly around our encampment unmolested. Two or three men will go hunting twenty miles from camp and last night two of our men lay out in the wilderness rather than ride their horses after a hard chase. Indeed if I do not experience something far worse than I have yet done, I shall say the trouble is all in getting started.

Our wagons have not needed much repair, but I cannot yet tell in what respects they may be improved. Certain it is they cannot be too strong. Our preparations for the journey, in some respects, might have been bettered. Bread has been the principal article of food in our camp. We laid in 150 lbs. of flour and 75 lbs. of meat for each individual and I fear bread will be scarce. Meat is abundant. Rice and beans are good articles on the road—cornmeal, too, is very acceptable. Linsey dresses are the most suitable for children. Indeed, if I had one it would be comfortable.

We are now 450 miles from Independence. Our route at first was rough and through a timbered country that appeared to be fertile. After striking the prairie we found a first-rate road and the only difficulty we have had has been crossing creeks. In that, however, there has been no danger.

I never could have believed we could have traveled so far with so little difficulty. The prairie between the Blue and Platte rivers is beautiful beyond description. The Indians frequently come to see us, and the chiefs of a tribe breakfasted at our tent this morning. All are so friendly that I cannot help feeling sympathy and friendship for them. But on one sheet, what can I say?

Since we have been on the Platte we have had the river on one side and the ever varying mounds on the other—and have traveled through the bottom lands from one to ten miles wide with little or no timber. The soil is sandy and last year, on account of the dry season, the emigrants found grass here scarce.

Our cattle are in good order ... none has been lost. Our milk cows have been of great service—indeed, they have been of more advantage than our meat. We have plenty of butter and milk. We are commanded by Capt. Russell— an amiable man. George Donner is himself yet. He crows in the morning, and shouts out "Chain up, boys! Chain up!" with as much authority as though he was "something

in particular". John Denton is still with us—we find him a
useful man in camp. Hiram Miller and Noah James are in
good health and doing well. We have of the best of people
in our company, and some, too, that are not so good.
 Buffalo show themselves frequently. We have found
the wild tulip, the primrose, the lupine, the ear-drop, the
larkspur and creeping hollyhock, and a beautiful flower
resembling the bloom of the beech tree, but in bunches large
as a small sugar-loaf and of every variety of shade, to red
and green. I botanize and read some, but cook a "heap"
more. There are 420 wagons, as far as we have heard, on
the road between here and Oregon and California. Give
our love to all inquiring friends. God bless them.
Mrs. George Donner

We plodded on through a vast expanse of flat earth—tree-less plains unbroken by bush or rock. The sun glared down with a pitiless heat, the distant blue prairie quivering under it. Here and there a crow, raven or buzzard circled languidly overhead.

"You know," mused Mr. Bryant, "someday this journey will be undertaken by railroad and what now takes four to six months will be accomplished in a few weeks."

"It don't seem likely to me," said Jacob, "where do you think they'd get the wood to run the engines? There ain't a stick a'wood fer miles around. An' who could pay the cost of travel that far even if there'd be a company that could build it?"

"I can't answer that, but I believe there'll be men who will find a way to do it. This is fertile country. In a few years there'll be people moving in to develop the fine resources that are here."

Jacob looked doubtful.

One day three men from another company came to Mr. Bryant, begging him to assist a boy whose leg had been crushed under the wheels of a wagon. Mr. Bryant had a constant call for his doctoring skills. He could not help the boy, telling the boy's mother that there was no point in causing more pain by an amputation, but she insisted. A man stepped forward to do the operation, but the boy died before it was completed.

"It is a problem," Bryant told Tamsen, "that those afflicted by disease will take medicines thinking that large quantities will more effectively cure. In most cases more harm than good is achieved. I believe the application of common sense along with a little knowledge of herbal remedies may work to relieve sickness and disease better than the practice and habit of bloodletting and strong cathartics. I think these methods are more likely to kill than to cure."

"Yes, I feel the same," said Tamsen. "A woman that I am treating had been taking large amounts of calomel and I believe she is now suffering from mercury poisoning as a result."

Tamsen was independent and not afraid to speak her mind. She grew up with the idea that a woman needn't be pinned under the thumb of a man, and hadn't experienced that treatment with her first husband, Tully Dozier, nor her second, George Donner. She'd been tempered by grief, losing two children and her first husband within a few months. That experience gave her a desire to learn all she could about the art of healing.

[Bryant]
June 13
Within the space of a few hours, there was a death of a boy and his funeral, a marriage, and the birth of a baby. Tomorrow the wagons will pass by the place of these events and soon it will be deserted and unmarked except by the grave of the unfortunate boy. Such is the checkered map of human suffering and human enjoyment.

The train ground on, the wheels of the wagons kicking up clouds of dust that entered mouths, noses, eyes and lungs, covering the people and animals so thoroughly they matched the brown-gray earth upon which they traveled. The alkali in the gritty dust inflamed their eyes. Tamsen treated her family with her medicines and doctored the eyes of the oxen too. Some oxen in the train were affected so severely by the dust that they became temporarily blinded.

"Colonel Russell has resigned his post," reported George at the evening fire.

"Again?"

"Yeah. That means the rest of us will resign also. I'm happy to give it up. I'm tired of all the vexations."

"I heard Bryant is going to leave the group," said Jacob.

"Yes, it's true," replied George. "He doesn't like the progress of the company. He an' some other men are planning to buy mules at Fort Laramie an' continue on packing. Mr. Russell wants to go with them."

"Who else?"

"Kirkendall, Miller, Buchanan, Nuttall, some others, 'bout ten in all."

"Well, they're single men," said Jacob. "I mind that's it's good to travel faster, but with families we cain't do it. If someone gets sick or injured, how could they be carried? Our wagons're slow, but it's the best way fer us, we couldn't pack our goods."

George got up and started kicking dirt over the last embers of the fire. "I've heard that if we're at Independence Rock by the fourth of July, we're doin' fine. I think we'll make it. I'm turning in. I'm some tired from fightin' the wind an' the dust all day. This is the damndest country for wind."

The company was now on the north bank of the south fork of the Platte. Large herds of buffalo were now seen on the march, and some approached so close that there was danger of them mingling with the livestock. At last the company had found the fabled buffalo. We were near an area where salt had accumulated on the ground and the buffalo herds came to lick the salt. Immediately a hunt was organized. James Reed and two of the teamsters participated in the hunt. When they returned with several choice parts of the buffalo, James felt compelled to do a little crowing.

"I was very successful. My purpose was that the hunters might see that a sucker had the best horse in the company and was the best and most daring horseman in the caravan. Well, I removed the stars from their brows."

James had constantly to prove himself as good as or better than the so-called professional hunters of the caravan. He'd been smarting because some of the hunters had critiqued him and pronounced him a green horn and a "sucker". His next letter home, addressed to his brother-in-law, James Keyes, reflected his satisfaction with the hunt.

....yesterday I thought to try my luck, as old buffalo hunters and many others, as they would permit to be in their company, have left the camp for a hunt, Hiram Miller, myself and two others, after due preparation, took a line of march ....every thing in camp was talking that Mr so and so had gone hunting, and we would have some choice buffalo steaks. No one thought or spoke of the two frontier hunters, and no one but the two asked to go with us. Going one or two miles west of the hunters on the bluffs, and after riding about three miles, we saw a large herd of buffalo bulls, and choice young game, which is the hardest to get being fleeter and better wind—we went towards them as coolly and calmly—as nature of the case would permit....

Closing upon a gang of ten or twelve bulls, the word

was given and I was soon in their midst, but among them, there was noise made enough for my taste to shoot, and upon seeing a drove to my right I dashed among them, a Craddock's pistol in hand—a fine instrument for Buffalo hunters on the plains—detected my victim and brought him tumbling to the ground, leaving my companions far behind....

The following Sunday was a half-day layover. Some were observing the Sabbath at morning services and others were engaged in repair and housekeeping matters.

The hunters were staying in camp, but I noticed that James Reed was heading out on Glaucus. I decided to follow him.

After traveling a distance he stopped several times to peer through his spyglass across the prairie. At last he appeared to have found that for which he was looking and he set off at a trot, covering a mile or more before dismounting. Taking his rifle from its holder, he left the horse and crept up to a small rise in the ground.

The object of his interest was a single bull buffalo, rolling in a wallow. It seemed that he meant to kill the buffalo. I thought it strange because the animal was obviously old. The meat would be undesirable, particularly since there was so much good tender meat in camp. I surmised that he was looking for a trophy.

James stood from his creeping stance, walking towards the writhing animal as he primed his rifle. When he judged he was close enough, he raised the gun and fired. The bullet found a mark, but not a fatal one. The buffalo lurched to its feet and lunged out of the hollow straight for the puff of black smoke that was still drifting in front of James.

I sensed the surprise and panic as James realized he could not reload and fire before the animal would reach him. He turned and ran. Jumping over prairie dog holes, dodging around hillocks of wire grass, he dispensed with the rifle, whistling frantically for the horse. But Glaucus only raised his head in the direction of his master's call, choosing not to leave the clump of tender grass on which he'd been munching.

Legs churning, James glanced back at the fast approaching buffalo, failing to see the edge of a gully dead ahead. He tumbled down its side, dirt and dust cascading over his body as it followed him down the slope. This, however unfortunate he considered it at the time, saved him. The enraged beast thundered along the top of the embankment, failing to see that James had rolled into brush at the bottom of the gully.

James scrabbled to his feet and looked at the plume of dust that signaled the departure of the buffalo. He limped up the gully, brushing dirt off his clothes and calling Glaucus. This time the horse decided to answer the call. I thought perhaps James was through with this little adventure, but I was wrong. I could tell from the set of his jaw and his body that he was furious. Furious at the buffalo, furious at the horse, and disgusted with himself for engaging in such a foolish enterprise.

He had some very cross words for Glaucus as he led the horse to where his rifle had been dropped. I'd discounted his pride and his determination to never be bested by man or beast. Now I saw that he was determined. Slowly, deliberately, he took his water container from his saddle and drank. Slowly and deliberately he cleaned his rifle and reloaded. Mounting, he began to track the buffalo, finding him two miles away in the bottom of the gully.

He crossed over the gully, the horse skittering down one side and lunging up the other. He worked his way downwind of the buffalo, keeping out of sight. When he was about 100 yards away, he turned into the gully and kicked the horse into a run.

The services had just ended and people were returning to

their wagons, others were completing their chores. The sounds of clinking chains, the mutterings of oxen and the men shouting out commands signaled that the camp was stirring in preparation for the chain-up.

Then, a bolt of movement in the middle of the camp. Pandemonium broke out. Crazed with fear, spilling and breaking camp gear and tents, a huge buffalo ran and lunged through the camp, James trailing it on his horse, trying to drive it away. People broke in all directions. James managed to turn the animal between wagons and it dashed off over the prairie leaving a pall of dust and baying dogs in its wake. Some of the men grabbed their rifles and mounted up, chasing after James. They reined in on the top of a rise and watched the buffalo disappear over a swell.

Several in the company complained about the incident to Mr. Boggs, now the captain of the company. He came to talk to James.

"I regret the incident, Mr. Boggs. I spotted a small herd in a draw about a mile out and gave chase. The bull broke from the herd, so I shot, but only wounded him. Unfortunately, he ran down the draw, which was in direct line of the camp. I did my best to drive him away."

"Nobody was hurt. They'll forget about it," said Boggs.

• • •

The ridge between the South and North Platte was crossed, a distance of some twenty miles. It was through some of the roughest country we had seen, all ridges, mounds, deep hollows, and sand, with sparse vegetation and the only water a stagnant pond or two. The road struck directly up a bluff, rising quite rapidly at first, then very gradually for about twelve miles when we reached the summit and a most magnificent view. Before and below us the river wound its way through broken hills and green meadows.

Behind us was undulating prairie rising gently from the South Fork over which we had just passed. On our right was the gradual convergence of the two valleys and immediately at our feet was Ash Creek, which fell off suddenly into deep chasms, leaving only a high narrow ridge that gradually descended until falling off sharply into the bottom of the creek. The entry into the hollow was particularly difficult. Ahead of us a wagon overturned, killing two oven and injuring several others.

The men double-rough-locked the wagons, wrapping the wheel chains around the wheels. Then they removed all but one yoke of oxen. The descent was begun with trepidation, but the wagons made it down with no serious problems.

In the hollow was a pure cold spring and patches of currants and gooseberries. The children were sent with pails to pick berries, emerging from the patches with blue stained hands and faces. That evening the company feasted on berry pies.

There were many Indians in the area, a sort of trading crossroads for the different tribes. Here sat a weathered cabin on the verge of collapse, constructed by trappers the previous winter and now serving as a prairie post office of sorts. Inside there was a niche where people would place letters waiting for anyone passing east to carry them on to the settlements. The party spent a goodly amount of time looking at all the letters and messages that had been left, adding some of their own.

For several miles after leaving the encampment the trail passed over a sandy soil and the wheels sank eight or ten inches. The bluffs that walled in the river valley were rugged and sterile with barren sands and perpendicular ledges of rock. The country was parched looking with very little vegetation.

The valley of the Platte was very rough, knobbed and hilly. A peculiarity noticed was that the knobs, or bluffs, were only to be found upon one side of the river at a time, sometimes on one side and then the other. One could imagine castles, towns and houses rising amongst the bluffs.

Still following the Platte, the wagons toiled on, now headed northwest. The scattered buttes and bluffs which had been growing common became a true badlands and the country lost its monotony, but now it was truly tough going. The formations were fantastic. Jail Rock, Courthouse Rock, and in the hazy distance, a spire known as Chimney Rock stood out in bold relief. Then Scott's Bluff reared up from the valley floor.

In sun and dust the wagons creaked on, the daily distance shortening and the country stretching out before them with no end. The grass was sparse, the water bad. The livestock suffered, many of them died. The higher altitude added to the strain and discomfort. The trail narrowed, becoming steep and precipitous. The dry air caused wheels to shrink—tires would roll off or spokes pull out. Delays were caused by the necessity of lowering wagons with ropes down the steep pitches or hauled up over boulders and gullies.

[From an Emigrant on the Trail]
Fort Bernard, June 25, 1846
TO THE ST. LOUIS REVEILLE
... the companies, generally speaking, have got along remarkably well. Some hundred head strayed away from the advance company—through sheer carelessness on the part of the company, however. We stopped but a few minutes on our arrival at this post, promising to return and partake of the hospitalities politely tendered us by its commander, J.F.X. Richards, Esq., we hastened on, in the midst of a heavy rain, to Fort Laramie, eight miles above.... the plains surrounding the fort were covered with the lodges of the

Sioux, who were preparing to send out a large war party against the Crows ... we ascertained that they had taken on their line of march for the mountains, and the achievement of their purpose—the thrashing of the poor Crows, or the plunder of the emigrant—more probably the latter.

Their cavalcade ... was imposing as well as grotesque ... riding as fast as horse flesh could possibly carry them. Following them, came a long string of pack animals—ponies, and a considerable many dogs, attended by women, whose duty it appeared to be to do all the drudgery of the removal. The queerest kind of go-carts, too, had been impressed into the service; long poles were lashed to the sides of the dogs, across which were bound their burdens, while many of the ponies seemed to be lugging an unnecessary pile of lumber after them, solely for the purpose of accommodating a few little light articles which were bouncing about on top.

June 27, 1846
Fort Laramie

The sun flattened on the horizon and disappeared in a ball of fire. Ahead, the much anticipated trading post known as Ft. Bernard. The crudeness of the half-finished post was disappointing, but it was the first glimmer of civilization in hundreds of miles. Traders from Taos were there and hundreds of Ogalala Sioux Indians, mostly denizens of Chief Old Smoke's village.

Later in the evening the cousins of these Sioux, the Miniconjou, began arriving. The emigrants gaped and marveled, marveled and gaped some more. They were dazzled. Hundreds of yelling Indians made up for war.

The group bound for Oregon that had separated off earlier in the journey, now led by Rice Dunbar, had already arrived. It became a reunion of sorts. Tamsen took her daughters to the other camp to visit people she knew.

"Mr. Thornton has been very sick," Tamsen reported that evening. "He still suffers greatly from asthma. Mrs. Thornton says sometimes he's coughing up blood and seems to have a complaint in every part of his body. To add to his distress, their driver seems to cross Mr. Thornton at every opportunity."

"Well, Thornton seemed a bit peevish to me. At this stage of the journey he better get along with his driver," said George.

Tamsen brought her bag of medicines from the wagon and sat down to look through it. "I can't think of what I have in my remedies that would help. Hmm, evening primrose, I think. Laudanum would help him sleep and ease his anxiety. I'll take some to him in a little while."

"Tamsen, you can't treat every ailment in this whole gol-durned wagon train," said Jacob.

Lines of campfires dotted the area, their flames glowing against the cottonwoods and shining in the Platte. The emigrants had hosted a banquet for traders and others of the fort and afterwards several people gathered around the Donner campfire. Toby went off, hobnobbing with the traders. When he came back he brought a man with him.

The last time I'd seen Jim Clyman was '24 or '25 and twenty years make a lot of difference in a man. He'd weathered into dry leather. Jim was a tall man, with a dignity and bearing that called for respect. I noticed he must have lost some teeth because one side of his mouth had a little twist to it. Toby introduced him to the gathering.

"Howdy," said Clyman. "I see one man I know. I was at Dixon's Ferry in Early's company with you, Reed. How you be?"

James brushed a mosquito away from his face, squinting at Mr. Clyman. Then he stood up, extending his hand.

"Ah, yes. When were you mustered out?"

Mr. Clyman's voice was raspy. He cleared his throat several times before speaking. "I was in Dodge's battalion for awhile, mustered out in Missoora in 1834." He sat down on the ground, cross-legged. "Y'all from Illinois, are you? What part?"

"Sangamon."

"That right? I spent some time there doin' surveyin' work fer Colonel Hamilton. 1821 'er '22, it was."

"You've just come from California?"

"That's a fact."

"What do you make of it?"

"Well, some're gonna like it, some not. Personally, I think it's a little short of paradise. It depends on what you're lookin' fer. We traveled in that territory for twenty-eight days, mostly through the Spanish settlements. There was only three places where we slept in a house an' those were owned by foreigners. The usual ranch is from six to twelve square miles, some're real large. There's one I passed which belonged to a Mexican gent that was thirty-three leagues."

"What would that be in acres?"

"Lemme think now." Mr. Clyman squeezed his eyes shut and concentrated. "That's close to one hundred forty thousand acres."

"The hell you say."

"Their ranchos are huge. Like nothin' you ever seen before. On this one they cultivate only four or five hundred acres, the rest is used for grazin'. There's twelve or fifteen thousand head of cattle an' seven or eight thousand head of horses. They don't feed their animals grain. You cain't find a single kernel to feed yer horse in California, but I seen the biggest field of wild oats on the globe, some two or three hundred thousand acres. It falls on the ground to seed the next crop."

Clyman hawked and spit, then wiped his mouth on his sleeve. "There's opportunities in the territory, that's a fact. There's a man, Yount, has a flouring mill, the only one in the province. Has a saw mill too, an' both are profitable. He's an American, been in the Mexican country thirteen, fourteen years."

"What be the situation with the Mexican government?" asked Mr. Stanton.

"Well, Fremont caused some alarm by raisin' the American flag at his camp near the Mission of St. John—suppose that would be Jose in Mex-speak—then the Mexican general, Castro, raised some four hundred men under arms at Monterey. You cain't tell what the truth is most times, 'cause the reports are carried by hearsay. But you can count on it, Frémont's bent on conquest and the territory will fly the American flag. But it's been some time since I was there. I left Johnson's ranch mid-April."

"You came over the mountains of California?"

"I did."

"There's a feller, Hastings. You heard of him? He says he knows of a route that's shorter than goin' by Fort Hall. Do you know anythin' of that?"

Mr. Clyman went through the procedure of knocking ashes from his pipe and refilling it.

"Yes, I came through there. I was *with* Hastings."

Getting up, he took a stick from the fire and held it to the tobacco, sucking on the pipe until it was going. Filling his lungs, he slowly breathed out the smoke.

"He's stayin' up by Fort Bridger waitin' so's he can direct emigrants back over this here route. You ask me, it's foolish. We came through packin' on mules. No wagons've ever gone there an' it will be difficult to do so. The country is rough, full of canyons an' choked with trees and brush."

Mr. Clyman picked up a stick and began drawing some lines in the dirt, his bony shoulders hunched against the evening chill, his eyes squinting against his tobacco smoke.

"See, now, this is the trail from Ft. Laramie to South Pass. Y'all have to follow the Platte north, northwest—there's a desert if you go west." He drew another line out from the first one. "Then you have to leave the Platte and strike for South Pass. Smith and Fitzpatrick and I explored that pass."

"Mr. Clyman, we're well advised on that route," said Mr. Stanton. "We want to know more about the country past Fort Bridger. It does not seem logical to have to take that big dog-leg north by Fort Hall."

"West a' Bridger the country is passable good. Here's Bridger," Clyman dug his stick in the ground, "an' here's that big butte west of there. You'll head west fer a spell. At the Big Muddy River you'll take a southwesterly direction. You'll keep on thataway twenty miles an' you'll come to Sulphur Creek. A ways more, you'll cross the Bear. It's a fair-sized river. There's good trout in that river. Then another five, six miles you go off to the northwest, twelve, fourteen miles an' its southwest fer twenty-five miles or so."

He punched the stick in the ground and stood up. "Then yer troubles are gonna start. Yer gonna say, now why didn't we listen to Clyman?"

"What trouble?"

"I been tellin' you. There's high mountains with a passel of canyons, real rough country. There's no road, mebbe a little Injun trail here an' there. The streams're filled with rocks an' boulders, there's places where there's cliffs on both sides."

"We understand what you are saying," said James, "but if there is a closer route, it is of no use to take a roundabout course. We trust that Mr. Hastings knows what he's about."

Mr. Clyman looked at James. "Uh-huh? Well, each man floats his own stick." He got up, his knees cracking as he straightened them out. He ducked his head towards Tamsen and then at the men.

"Thank you fer the coffee, ma'am. Good evening, gentlemen." He placed his hat on his head, picked up his gun, nodded to

Toby and strode off into the darkness.

Jacob hadn't spoken during Mr. Clyman's discourse, but now he stood up and threw his cold coffee on the fire. "Do you believe that? Fifteen thousand cattle on one ranch, an' that bein' one hundred an' forty thousand acres? Thousands of acres of oats jes' growin' on their own? I think the man's a liar. We cain't put no stock in what he says."

Toby was indignant. "Clyman's just about the best there is when it comes to knowin' country. He went to the mountains with Ashley, that's where I knowed him, an' with Fitzpatrick too. He was with Jeb Smith an' Tom Fitzpatrick when they found South Pass. He's been around that big Salt Lake. You just heard him telling of comin' through from California on that route that idiot Hastings feller's talkin' about. I knew you all was stupid greenhorns an' now here's more proof."

It was the longest speech Toby had ever made in his life. He led his mule out of camp that night, and that was the last we saw of Tobias Smithson.

• • •

Fort Laramie was situated near the junction of Laramie Creek and the Platte, central to the fur trade and within reach of a number of Indian tribes. As we approached the fort all eyes turned to a great spectacle stretched out over the plain.

"Mother, Mother! Look! Look at all the Indians!"

The girls pointed across the plain and gazed in wonder at the hundreds of conical shaped tents spread out across the valley. The area was alive with activity and horsemen galloping back and forth, showing off their prowess and their exotic costumes. A constant stream of people walked to and from the large mud-walled stockade in a tableau of savage dignity.

I'd been at Fort Laramie many times over the years. In the

first years it was called Fort William, named after Bill Sublette. When the American Fur Company took it over they called it Fort John, but most of the traders and trappers knew it as Fort Laramie. Bordeau was in charge when we got there. Papin, the bourgeois, was off to St. Louis with hides and furs.

The fort was now the principal trading post of the American Fur Company, a square shaped structure with outer walls of mud bricks around a center area of about one-half an acre. On three sides there were various rooms in which the living and working aspects of the fort were carried out. The fourth side was a main building of two stories with towers guarding the corners of the quadrangle. Although there was always the possibility of a war attack, the gates were closed more often against constant carousing and stealing by the Indians.

Thousands of Sioux surrounded the fort preparing to go to battle with the Snake and Crow Indians. They were holding war-dances, working themselves into frenzy helped along by the effects of whiskey. They obtained some whiskey from the emigrants who were eagerly bargaining for buffalo skins, moccasins and other products, such as pemmican, a food made from pounded dry berries, seeds and meat.

Mr. New, the Santa Fe trader that had swapped mules for wagons with Mr. Bryant at Ft. Bernard, came to Fort Laramie to complete the transaction and to help Mr. Bryant and the others learn the business of packing and dealing with mules. They didn't learn much, except that experience was the best teacher.

The emigrants bought supplies, repaired their wagons, wrote letters back home, and gawked at the Sioux. The Indian braves were loathe to waste an opportunity to show off in front of such a dropped-jaw audience. They had recently returned from an excursion against the Pawnees and had twenty-five scalps to brag about, and many captured horses. Tamsen, like the rest, was fascinated with the culture, dress and living quarters of the Indians, but there was something deeper. She knew the Indians had extensive knowledge of the healing properties in the herbs and shrubs in their natural environment. She questioned Mr. New, asking if he could arrange for her to visit one of their healers.

"Do you speak the Sioux language, Mr. New?"

Mr. New's faded blue eyes squinted out from under brows as thick as a bird's nest. "Yes, ma'am. I been with and around the Injuns fer twenty years or more."

"I would like to visit one of their doctors, a healer."

"No, ma'am, that wouldn't be likely."

"Why not?"

"Well, they don't have doctors like you're thinkin'. Their doctors are called shamans. The shamans, they do, well, I guess you might call it hocus pocus. They shake rattles, spit stuff out'a their mouths, sing and dance around, such like."

"Do they effect cures?"

"Sometimes the patient gets well, dependin' on if the shaman knows his potions and cures. These here Injuns know a passel 'bout what plants and such can cure certain things."

"I have an interest in botany and plant cures. I would like to learn what plants they use."

Mr. New knocked the ashes from his pipe. "No, it ain't likely they'd allow it, you bein' a woman, an' a white woman to boot. The shamans, they're real touchy. You see, they depend on fear an' mystery to keep their power, their medicine. They have to convince the Injun that comes to 'em fer a cure that they have the medicine to drive off the bad spirits that's caused the sickness. That's why they do all their hocus pocus, to make the patient believe the shaman has somethin' special that'll make a cure. It be a tough job, sometimes if the patient isn't cured, the family will kill the shaman or he loses his standin' an' he don't have a practice no more. Now, in any Injun camp thar's gonna be a woman or a man that knows how to use herbs an' plants fer certain things."

"Would one of those people speak with me?"

"Ma'am, I wouldn't know who those people would be. There's thousands of Injuns here. I ain't lived in a Injun camp fer many years."

"But perhaps you know of some of their cures."

Mr. New took out his tobacco pouch and refilled his pipe, tamping down the tobacco. He leaned over, took a stick out of the fire and held it on the tobacco while he puffed on the pipe to get it started.

"Now, a partner a' mine—Henry was his name—a long time back, had a broken leg. We was stayin' with the Sioux fer the winter. We sent fer the head shaman an' he came, but he said that broken bones warn't his line of work. He sent in this old Injun who said he was a Bear Dreamer. It seems the Bear Dreamers specialize in broken bones an' such. He looked at the break—it was a bad one with the bone comin' through the skin. He said he could fix it, but we'd have to give him a horse in payment before he'd start the work. Course we were in no position to dicker. After some hoopla the Injun mixed up a salve an' smeared it on my friend's leg."

"Do you know what the salve was made of?"

Mr. New looked down into his coffee cup, reflecting. "It was bear grease an' somethin' else he called hu-hwe-han-pe-zu-la. This here salve kind'a relaxed him, an' then the healer pulled the bone in place an' laced a wet rawhide 'round the break."

"Your partner didn't seem to have pain?"

"Well, he'd drunk a pint a' whiskey before the healer got there."

"Was the break cured?"

"He was up an' walkin' around not too long after that. Had to use a stick to walk with fer a time. Henry got hisself drowned the next spring. I'll allow that if'n we'd been in the white man's camp when he broke his leg, they'd of cut it off an' he'd a been a cripple or died from the gangrene."

"Mr. New, I would like to know more about the cure."

"Well, mebbe I can find out for you."

Mr. New puffed on his pipe for a moment, then took it from his mouth. "Now, if'n you had gut pains, you'd look fer some horsemint an' drink a tea of it. Fer the trots some take a concoction of lambsquarters, an' fer stomach pain a tea made of verbena's good."

He put the pipe in his mouth again, but then removed it and pointed it for emphasis as he thought of something else. "I mind that the root of calamus could help a toothache. Some claimed it, but it never helped me none."

"I'm familiar with the plants and cures that you've mentioned, but not calamus. Do you know what it looks like?"

"It's the root you use. The leaves are kind'a narrow like, yellowish an' green. It has a yellow pod that comes out at a' angle an' kind'a a spicy smell."

Tamsen handed Mr. New an open page in her notebook and a pencil and asked him if he would sketch the plant.

"Well, I ain't much hand at this, but I'll give it a try."

He sketched for several minutes, then handed the things back to Tamsen. "Best I can do, ma'am."

"Why, Mr. New, that is very good. I think I recognize this as sweetflag. Now, the other one, hu hwe—"

"Missus, I'll ask around an' see if I can find out."

"Are you sure I can't arrange a visit?"

"Ma'am, it don't pay to get too close to them Injuns. They might just hold you fer ransom. The Sioux're not too bad right now, but you never know."

After dinner we went to watch the shooting demonstration.

The Indian archers showed much skill and proficiency with the bow and arrow, attaining great distance with accuracy.

We didn't stay long as it was hot and the children soon became restless. I didn't care to hang around, even though I knew Bill Williams, one of the competitors. It was sad to observe a formerly fine mountain man reduced to a drunken fort hanger-on. There was kind of a comparison there: the present condition of Bill Williams and the past glory days of the mountain men.

That evening the men were all abuzz talking about Bill's rifle bursting as he fired at a target. "See, this is how it happened," related one of the men. "Old Bill was wantin' a new rifle. He looks at ever' rifle in the camp 'til he found one he considered the best of the bunch. Someone tried to talk him out'a the purchase, tellin' him it was a unlucky gun an' that with it the owner had accidentally shot an' prit' near killed a man an' had clipped a piece off the ear of another.

"Old Bill didn't cotton to this suggestion that he did'n know a good gun when he saw one, 'specially from a greenhorn all decked out in a brand new buckskin suit. So he says, 'See here, I've hunted an' trapped in these mountains fer sixty years an' you needn't think that you kin teach me anythin' about a rifle. Just get back under your wagon an' mend your moccasins an' don't bother me.' So he paid fer the rifle an' marked off a hundred'n fifty yards an' put up a mark. He loaded the gun heavy to see how she would carry fer the distance."

The story teller raised his arm in demonstration, pulling an imaginary trigger. "He aimed at the mark an' fired. Blowie! The rifle burst the breech, a piece a' the barrel split out, the stock blew to pieces, an' the lock flew fifty feet away. The blast knocked Ol' Williams flat on his back, full a' splinters. They thought he was dead an' carried him back in the fort. Bridger poured some whiskey down his throat an' he comes to proclaimin' that nothin' could kill him, much less a blankety-blank rifle."

The emigrants began unloading weight from the wagons, some people trying to trade off treasured relics to traders at the fort, mostly with little success. The trail was a forlorn scene of claw-footed tables, carved bureaus, and other furniture, their noble feet covered with drifts of sand.

• • •

We traveled on through plains dotted with box elders, willows, and alders. Mr. New caught up with us. He'd found an Indian woman who gave him some cures to give to Tamsen. The medicines were wrapped in squares of thin hide. Tamsen carefully unwrapped the packets, and Mr. New patiently explained what the Indian woman had told him about the use of each one.

We were passed by a steady stream of mounted Sioux warriors resplendent in war dress and paint. The Indians put the company on edge. The warriors were very interested in Virginia Reed's pony. At the fort they'd brought buffalo skins, tanned buckskin, beaded moccasins, and several horses, offering the gifts as exchange for Billy, Virginia's pony, but it was to no avail. Now, as the braves passed Virginia riding her pony, they kept pestering her. Finally, James put her in the wagon and handed her horse to one of the teamsters.

This annoyed Virginia because she enjoyed riding her pony when the wagons were moving. She was annoyed more when the Indians swarmed around the wagon to get a peek at the looking-glass that hung outside. As she was fretting about being confined to the wagon she remembered how her father had startled some Indians by pulling out his field glass with a loud click and pointing it in their direction. Virginia took the glass off its rack and whenever Indians approached the wagon she took her revenge by scaring them with the field glass.

The company stopped for the night in a depression of a ridge we had climbed in early afternoon. As supper was being prepared, an Indian man who had an imposing presence entered the camp, followed by three others. Letting fall their robes, they sat down beside the fire. They had with them their food bowls and grunted in appreciation as Tamsen filled the bowls with sweetened coffee. After everyone had eaten and the men had smoked, the Indians departed the camp.

"The older one, now," said Mr. New, "has a standin' in the tribe. He's proven himself by killing in battle, stealin' horses an' such like. That's why his face was painted black. He's killed a Pawnee an' taken a scalp. But those others, you noticed how they seemed bashful-like an' kept back? They ain't distinguished themselves yet an' they have no standin'. The Injun men're required to be great hunters, an' make war, or they can't achieve a place amongst the warriors of the tribe. An' the women requires it too. A brave without some honors is less of a man to the squaws."

"It's fascinating to observe their ways," said Mr. Stanton. "They have such a child-like nature."

"Injuns're as intrigued with the white man as the whites are with them. They're curious about things they can see an' somewhat comprehend, but they don't trouble themselves with what they can't—they just say it's 'medicine'. An Injun never has to worry himself with thinkin' things out."

Gritty billowing clouds of dust were raised by the wheels of the wagons. We noticed more and more rocky and fantastic terrain with deep ravines and chasms. As we topped a slightly higher point, we observed, far away, high mountains covered with snow.

In the ladies circle, the topic of conversation turned to the rugged scenery.

"I will be so glad when we're out of this country. It's the ugliest, most God-forsaken place I've ever been, or could even imagine," exclaimed Mrs. Dunbar.

Mrs. Dunleavy pointed towards a particularly grotesque formation. "Do y'all know what has caused the earth to be so torn up, so shook to its center?"

"No, what has done it?"

"Sin! Sin has caused these rocks to reverberate, to be upheaved that they may be eternal monuments of the curse and fall of man. These fantastic formations are symbols of Divine Wrath."

"I allow they do make you feel a little humble, the castles and domes an' all," replied one of the ladies. "But you figure it's the Injuns that done the sin you're speakin' of? I thought it was white people's sin that the Almighty cares about an' there ain't been no white people out here to speak of. That's like saying the animals sin, if'n you think it's the Injuns been doing it."

"Man's sin. All of mankind is sinners."

"I heard tell that missionaries have gone out to the Oregon country to bring the word to the poor savages there," said Mrs. Quincy.

"Seems like they should first finish the job with some of these white folks we been travelin' with. Not keepin' the Holy Sabbath like we been doin' just boils my blood," said Mrs. Dunleavy. "The Reverend is fit to be tied about it but nobody's listenin'."

"My husband is very concerned that we are proceeding too slowly," said Tamsen. "We've had so many delays of one sort or another. If we stop every Sabbath, it will put us farther behind. We must accept that there is a necessity—God will understand."

Mrs. Dunleavy was indignant. "It's in the scriptures, Mrs. Donner. You don't go against the written word or the commandments."

"Yes, ladies, thank you for the pleasant company." Tamsen excused herself from the group and walked back to camp, her chin up and her back stiff.

After leaving Fort Laramie progress became much slower. The animals were considerably weakened by the work and lack of good water and forage. We traveled only thirty-two miles in the next three days. Everyone chafed at the slow pace, aware the train was falling behind the main emigration and the days of travel before the snow would close the Sierra were getting fewer.

On the third day, just after starting off after the noon stop, Tamsen and the girls were walking a distance away from the caravan when it was noticed that the wagons had stopped. The air was so thick with dust we couldn't see what had stopped them. I could sense that Tamsen was uneasy.

She called to Elitha and Leanna. "Girls, let's go back."

As we waited for Elitha and Leanna to come up, George

came running toward us, shouting, pointing to the wagons. Everyone started to run. As we got to George, he grabbed up Eliza, Tamsen pulled Georgeanna along, calling back to Elitha and Leanna to help Frances.

"Hurry! Get under the wagons!" George yelled.

As we neared the wagons we felt a throbbing in the air that turned into a vibration of the earth. People in the train were screaming. George pointed toward the north where a huge yellow-brown cloud was bearing down on us.

"Oh, my God, a buffalo stampede," cried Tamsen. "They're going to come through the wagons."

The noise was incredible as the mass of huge beasts pounded toward the wagons. A wagon was knocked over and the oxen were swept under the thundering bodies. Everyone scrambled under the wagons, choking from the dust, hearts pounding heavily. The ground shook violently.

Our oxen were frantic—bucking and yanking in the bows, causing the wagon to jerk forward and sideways, forcing the family to scramble on all fours to stay underneath.

A crazed buffalo ran between the wagon we were under and the next one, smashing against the pole of the wagon, splintering it. The huge beast collapsed on its front legs only a few feet from us, bellowing horribly as it struggled to get up, pushing itself forward with its hind legs. The oxen, now released, frantically pulled each other one way and then another, dragging part of the broken pole behind them. We were so stricken by fear and shock that it was a few minutes before we realized that the din was receding and the trembling of the ground had moved off.

We heard gunshots very close. We crawled out from underneath the wagon, and saw several of our company standing over the heaving and groaning buffalo that had ran between the wagons.

"Mr. Donner," said Noah, "he broke his front legs on that pole, an' the pole's a goner."

"Well, it could have been a lot worse. We saw a wagon break up right before they hit us. Let's go see if we can help."

The men came back with bad news. The owner of the wagon had been killed while attempting to turn the beasts away.

The women gathered around the family, a mother who had given birth a few weeks before and was feeble in health, and several children, one of whom had been injured earlier from falling under the wheels of their wagon. The mother hired one of the single men in the company to drive her wagon.

The next evening, the hired hands and single men were sunning by the stream after they'd made an attempt to wash themselves and their clothes in the tepid brown water.

"Jeez, that soap burns!" Sam Shoemaker looked at some raw sores on his legs.

"You should get Miz Donner to look at those sores. She fixed me up with some stuff, it worked good."

"Yeah … mebbe. But I got some on my butt too, and I ain't showin' her my butt!"

"An' she don't wanna see it, neither." said Noah.

Samuel pointed to a wagon down the stream where a woman and several children could be seen.

"I could'a got that job, drivin' for her, if'n I'd a wanted it," said Jim. "You know, the lady … husband got killed in the buffler stampede?"

"Well, why would you have wanted it?" asked Noah. "Mr. Donner treats you good."

"Did you see the daughter?"

"No, can't say as I did."

"A looker. Too young though. Still …"

"Who ended up with the job?" asked Denton.

"You know that man? The one that looks like a hound dog, his face? Can't think of his name."

"Oh, yeah, I know who you're speakin' of. I feel sorry for that woman, he's a lazy son-of-a-bitch."

We celebrated Independence Day at Beaver Creek, meeting up with many friends. We were quite surprised to find Mr. Bryant and Mr. Russell there. Mr. Bryant had stopped to await our party as he needed another man to fill out his company.

We feasted on buffalo meat, bread, beans, and greens. One of the ladies provided a pie made of sage hen and rabbit with a crust as light as a feather. Toasts and speeches were made, punctuated by blasts from muskets. Mr. Bryant stopped by the camp before starting out again.

"Have you made up your mind on which route you will take?" he asked George.

"We're arguin' about it, but we haven't decided one way or the other. I'm takin' a wait an' see attitude."

We lay by for two days to rest and repair, then headed out again towards the setting sun. The wagons inched along under clouds of brown dust through a barren landscape.

Most of the water that was found had a terrible taste, and was bad for the animals and the people. There were more and more dead oxen on the trail and some alive but too exhausted to continue.

Tamsen and the little girls stopped beside a dying cow. She was too weak to lift her head, but rolled her eyes as they approached. There was a note pinned on her head.

"Mother, what does the paper say?"

"That she is the best of cows and she was left to die, but if anyone wants her they may have her."

"Can we take her? You can make her well."

"No, she is too far gone." Tamsen called to Noah to stop

the wagon, and she walked to it and got the water bucket. Kneeling beside the cow, she poured water from her hand onto the cow's lolling tongue and into the corner of her mouth.

"She can't take enough to do any good. Let's pull that bush and put it over her head to shade her eyes. Then we must go on."

We were now approaching a monument known as Independence Rock.

"I was led to believe this was some gigantic mountain but it looks pretty small and tame," said Jacob. "I 'spected to see a rock so high you could hardly see its top."

"It will probably look more dramatic when we get closer. From this distance it does look small with the mountains behind it," said Tamsen. "We were supposed to be here by the fourth of July."

"I calculate that today is the fourteenth," replied Mr. Stanton. "It would be advisable to spend more time moving and less time in camp."

The wagons were spreading out, as the country was wide and mostly flat. We were now close to three other wagon companies.

A number of people in the camp were sick and the livestock too. I knew from experience that it was a combination of bad water and the effects of altitude. A body not used to exertion at high altitudes must suffer some consequences as it attempts to make an adjustment. The mountain men know of this condition and call it mountain fever. Most who have been in the mountains for a time have acclimated to it and sickness is rare.

"They seem never to suffer from sickness an' a wound that would kill one'a us don't bother them," said Noah.

"They's tough as hide leather, them boys. I mind that mountain man, Smith, was it? Cut his own leg off. He was shot by some Injun, breakin' the bones in his leg. There was nothin' to do but cut 'er off, but nobody would do it, so he ups and does it hisself. An' lived to tell about it."

"You know about that mountain man, the one that was clawed and mangled by a grizzly an' left by his friends fer dead? He made it back to civilization after months of crawlin' through the wilderness, livin' off'n bugs and rotten carcasses."

"I reckon you're thinkin' of Hugh Glass. The mountain men seem to get tough from livin' as savages. An' wasn't Jim Bridger one a' the ones that left him fer dead?"

"I allow you're right, I heard that."

"You know," said Charles, "I've observed some of these mountaineers and I marvel at how easily they lapse into being an Indian, yet the Indian does not easily become a white man."

"I mind what Toby said about Injuns," said Solomon. "He said the way they live is better'n our way, all cooped up inside a house an' never beathin' the natural air, wearin' clothes that itch and shoes that hurt your feet."

We met the Sweetwater River and followed it, coming abreast of a cleft in the mountains called Devil's Gate. A sense of urgency finally became general amongst the company, but the animals were in poor condition and could not be pushed beyond their limits.

The wagons creaked and groaned onward, swaying over ground that was sometimes rolling, sometimes flat. We came upon throngs of insects resembling the cricket. They covered the road, the wagon wheels rolling over them with a crunching sound that reminded the girls of a buggy rolling through snow. The insects flew about, clinging to clothes and hair. The girls shrieked and jumped around, trying to bat them away. Noah stopped the wagon and they got in, giggling in relief to be away from the buzzing hordes.

That night, the fires had burned down to embers and the folks were making ready for bed when a sound was heard that was not part of the desert. At first it was soft and distant, then grew louder and all heads turned when a horse and rider entered the campsite.

It was a young man by the name of Bonney, traveling east alone and bearing an open letter from Mr. Lansford Hastings directed to all emigrants on the road.

The letter invited those bound for California to concentrate their numbers and strength and take a new route that he had explored. He wrote that the distance to California would be very much shortened. Everyone gathered in our camp when word was passed that Bonney had brought a letter from Mr. Hastings.

"George," said Mr. Reed, "this is a practicable route for us. Time is getting short. It makes no sense to take a round-about course."

"Well, it might be. I'm going to reserve judgment until we meet up with Hastings."

"George," exclaimed Tamsen, "everyone we've talked to has said there's no wagon road. It's got to take more time if a road has to be made. Why take a chance on an unproven short-cut?"

"I expect we'll have plenty of time to decide."

"There's no advantage in going the longer way," insisted James. "Mr. Hastings has been over the route and will guide us. There'll be less worry about running out of provisions. Let's not let the nattering of nervous women affect our better judgment."

Tamsen's mouth tightened and she looked at George. He got up, stretching his back and flexing his arms several times.

"Mother, I think we'd better turn in. James, there's good to be said about stickin' to a known road. I'll keep an open mind. We got a long ways to go before we have to make a decision."

Tamsen hung the lantern on the outside of the tent and crawled inside beside George.

"George, I just have a premonition about this that keeps me fretful—"

"Honey, I respect your feelin's. Let's not worry over this any more until we get to Fort Bridger." George grunted as he pulled off his shoes. "I'm worried 'bout that brown ox, he's mighty weak. I'm lookin' to buy one or two at Bridger."

A wolf howled in the distance and an answering call came very close by. They heard the sound of a child whimpering. Tamsen crawled out from the tent.

"It's Eliza. She's terrified of the wolves. I'll have to sleep with her in the wagon."

In the morning George perched Eliza on his knee. "Don't worry 'bout those wolves, honey, they aren't going to bother us here in camp. They ain't goin' to hurt you."

"Papa, you're not supposed to say ain't."

"Now who told you that?"

"Soon we'll be on the crest of the Rocky Mountains. From

there on, the streams will be running west. Surely we'll have better water," said Tamsen.

"How long since we left home?" asked Frances.

"Forever," said Leana.

"Hmm. Let me think," said Tamsen. "Today is the nineteenth of July. It's been three months, about half our journey."

"You mean we have three more months to go?" cried Elitha. "I'm tired of the dust, the horrible water, and the same food."

"Are you also sick of the dancing and singing and merriment with all your friends at night?" asked Leanna. "And all that sparking from Charles and Laon?"

"What sparkin'?" asked George.

"Leanna, shut up!" yelled Elitha.

"Didn't you like the berry pie? And the onion stew was a change, wasn't it, Elitha?" asked Tamsen.

"It gave me the trots."

"Yeah, me too, honey," said George, "but the life we'll have in California will make up for these little discomforts."

[Charles Stanton]
South Pass, July 19, 1846

> *A week's hard travel from the date of my last letter on the Sweet Water, has brought us to this most interesting point in our route. Yesterday at noon we arrived at the "culminating point," or dividing ridge between the Atlantic and Pacific. In every step thus far there has been something new, something to attract ... should the remainder of my journey be as interesting, I shall be abundantly repaid for the toils and hardships of this arduous trip....*

> *In the morning, Saturday, we got an early start, and drove about ten or twelve miles and "nooned" without finding water for our cattle. This place was on a ridge.*

There was a large table mound on our left, covering an area of about a mile square ... the wind was strong from the west, and the day quite cold.

... we passed Bogg's company on the Sweet Water— a mile further up, Dunlavy's—a mile further, West's—and about two miles beyond that was Dunbar's. We encamped about midway between the two latter. Thus, within five miles were encamped five companies. At Indian Creek, 20 miles from Independence, these five companies all constituted one, but owing to desertions and quarreling, they became broken into fragments; and now by accident we all again once more meet and grasp the cordial hand—old enmities are forgotten and good feeling prevails....

After our usual delay we were again on the road ... and came to a fine spring, with the grass looking green about it but found no wood or water; and it was not till the middle of the afternoon, that we reached a small stream where we encamped. This stream was of a swift current and sandy color, and its general course was westward. This surprised the most of us, as now they were willing to acknowledge that they had crossed the dividing ridge without knowing. But it was true. The place where we had "nooned" the day before ... was the first water that flows westward.

• • •

It was near the Little Sandy that the four wagons of the Breen family joined our caravan. With Patrick and Margaret Breen were their seven children and their friend, Patrick Dolan. The children were the first to get acquainted.

Levinah Murphy straightened up from the fire and gazed out across the plain, swatting a swarm of gnats and mosquitos away from her face. Her attention turned to her eight year old son, Simon, as he approached the camp. *I need to get him to the stream and wash off some of that dirt.* Then she noticed the other boys with him.

"Mother, these are my new friends. This is Patrick, and that's Simon. He has the same name as me."

Simon pointed to the four wagons that had pulled next to the Murphy camp earlier. "That's their camp over there. They have a pony and Patrick said maybe I can ride it sometime."

The older of the two boys nodded his head.

Simon's brother, William, had been on his knees breaking up wood but he got up and moved to stand beside Simon, staring at the new friends.

Simon shrugged his shoulders, as though he needed to make an excuse for having a brother. "This is Will. He's ten."

The two boys nodded in William's direction. "Patrick's older'n you, he's eleven already," said Patrick's younger brother. The age-old challenge, boy to boy. Older'n you.

"Well, look," said Patrick, "c'mon with us and you can meet my folks."

"I'll come too," said Levinah. "Wait, I need to change my apron."

"Naw, it's o.k.," said Simon Breen, "Ma's apron's dirtier than yours."

Levinah liked Margaret at once. *There's a stern set to her mouth but softness in her eyes and face,* was Levinah's first thought. Patrick Breen looked tired, with baggy dark circles under deep set eyes in a high cheek-boned, narrow-jawed face. Levinah guessed that he was in his fifties, and wondered how he would hold up on the journey because he didn't look real strong. *Mrs. Breen seems so hale and hearty to have all these kids, a nursing babe and no female help at all.*

"Where're y'all from?" asked Levinah. "I hear a brogue and I suspect that it's Irish."

"Yes, my husband and I were both born in Ireland. We immigrated to Canada, and then to the States. Our last home was near Keokuk, in the Iowa Territory," replied Mrs. Breen.

"Are y'all fer Oregon or California?" asked Levinah.

"California, God willing," said Patrick.

Levinah looked at Patrick Dolan, thinking he was a nice looking man with a pleasant manner. She had a brief thought that maybe he was a prospect as a husband, but her second thought was of all the young, pretty girls in the company that would be far more likely than a thirty-six year-old widow to catch his eye.

"And, Mr. Dolan, are you also from Ireland?"

"Yes, ma'am."

"Mr. Breen, you might be interested to know that tomorrow evenin' they're planning to hold a meetin' to elect a captain. It's at the wagons of Mr. Donner." Levinah pointed across the camp. "See the blue—well, used to be blue—wagon with the man in the red shirt standin' beside it? That's his camp. Y'all are welcome."

"Thank you," replied Patrick Breen, "we'll come."

Some people attending the meeting, like the Donners, still had not made up their minds whether to follow the new route. They would continue on to Fort Bridger and make a decision upon reaching that outpost.

Others, both those to California and those to Oregon, would take Sublette's Cut-off to Fort Hall the next day. After Fort Hall they would decide to branch off to the southwest to California or proceed northwest to Oregon. Those going to Bridger would still be able to turn north on the old trail to Fort Hall.

When the wagons for Oregon turned off on the right, sorrowful good-byes were said. We watched the line of white topped wagons going off through the sagebrush-dotted desert, appearing and disappearing in the rolling landscape.

We'd been on the road only a short time when we were forced to pull around a stopped wagon, our team almost walking over a woman on the side of the road. She was crying and wailing piteously. It seemed that the woman was distressed and angry, refusing to continue, trying to hold her children with her.

Some men came up and put the children in the wagon. Then the husband drove off, leaving his wife sitting there. Some of the women tried to console her, but the woman's mind was deranged and they could do nothing for her.

George was exasperated. "Tamsen, you can't do anythin' for that woman. Her husband's at the end of his rope dealin' with her craziness."

"That poor soul," exclaimed Betsey. "She came to our camp last night, talkin' crazy, walkin' around like she didn't know where she was. I know what set her off. They was travelin' with her folks an' her daughter's family, an' they'd decided for Oregon an' they aimed to turn off to Fort Hall. The woman's husband said no, he was goin' to California. She couldn't bear to part with her daughter an' the little granddaughter an' the rest of her folks."

As we approached the evening camp we saw a wagon burning, the same family of the left-behind wife. There were several men helping to put out the blaze so we went on looking for a good spot away from the crowd.

That evening George reported the news about the unfortunate family.

"That woman got up, cut across the country, an' when her husband came up she tol' him she'd knocked her oldest child in the head with a rock when he'd come back to get a horse. The man believed her a'course, she'd been actin' so strange, so he took off to go back an' find the boy. When he left she set fire to the wagon. It burned the cover and some store goods."

"Was the child hurt badly?"

"No, he hadn't even seen his ma."

"She's likely goin' to come to her senses now or get another flogging," said Jacob.

"He beat her?"

"What else could he do?" answered Jacob.

"I know how that woman feels," said Betsey. "Her husband told her they'd be with her family so she'd agree to go an' then he ups and takes off for California instead. Don't you men think he should keep his word?"

"If'n he decides a thing, it's the duty of his wife to go along with it without making a fuss an' causing trouble fer him. I'd do the same thing," said Jacob.

"Not if I'm your wife, Jacob Donner, an' if'n you tried, I'd do more than burn your damn wagon!"

Jacob tapped Tamsen on the knee with a stick he was fiddling with. "Mrs. Donner, didn't you just hear Betsey utter a curse word? Git on yer high horse, woman!"

Tamsen hadn't been paying attention to the talk. Of late, she'd been moody and preoccupied.

Charles Stanton came to talk to George. "It's necessary that a captain be elected. Most of us feel that you are the best qualified."

"Most venerable perhaps," George replied, "qualified, no. That post requires a man that don't care about bein' nice to people, that can hold himself away from formin' friendships. You'll have no friends once you agree to take the job."

"I agree, the position is a thankless one. If you don't take it, who do you feel would be a good man for the job?"

"Well, James has been leading our group most of the time. He's proven himself as a leader in the war."

"Or so he says. I wouldn't know about that. I do know that

he is not liked by some in our group."

"I think it's mostly jealousy, Charles."

"Perhaps, but he has an attitude that rubs people the wrong way. He won't be accepted as leader."

Margaret Reed was sitting in her "parlor" doing needlework with Patty an eager student. Virginia didn't like to do anything involved with sewing.

"Virginia, I certainly hope you find a wealthy man to marry," said Margaret. "You'll have to have a seamstress do all your sewing and mending."

"You had a seamstress make our clothes."

"Yes, there's not many men as well off as your father."

The canvas door was pushed back and James cursed as he stubbed the toe of his shoe on the sill. "Damn!" He looked at the scrape disgustedly, then sat down across from Margaret, tapping his fingers on his knees. She was slow to see that he was agitated.

"James, the girls shouldn't hear such—"

James held up his hand. "I'm sorry. I'm upset. Can you guess what just happened?"

"No, what? At the meeting?"

"Yes. The idiots just elected George leader."

"I thought he wouldn't take it."

"Well, they insisted, and he did."

"He's not a good leader, James. He's too soft with people. You would be a much better captain."

"I would. But several are dead set against me, especially those Germans that all hang together. In actuality—and George and I talked about it—he'll have the designation as captain, but in truth, I will help make the decisions."

"What if George decides for Fort Hall—he doesn't take Mr. Hastings' route?"

"He'll take it—if he doesn't give in to Tamsen. He's got to

stand up and be a man! Why he allows Tamsen to lead him around by the nose I'll never understand."

"I don't think that's true at all, James. He gives her credit for having a mind, and if you ask me, more of a mind than most of the men." James frowned. "Of course, I don't mean you, James."

A discussion on the same subject was being carried on in the George Donner tent.

"George, you said—"

"An' at the time I meant it. But who do you think could take the job an' carry it out? James would be a good leader because he feels superior anyway, but the people flat don't like him an' most likely wouldn't take direction from him. He knows it, we talked about it. An' really, the position is in name only. James will take responsibility too."

"But, George, now you're going to feel duty bound to stay with James and he's going to follow that Mr. Hastings. I just have a bad feeling about it. Something is weighing heavily on me. I am very apprehensive. George, I just don't want to go off on that unknown route. It will be a mistake."

"Honey, you know I respect what you feel, but godamighty, why're we talkin' about it, nobody's made the decision yet. We just got to wait until we talk to people at Bridger, find out more. Will you quit frettin'?"

Just before nooning the next day we spotted a dust cloud on the horizon. As it drew nearer we could make out a large group of horses. The wagons stopped and gathered up, thinking it might be Indians. Men on horseback went out in advance of the train and reported back.

"It ain't Injuns, it's some men drivin' horses."

The man in charge of the horse herd was Joseph Walker, a man I knew well from my days in the mountains. A fur man early on, he'd worked for Bonneville who'd sent him to California to explore the country and look for beaver.

Walker signaled his riders to keep pushing the herd and rode over to our stopped wagons, dismounting stiffly. His horse had the skittishness of a half-broke mustang. Joe's face had been burned by wind and sun into dark brown leather, his red-rimmed blue eyes the only color other than the gray-brown desert dust that covered him from head to toe.

"I'm Joe Walker. I ran into some of yer feller travelers," he said, jerking his thumb to the west, "back at Fort Bridger. You'd best hurry along, they're formin' up."

"Seems like I've heard of you, Mr. Walker. I'm George Donner. Do you have time to stop and palaver just a bit?"

George dipped a cup of water from the water bucket in the wagon, handed it to Walker and then introduced him around the group that had formed.

"You drive those horses all the way from California?" Mr. Pike asked Walker.

"Yes, sir. I was with Captain Frémont there. I got disgusted with what was goin' on an' decided to get in the horse acquiring business. There's thousands a' horses in California, runnin' wild."

"You know anythin' of the short-cut route that Hastings is talkin' up?"

"Mr. Donner, I've been asked that question several times from people I been passin' on the road. I'll tell you the same thing I told them. It's rough country, some of it without water. Indian trails, mebbe, but sure as hell no wagon road."

"Did you see Hastings?"

"He's back at Bridger, gatherin' up wagons."

Mr. Walker tipped his hat to the ladies, placed one hand on his saddle and swung up, the saddle leather squeaking under his weight. His horse danced sideways and then bolted away, a plume of dust rolling up behind.

It was only an hour or two later that a group of Shoshoni Indians, returning from a buffalo hunt, overtook us. They'd been told by someone on the trail that the Sioux were singing war songs against them and they were making haste westward.

THE MISSOURI REPUBLICAN
A Letter From An Emigrant To A Friend in St. Louis
Fort Bridger, July 23, 1846

The letter ... was brought in by Capt. Walker, who was returning from California.

At Fort Laramie, col. Russell and many others of the emigrants, sold off their wagons, and with a pack containing a few articles, pursued their journey on horseback.... Col. Russell and his party, by hard travelling, reached Fort Bridger two or three days before the others, but his horses had their backs badly worn, and he remained there four days to recruit. At that place they were met by Mr. Hastings, from California, who came out to conduct them in by the new route, by the foot of Salt Lake, discovered by capt. Fremont, which is said to be two hundred miles nearer than the old one, by Fort Hall....

Fort Bridger is said to be a miserable pen, occupied at times by Messrs. Bridger and Vasques, and resorted to be a number of loafing trappers to exchange furs and moccasins with the emigrants for flour, bacon and whiskey. The latter sells at two dollars a pint.

July 28, 1846
Hastings Shortcut

Fort Bridger was a small trading post established by Jim Bridger and his partner, Luis Vasquez. It consisted of three crude log structures, redeemed somewhat by a beautiful setting in a fertile valley with clumps of cottonwood trees along the stream. I knew both men from my days in the mountains. Jim was highly regarded amongst the men in the mountains, Vasquez not so much so.

Our wagons made a circle some distance from the fort. After the animals were looked after and things put in order, the men walked to the fort. There was a group of men lounging by the gate. As we neared them, a man stepped out of the group and approached us.

"How come y'all are so late gettin' here? That Hastings feller already been and gone. He took 'bout sixty wagons of emigrators out a' here a week ago."

"The hell you say! He promised to wait. Now how can we find our way through there?" cried Jacob.

"He left word fer the people on the trail to follow after him.

If you hurry along, you might catch up. But if I was you, I'd just go on up to Fort Hall. Take the old trail, you'll be better off."

George stopped to talk, but James pushed past him to go inside the fort. "Let's go in and talk with Mr. Bridger."

The next morning, some of the women sat beneath a cottonwood tree, fanning away flies and insects that buzzed around them. A light breeze rustled the leaves of the trees, wafting fragrance from the grasses and flowers that carpeted the meadow.

Tamsen made a quick swipe at a fly with her fan, knocking it to the ground where it buzzed upside down in a circle.

"At least we're not besieged by gnats like we were yesterday," said Mrs. Murphy.

A huge crow circled overhead and then coasted down, landing lightly. With a stiff-legged hop he came close, side-stepping, first one way and then another, twisting his head around and staring at the fly still buzzing at Tamsen's feet. Two more crows spoke their caak-caaks from branches overhead. The first crow looked up, twisted his head around and flew off.

The crows give me such a morbid feeling, thought Tamsen. *They remind me of when Tully was buried. Crows were in the trees near the grave ... and when we buried our little boy, too. North Carolina seems so very far away now. I'll never be able to visit their graves again ...*

Mrs. Murphy tapped Tamsen on her shoulder with her fan, startling her from her reverie. "Mrs. Donner, is your husband goin' to hold a meetin' this evening about takin' the new route? I'm confused about what to do."

"Everyone is confused. I believe there will be a meeting after supper."

"What is Mr. Donner proposing that we do?"

"Most of the men in our group are for following Mr. Hastings. I wish that we weren't but they seem to be set on it."

"Well, they aren't always right, but a woman had best not question them, it kind of puts their teeth on edge. My husband, bless his soul, couldn't stand for me to even make a suggestion. I always had to work my way around it."

"Don't you think they know best?" said Margaret Reed. "I know that James—"

Margaret's impending discourse was interrupted by several of the children running towards the group, swinging pails filled with berries.

Tamsen stood, picking up her chair to carry back to the wagon. "I see the children have found some berries. Maybe we'll have enough for pies to share around this evening."

When Margaret Reed and Eliza returned to their wagon they found James writing a letter. He looked up at their approach.

"Margaret, if you want to write to back home, this is the last place we can leave a letter. At least with any assurance it will be carried east."

"If you're writing to Springfield, then I don't really need to," Margaret replied.

James looked at Eliza. "Do you want me to write something for you to send back?"

"Naw, me an' Baylis, we ain't got nobody." Eliza began tying her skirt up around her legs. "I'm gonna go pick some berries."

"Eliza! Don't go around showing your legs like that," cried Margaret. "You don't have a lick of sense."

"Ma'am, you want this last dress to get all tattered up? It's fallin' apart as it is." Eliza glared at Margaret, picked up a bucket and went off.

"Oh, what I have to put up with," moaned Margaret.

James completed his letter and walked over to the fort to leave it with Jim Bridger.

Fort Bridger, one hundred miles from the Eutaw or Great Salt Lake, July 31, 1846.

We have arrived here safe with the loss of two yoke of my best oxen. They were poisoned by drinking water in a little creek called Dry Sandy ... Jacob Donner also lost two yoke and George Donner a yoke and a half ... The new road, or Hastings' Cut-off, leaves the Fort Hall road here and is said to be a savings of 350 or 400 miles in going to California, and a better route. There is, however, or thought to be, one stretch of 40 miles without water; but Hastings and his party, are out ahead examining for water, or for a route to avoid this stretch. I think that they cannot avoid it, for it crosses an arm of the Eutaw Lake, now dry ... there is plenty of grass which we can cut and put into the wagons for our cattle while crossing it.

We are now only 100 miles from the Great Salt Lake by the new route—in all 250 miles from California; while by way of Fort Hall it is 650 or 700 miles—making a great savings in favor of jaded oxen and dust. On the new route we will not have dust, as there are but 60 wagons ahead of us. The rest of the Californians went the long route, feeling afraid of Hastings' Cut-Off. Mr. Bridger informs me that the route we design to take is a fine level road, with a plenty of water and grass, with the exception before stated. It is estimated that 700 miles will take us to Capt. Sutter's fort.

I have fine times in hunting grouse, antelope or mountain goat, which are plenty. Milford Elliott, James Smith and W. Herron, the young men who drive for me, are careful, first rate drivers, which gives me time for hunting. We are beyond the range of buffalo. The independent trappers, who swarm here during the passing of the emigrants, are as great a set of sharks as ever disgraced humanity, with few exceptions. Let the emigrants avoid trading with them. Vasquez & Bridger are the only fair traders in these parts.

James F. Reed

James talked with Bridger for a few minutes, then stopped in the trade store and bought a few items, including some sweets for his children. When he left, Jim Bridger went to the blacksmith shop to find Luis Vasquez.

"I still got that letter Mr. Bryant left here for those people— Reed 'n Donner. He tol' me he was tellin' them not to take the new route. Should I go ahead an' give it to them?"

"Hell, no. How does Bryant leave off tellin' them not to go? This route gets developed, we get more emigrants through here. Business has been bad since Sublette opened up that cut-off. Reed's got a lot of influence, if he goes, others will too."

The debate raged within the camp. That evening the children were put to bed and the group gathered around the fire. It was cold. The women covered themselves with their shawls, the men hunched up in their homespun coats.

A breeze was blowing and the fire glowed and died and glowed again as the wind played with it, the orange light flickering on the solemn faces of those assembled around it. George started the discussion.

"Y'all know there are sixty wagons ahead of us breakin' the trail, led by this Hastings fellow. Time is getting' short an' this here route may cut many days off our travel. The men here at the fort say there's a forty-mile stretch without water but with good plannin' we can overcome that."

"Do you remember what Mr. Clyman said?" asked Mr. Stanton. "He was against it in no uncertain terms."

John Denton spoke up. "That other bloke that came through, the one that had been with Mr. Frémont, he spoke unfavorably of the route too."

"Sublette? I heard he told Cap'n Davis that the southern way of goin' was the same miles as goin' north an' had sixty miles of desert."

"No, it warn't Sublette."

"You must be thinkin' of Joe Walker," said Noah. "He's the man we met drivin' those horses. It's said of Walker that he don't follow trails, he makes 'em."

"Walker's a puke and a thief, stole those horses from the Mexicans. You can't trust what a man like that says," someone exclaimed.

"Walker's well thought of. Who are you callin' him a puke anyway?"

"Now, let's keep to the subject," said George. "Hastings is openin' this route an' we can follow him. It's already late in the season an' we still have more'n a thousand miles to go."

Tamsen spoke up. "If we go the old route we will still arrive at the peak of the Sierras in mid-October, in plenty of time before the snows. Everyone we ask about the new route is against it, except for these men at the fort, and of course, Mr. Hastings. Their motives are questionable. Why take a chance on the unproven?"

George cleared his throat and shifted his feet nervously. "Yes, there is another side to this. We can head north and go by Fort Hall. It's a longer route, but a proven one."

"One of the hanger-ons at the fort was tellin' me Hastings had some kind of a arrangement with Bridger an' Vasquez— Hastings is wantin' to get men in California to help fight for independence from Mexico an' Bridger an' Vasquez is wanting more emigrants to pass by the fort. He said business has been slow since the cut-off was opened."

James stood up and took a few steps back and forth, placed one foot on a log and leaned forward. "I am going to follow the new route. There is said to be a savings of three to four hundred miles and a better route. And we won't have the terrible dust since there are but sixty wagons ahead of us. And another thing we need to think about is that some are getting low on provisions."

"It would be good to get away from the dust," said Mrs. Murphy.

Mr. Stanton leaned forward, pushing a piece of wood into the fire with his foot. "Provisions can be bought here at the post."

James made a gesture of exasperation. "The prices are exorbitant. These traders here will take your last penny in trade." He took his foot off the log and sat down again. "I grant you, there are some difficulties, but I think we can make Sutter's fort in seven weeks from this day."

"Whoopee! Only seven more weeks!" exclaimed Mr. Pike. "I'm all for that. No more sleeping on the ground, eating dust, dying of thirst and all the other things that have been so intolerable. Mother Murphy, what do you think?"

"I'm all for cuttin' off some miles. Our animals are 'bout to give out an' we're runnin' short on some of our provisions."

"Aye, it hae the ring of reason," said Mr. Breen. "With yon party makin' the road, we'll not have the problem gettin' through the mountains. I have provisions enough, but a shortnin' of the journey is welcome."

George stood up. "Y'all make your decision. The Donner an' Reed wagons are goin' to follow Hastings' party."

The fateful decision was made. The next day the wagons left Fort Bridger. Under the captaincy of George Donner were now 74 people in a caravan of nineteen wagons. We'd picked up some additional people at the Little Sandy and Fort Bridger: A Mexican named Antonio; the son of a French trapper and a Mexican mother, Juan Baptiste Trudeau; William McCutchen and wife Amanda with a baby daughter; and a consumptive man, Luke Halloran. Mr. Halloran had been in the Russell party and was left at Fort Bridger by his companions, too sick to proceed. Tamsen felt sorry for him, and he was placed in one of the Donner wagons.

There was a group that tended to camp with the Keseberg

family—now a family of four since Mrs. Keseberg had given birth—who were mostly of German heritage. In the group, a seemingly wealthy couple, Mr. and Mrs. Wolfinger, and Karl Burger, their driver; Augustus Spitzer; Joseph Reinhardt, and an elderly man from Belgium, Mr. Hardcoop.

Juan Baptiste had come to Fort Bridger with a man named Hudspeth, who was now with the Hastings group. He'd told Tamsen that he'd been with Frémont, but had left the group at the Green River, tired of the hard work and less than kind treatment. He'd gone to different families in the company asking for work in exchange for food and a way to California, but so far had been turned down.

There had been desperation in his manner when he'd approached George, his mouth dry from apprehension and fear. Baptiste looked European, with a wide brow, deep-set eyes, long narrow nose and a sparse moustache. He wore a coat of fringed buckskin, in the manner of the mountains, and carried a rolled-up Indian blanket.

"Have you traveled in the country south and west of here at all?" George asked him.

"No, *Señor* Donner, I no travel that country. I no think it a good idea, but if that is the way you will go, it is my wish that I go with you. I will trust in *Dios*."

George chuckled. "Yeah, we will too. How old are you?"

"I have sixteen years, *quizas* seventeen. *Mi Abuela*, she lost the count. I am a man. I know the ways of the *animales* an' I know the hand-talk of the Indians in the country you will cross. I will be of much use to you."

"Well, look, you don't look like you'll eat very much—you might turn out to be a bargain," said George. He looked down at the worn-out sandals on Juan Baptiste's feet.

"Son, you've got to have somethin' better on your feet."

George went to his goods wagon, rummaged around in the boxes and came back with two pairs of brogans. "One of these is likely to fit you."

"Am I to go with you then?" asked Juan Baptiste.

"Yeah. You can help Mrs. Donner, whatever she wants you to do, an' you can help the other men with the livestock."

"Which wagon will carry my pack?"

George pointed to the supply wagon and Juan Baptiste threw his blanket roll into the back.

The wagons creaked and groaned their way past a remarkable butte and the northward turn of the road which headed for Fort Hall. We were following Hastings' two-line trace heading south and west.

Wagon covers snapped in a stiff breeze that peppered wagons, beasts and people with gritty sand. The emanations of energy were diverse. Most of the people were excited, anticipating the end of the journey, but Tamsen was gloomy and dispirited, convinced that following the Hastings route would be a mistake.

Tamsen, with the little girls, lingered at the turn-off, gazing off to the north. Georgia tugged on her sleeve.

"Mother, the wagons are leaving us."

Tamsen sighed. "Well, we can't go to California by ourselves, can we? Come along girls, it's a fine day, let's enjoy it."

By that time I knew the fate of these people and I had seen what was before them. They had no way to know what factors were working to change their lives forever. They headed into an unknown, thinking it was known. By that time I was such a part of them that I could not leave them even had I wanted to.

• • •

The country took on a more favorable aspect as we crossed several plains which had good grass. The bordering hills had bright green patches of growth with clumps of aspens in the hollows.

Not too far from Fort Bridger, one of the Breen boys, Edward, suffered a broken leg. He and Patty Reed were running their ponies when his horse stepped into an animal burrow and took a hard fall. Edward was thrown from the pony, knocked senseless, his leg broken between the ankle and the knee.

Someone was sent back to the fort to fetch help, and after a long time a bearded mountain man appeared riding a mule. He dismounted, removing a small rolled-up canvas pack from the back of his saddle.

"How'ye, they call me Jim," he said. "Whar's the one with the broken leg?"

Mr. Breen pointed to where Edward had been placed on a pallet in the shade of his family's wagon. Jim ambled over to the wagon and peered down at Edward, who was wide-eyed in apprehension.

Jim looked at Mrs. Breen, who was kneeling at Edward's side, then to the people standing around. He spit a stream of tobacco juice on the dusty ground. "Wal, git the boy up on a wagon gate," he said, as he unrolled the bundle, taking out a meat saw and a long bladed knife.

Mrs. Breen didn't like the looks of this rough man. "Mister," she asked in a shaky voice, "have you experience in doctorin' a break like this? Have you any surgical trainin'?"

"Har! Surgical trainin'? A'course I have." He looked defiantly around the group. "I've killed an' skinned out mebbe a hunnert buffler an' as many deer, to say nothin' of all t'other game. I've done more cuttin' on animals an' folks than nine out'a ten surgeons. I've cut arrows out'a people many times an' cleaned up bad wounds a'one kind or 'nother. I opine I've more experience than any ye so-called doctors."

Jim glared at the assemblage, wiping his mouth and looking down for the chaw that had fallen from his mouth during his indignant oration. Pushing dirt over the chaw with his moccasined foot, he pointed to the back of the wagon.

"Git him up thar, I ain't got all day. Missus, you needs to git those pants off him, jes cut 'em off, it'll hurt him less."

Edward commenced to pitch a fit as the man approached him with his tools. "No! Let me be! No. Ma, no!"

He howled louder as they lifted him to the wagon gate. Someone brought a flask of whiskey which Jim commandeered, taking a long swig and then holding it to Edward's mouth.

"Here, young'un, this'll help ye stand the cuttin'."

Eddie's cries were pitiful. "Get him away from me! No! No! I don't want it, I don't want it."

Margaret became more nervous, her normally soft and musical voice becoming screechy. "Aye, Patrick, the boy is terrified. Maybe it's not the thin' to do."

Finally, not having any confidence in the dirty rough looking mountain man, they told him they would let the boy have his way. They gave Jim five dollars and sent him back to the fort, stiff with indignation that he wasn't allowed to demonstrate his skills.

Margaret asked Tamsen if she would help with the straightening of the boys leg.

"Clean his leg well with the whiskey. I have a medicine for broken bones. I'll be back in a few minutes."

By the time she returned, Mr. Breen had made splints. Tamsen gave Edward some willow bark to chew and gently pulled off his trousers. She'd brought scissors, but Mrs. Breen had wanted to save the trousers if it wouldn't hurt Edward a lot to take them off. Edward was embarrassed and tried to cover his privates with his shirt. Tamsen began to spread a salve on the boy's leg.

"What is that you're puttin' on?" Margaret asked.

"This salve is made from a root that Mr. New obtained for me from an Indian healer. He told me that his partner had been treated with it when he'd broken his leg and it seemed to effect a cure. There's no harm in trying it."

Tamsen placed a pillow under Edward's head. "I think we'll wait to give the salve a chance to work. Keep chewing on that willow bark. We'll straighten your leg and bind it up in a few minutes."

"Is it gonna hurt?"

"Yes, but perhaps not a lot. I was told the salve will relax your leg. You might even become sleepy."

Georgia and Eliza edged up to the wagon gate, Frances behind. Eliza was too little to see Edward, so Frances put her arms around her waist and lifted her up. Eliza patted Edward on his arm.

"Does it hurt a lot?"

He turned his tear-streaked face towards the girls. "It's not so bad. Is that man gone?"

"Your mother sent him away. Our mother's a healer," said Georgia. "She'll help you."

"Girls, go back to our wagons and tell Father we can't go on today. We'll need to make camp."

When Tamsen returned to our camp she told of Edward's treatment.

"It's fortunate that the bone had not broken through the skin. It was painful for him, but easier than I expected."

"Do you think we can move on tomorrow?" asked George.

"Yes. They've placed Edward on a hammock arrangement in their wagon. He'll be jostled some, but he'll be fairly comfortable."

Edward suffered for a time with the jolting and jerking, but in a few days he could sit up and in a month he was riding his horse again.

Baptiste proved to be very helpful. Tamsen and the little girls became very fond of him, and he with them. He liked to tell them stories and show them things when they were walking. One day they saw two lodge poles lying on the ground.

"*Señora* Donner, a company of Shoshone Indians, they go this way. They were in much hurry."

"How do you know?"

"You see the poles for the lodges? The poles no easy to find an' they have much value. The Indians they move fast, their soldiers no let them stop for the poles that drop off from the travois. You see the dung of their horses? It is much scattered an' that means the horses are moving fast. I think they get away from other Indians. The people, they move with all the village, the women an' children an' the old ones."

"How can you tell they are Shoshone?"

"I see the tracks of moccasins. Each kind of Indian, they have ways of doing things. The way they make the moccasins, even so."

Juan Baptiste turned to the girls. "Little ones, do you know the hand talk that mean the Snake Indians?" Baptiste moved his right hand in an up and down waving motion. "See, it is like a snake moving. If I want to tell you that I saw a Snake Indian, I do this." He placed two fingers outward from his eyes. "You see, *niñas*? I know something more. Soon we are going to have rain."

Frequently we were bothered by squalls of rain and when the clouds lifted, we could see snow on the mountains.

We crossed the Little Muddy, camping in a valley covered with fine grass and clumps of cottonwood trees and willows. At one point we descended into a narrows enclosed by high yellow and red cliffs and lost the road. At the end of the hollow was an impassable barrier of red sandstone and the company had to reverse course to find the road again. Ascending a high elevation on the left, we passed through a plain with sage so thick it was difficult to force a way through.

Entering a deep and broad valley the road took a southwesterly course for two or three miles, passed through a gorge and came to the Bear River. The river bottom was well covered with grass, and everyone marveled at the blue fields of wild flax. After a difficult ford over a very uneven and rocky river bed Tamsen asked George if they could stop and camp.

"Mr. Clyman said there was good trout in this river. It would be so good to have the fresh food."

George looked down the line of wagons, some still waiting to ford the river. "Yeah, time everybody gets over ... might as well. But who do you think's gonna catch the fish?"

"I will, if I have to."

The children were sent out to catch grasshoppers to use as bait, and several people went to the stream to fish. There were numerous sagehens in the area and quite a few were bagged before supper.

We traveled over ridges where the western slopes were abrupt and precipitous. The wagons were eased down, skittering and bumping over the rough terrain, rocks and dirt bouncing down the slope. Then the wagons clattered and jolted over rocks littering the floor of the canyon. Red cliffs towered on each side. The sounds of people talking, the clatter of hooves, and the blows of hammers as wheels were tightened echoed back and forth across the defile.

After leaving the canyon we followed the trail along a stream for several miles. The lead wagons halted. George went forward to see what had happened.

"We found this paper stuck in a bush," said Mr. Eddy. "It seems to be from Mr. Hastings."

"Here, let me have it," said James. He read what was written, then slapped the paper against his palm in frustration. "He's telling anyone that comes through not to follow him."

"What? That can't be. We don't know any other way to go." Jacob slumped down against a wagon wheel. "He was tellin' how good a road it is an' now he's sayin' it's no good."

"The bastard," muttered Mr. Eddy.

"He says that the canyon will be too difficult for us," said James, "and to send a messenger ahead to find him. He'll return and show us a better route." James looked at George. "We'll have to decide on a course of action. Let's camp here, no point in going ahead for now."

This was the first of a series of tragic events, and I now knew it was an inexorable first step to the scene that I had witnessed in the snowy mountains of California. The fate of these people would play out in the coming weeks and there was no way to change it.

The company made camp, and that evening a meeting was held. James Reed, William Pike, and Charles Stanton volunteered to go ahead on horseback to find Hastings. We expected that they would be back in a few days, but the days dragged on into almost a week. The opportunity to rest was welcome, but everyone was anxious, thinking about how short the days were becoming until snow would start falling in the California mountains.

The first Indians that the group came across after leaving Bridger described themselves as Utah, but one man told Baptiste with hand talk that he was a Snake Indian, married to a Utah woman. Most of the Indians were armed with bows and arrows, but had among them an old rifle and musket. The ragged fellow with the musket held it out for inspection, saying *"carabina … carabina … no ke too ch, no ke too ch."*

"Carabina, es Español. I think they have the guns from traders from Mexico. This man, he wishes to trade for powder and lead."

The Indians were extremely curious about everything, especially the utensils and procedures of cooking. They made it known they expected to receive food and Tamsen prepared an antelope stew, offering some to the Indians. They tasted of it, immediately making dramatic grimaces, drawing in and blowing out their breath as though they had been burnt. They seemed to feel that a trick had been played on them.

"Oh, dear, it must have been the pepper. Baptiste, please tell them that I meant no harm."

Tamsen handed out bread and lumps of sugar which delighted the Indians and all was forgiven. The Indian women had with them cakes made of ground seeds and Tamsen traded some cloth for a basket of the cakes.

During the visit it was noticed that the females would hunt for vermin in the hair and on the bodies of the children, which upon finding, they ate with great relish. Tamsen whispered to her girls that it would be best to stay a distance away from the children. She took the basket of cakes back to her wagon and inspected the food closely.

On the fifth day the children came running to report there was a horseman coming.

"Just one man?"

"Yeah. It's not one of our horses, but the man's wearing a hat like Mr. Reed wears."

It was James Reed. He looked very tired and dejected. Everyone gathered around.

"Where're the other men?" asked George.

"Their horses gave out. The country we went through was very rough. They'll meet up with us. Milt, see to my horse."

Margaret brought water for her husband. After drinking he poured the remainder over his head, drying off with his handkerchief. He found a stick, squatted down on his heels and began to draw lines in the dust.

"This is about where we are and this is the Salt Lake. Between here and there are a maze of canyons that are steep, rocky, and filled with growth." James drew in several wavy lines and triangles to indicate mountains. "The group ahead took a route other than the one Mr. Hastings wanted while he was ahead scouting. This canyon here is the one they took."

James tapped the stick on one of the lines. "This is the canyon Hastings pointed out to me—the one I followed back. When the other men and I left here, we followed their trail through the canyon and we could see where they had trouble. That canyon is extremely narrow, in places just barely wide enough to get by on the side of the river. Other places they were into the river. They had to move huge boulders and in some places had to fill in with rocks and brush."

"I don't understand why we can't follow them. The road's made now," said Mr. Eddy.

James threw his stick aside and stood up. "What they could do and we cannot is lift the wagons up the steep cliffs. We don't have enough men to do that. Even so, they lost a wagon and two oxen over a precipice. Look, if you men want to go on up by horseback and look it over—"

"It's my opinion we haven't the time," said Eddy. "We've already lost five days sitting here."

"Hastings would only point out to me the way he thought we should go," said James. "He wouldn't come back all the way. I blazed the trail so we could find it again."

Jacob made a bitter snort. "I knew we shouldn't've hitched our wagons to that no-good Hastings."

"How much time will we lose if we go back to Bridger?" said George. "An' if we go ahead, how much time will it take? We need to study on it. We'll meet at my camp after supper."

The group gathered just before dusk, the women sitting off to the side or behind their men.

"I'm reminded of people gathered around a body waiting for the preacher to begin," murmured Betsey.

James looked around at the group. "I recommend that we proceed. It will be hard work, but with every man doing their part we can get through in a week or so. We will then pick up the trail of Hastings' company."

The men shifted around, drawing circles in the dirt with their feet, spitting into the shadows, muttering curses.

"Hastings got us into this mess. The man's a coward, not comin' back."

"I don't think we can blame Hastings," said James. "They

got through, but he knew we didn't have enough men to do the heavy work in that canyon. He was trying to help us."

"Well, I can blame him," said Mr. Eddy. "He promoted this route as if it would be easy and we believed him."

Hot arguments and purple recriminations circled the campfire, but finally everybody agreed to proceed.

It was a maze of canyons, at times leading to dead-ends. The men hacked tunnels through the dense thickets, heaving the wagons over gullies and through riverbeds thick with boulders. Wagons would be pulled up inclines and over ridges, only to face another ridge, another canyon. It was slow going.

"We're spending more time than I thought we would," James told Margaret. "Some of the men aren't doing their share, they're slackers. Those Dutchmen just sit around and wait for the way to be made, hardly lifting a hand. We didn't clear a mile today, less yesterday."

"James, my head is just splitting. Please ask Eliza to bring me some tea."

"All right. I'm going over to talk to George. Something has to be done about these men that won't work hard."

George looked up when he heard James' boots crunching on the rocky ground. "Evenin', James. Coffee?"

"Yes, thank you." James took the coffee and leaned against a wagon wheel.

"George, we've got to get everyone to do a fair share of this work. Those German men aren't putting in a full day. Today Burger stayed behind after the noon break. Then Wolfinger left the work detail and then Reinhardt."

"Well, Burger's hurting bad from that big rock that rolled on him yesterday," said George. "Tamsen thinks he might have a splintered rib. Hardcoop is old, he's too weak for this work, can't walk more'n a mile or two before he gives out. Reinhardt, now, I reckon he could do more."

"There's Spitzer," replied James. "He worked for a couple of hours yesterday and today he lay in camp. There are several others that aren't pulling the weight they should. Jacob sits down more than he works."

"Jacob is not well," said Tamsen, "but still he works as much as he's able. Betsey, her boys and I and our two girls have been working, pulling off brush and whatever we can do. You could send Baylis and Eliza to help—they can do something."

"Baylis can't work in the daytime afflicted like he is with his white skin. He does his share standing guard at night. Eliza has to help my wife. Margaret can't be expected to do the cooking and chores."

"Perhaps Virginia could help Margaret with the chores. That would free Eliza to work," said Tamsen.

James frowned in annoyance. "Women should not do this kind of work."

George tried to smooth things over. "Tamsen, the men'll get it done. There's no call for the women to work. I'll go talk to those men."

"I'll go with you," said James.

"James, I think it's best if you don't. There seems to be some hard feelin's between you and them."

"I've done nothing—"

George wearily held up his hand. "Let me do this. I'm too damn tired to argue."

The German men were eating supper. Mr. Keseberg nodded his head at George. "Greetings, Donner." He pointed to a stump and George sat down. Nobody spoke.

George cleared his throat and looked around the group.

"Well, it's been a back-breakin' job an' we got a long way to go. We're goin' to have to put in more effort. Each one has to do his share as best he's able. Now, Burger's hurtin' from yesterday. He needs to lay off for awhile. Mr. Hardcoop, I know you can't do much. Wolfinger, Keseberg, I ain't complaining, you been working like the rest of us. Spitzer, you didn't work at all today. Reinhardt, you quit early."

"You expect us to work harder than the others?" Mr. Keseberg spoke angrily. "Some of those teamster men are not working full out. And who gave Reed the job of boss-man? He stays on his horse, telling us what to do."

"Let's not get into petty bickerin'. I'll be talkin' to the rest of the men too. All we want is for everyone to do their share, best they can." George looked around the group. "What do you say?"

"Ve vill verk, but Reed and the others, they do the same verk as us," said Mr. Reinhardt.

When George returned to camp, he leaned against the wagon and watched Tamsen knead bread dough.

"I'll bake this tonight and share it around in the morning. How did it go?"

"They're all as sour as can be, but they'll do the best they can. I wish we had more men."

"James's attitude bothers me, George. He acts as if he's ordering his own workers around. He reminds me of a slave owner thinking about using his whip."

It was beastly hot in the canyon, no breeze at all. Dirt and dust from the clearing work hung in the air, choking man and beast. As the tools were gathered after the day's work, an altercation broke out between James and his men and the German men.

"Iss goot you join the peasants to verk today, Reed," said one of the men. "Oh, iss pity, you got your boots dirty."

James swung around. "Who said that?"

No one answered. James stood with his feet spread, hands tight in fists. "Are you afraid to speak to my face?"

George came up, placing his hand on James' shoulder.

"There ain't no call to get upset."

"He's right, Mr. Reed," said Milt. "Those Dutchmen aren't worth spit. They ain't worth getting' riled up about."

James wiped the sweat and dirt off his face with a handkerchief. "I'll not be braced again."

The next day some of the children came running to tell of wagons coming. Everyone gathered around, curious. In front of three wagons was a tall, raw-boned, barefoot man with a shambling walk and a face of leather.

"We was a'feared we weren't gonna catch up with you people," he called. "We were told back at Bridger you were a week or more ahead. I'm Franklin Graves, from Marshall County, Illinois."

Mr. Graves had a large family; his wife, Elizabeth, and nine children, including a married daughter and her husband, Jay Fosdick. With the family was John Snyder, a congenial young man, a neighbor of Graves. They had intended for Oregon, but changed when they got to Bridger.

The back-breaking task continued, a little easier now with the men of the Graves family added to the work force. In the evenings the men would gather, talk about the day's work and the next day's work.

"We made two miles today, seems like it's goin' a mite faster. At least I hope it is," said Milt.

"Ahh, it was only a mile-and-a-half," said John Denton. "It's wishful thinkin', man."

"Well, tomorrow evenin' we can take the wagons up, I'm thinkin'," said George. He turned to Mr. Graves. "Where you from, before Illinois? Seems like you have a New England way of talkin'."

"I'm a Green Mountain boy, born in Vermont."

"My wife is from New England, an' she picked out that you had some connection."

"That right? Where from?"

"Newburyport, Massachusetts. A blue nose from the land of steady habits."

Mr. Graves chuckled. "That's about it—but I guess I left from there too early to get a blue nose."

A section of road would be made, a mile or two or three, and then the wagons would be brought up and camp would be made again. In one canyon the wagons crossed the same stream nineteen times in five miles.

The land rose steadily, the trees becoming larger. After ascending a high ridge there could be seen, far off, over lower mountains, the valley of the Great Salt Lake.

The wagons rattled and jerked down the other side of the ridge. A steep ravine was bridged by filling it with trunks of trees and brush. At the foot of the mountain, while crossing a steep banked stream, the wagon of James Reed broke an axle. Mrs. Reed and little Tommy were tumbled around, but they had only a little bruising for the experience. They were helped out and taken to the Donner wagon as the men assessed the damage.

"I'm surprised it's held up this long, the country we been through," said William Eddy. "He's got no spare?"

"No, we're gonna have to find a good tree to make one," replied Milt. "Don't look likely around here."

"I'll help," said Eddy, "the quicker we get about it—"

"Why are we stopped?" James had just come up. He'd been riding ahead scouting the area. With James was Charles Stanton and William Pike, the men who, weeks earlier, had gone with James to find Hastings.

"Sure am glad to see you men," said George. "You look pretty drug out."

"We were just about to kill my horse for food when Reed came on us," said Charles.

"Go on to my wagons an' Mrs. Donner will give you some dinner. We'll be along after we figure out what to do with this broken axle. We sure want to hear what y'all have to say."

James dismounted and squatted down to look at the broken axle. "Damn it!"

"I figure that if you'd had a jointed pole this would not have happened, Reed," said Eddy. James straightened up, staring at him. George put his hand on James' shoulder.

"Eddy here's a coach maker an' has offered to help make a new axle. Others will help too."

James' stare had become a glare. George shook his shoulder. James slowly turned and looked at George as though dazed.

"What?"

"We'll all help with the repair. Send your men to scout for a tree an' bring it back. We'll start on the work as soon as they get back."

James staggered to the door of his wagon and looked inside.

"Where is my wife? My children?"

"They're all right, they're with Tamsen."

"Mr. Reed, we'll go fetch the tree," said Milt.

James stood for a few moments trying to collect himself, then walked to his horse, taking the saddle off.

"Milt, take care of my horse. Put my saddle on the dun. We'll leave after I've seen to Mrs. Reed."

"Yes sir, I'll do it. Are you all right? You know, we got plenty of help. There's no need for you to go."

"Damn it, Milt, do what I told you!"

Milt stood for a moment with a shocked face, then led the horse away.

James glanced around at the men, his face red, his breathing fast. After a moment, he headed down the line of wagons.

"Seems he's swallowed a prickly pear," said George. "Mr. Eddy, shall we commence to get that axle off? An' let's see if we can get the wagon propped up secure enough that Mrs. Reed can use it tonight."

"Yes, I'll commence," replied Eddy, "But it won't be for that son-of-a-bitch. I'll do it for his wife and children."

As we sat around the campfire that evening, Mr. Stanton and Mr. Pike told a harrowing tale of getting lost and almost giving up hope of finding the company.

"We might never have come on to you. No telling where we were nor where you might be," said Stanton, "but we do know that we can't get to the Salt Lake by the direction you're heading."

"The hell you say! We saw the valley from the mountain we just came over. We figured this here stream would take us there."

Everyone was disheartened. More thickets, streams, and boulders. More hacking and chopping. They were at the limits of endurance. But the pause to repair the Reed wagon had allowed some rest and on they struggled. More clearing, filling, rolling of boulders. Six long days, another ridge topped and descended. We came out into a meadow leading into a canyon and beyond was the valley of the Salt Lake. Finally, the nightmare of the Wasatch was almost over. We camped in the meadow and riders went out to assess the last canyon. The news was not good.

"The canyon's choked with growth, thick as what we done come through, mebbe worse. It's gonna take several days of clearing to get through it, I'm thinkin'," said George.

It was too much. They simply could not do it, could not face more hard labor. The decision was to go up and over the sheer north face of the canyon wall. The first wagon was triple-teamed and the pull over the mountain began.

"There's a powerful right chance the oxen'll slip and the wagon'll come back on us," said Mr. Graves. "Hey, you there, Smith! Stick some more wood under those wheels!"

The men chocked the wheels after every few feet and the oxen were prodded to their limits.

"It ain't workin', Mr. Donner. We've got to have more oxen to pull. What if we took some of 'em to the top and put some ropes down?"

"We ain't got any ropes that long. Nothin' but slope all the way up."

Mr. Graves came over to George, pointing up the hill.

"You see that tree 'bout half way up? Mebbe we can get a rope around it and get some extra pull."

They wrapped ropes around the tree and several men pulled the ropes as the oxen were urged upward, gaining about fifty feet when the tree pulled completely out, slacking the rope. The oxen started slipping.

"Chock the damn wheels," roared McCutchen. Two more teams were brought up and connected, and the pull began again. Finally, all the wagons were brought up the ridge and the wagons descended to the valley of the Great Salt Lake.

August 22, 1846
The Deserts

The delay of waiting for Reed to return, the strenuous work, and the worry that provisions were going to run out had taken a toll on the group. Each day the cursing and bad talk increased and quarreling was a daily occurrence.

The wagons, now almost shook to pieces, groaned and rattled on. We came across the traces left by the wagons led by Lansford Hastings. Mr. Halloran's condition had worsened in the mountains and he died a few days after reaching the valley. It was found that he was a Mason, and James Reed conducted full Masonic rites and then he was lowered into a salty grave.

The road led off in a northerly direction, bending around the point of a mountain, leaving the lake off to the right. We passed into an area where there were many natural wells filled with cold pure water.

The next day we made a long drive and camped where there were more wells and good grass. The trail swept off to the west along what must have been a beach from a vanished lake high above the present. After crossing a sagebrush plain, we came to a good meadow and here we found shreds of a note that had been mounted on a board but had been torn apart by birds. The scraps were collected and everyone gathered around as Tamsen sat down with the board on her lap and pieced the scraps together.

"It's not complete but from what I can make out this paper was left by Mr. Hastings. It says we have a desert crossing ahead—two days and two nights—no water."

"Our oxen are in terrible shape," wailed Mrs. Murphy. "We can't get through without water."

"We'll fill every container we have. There's good grass here, we'll cut as much as we can," said George. "We knew we were goin' to face a desert."

The company proceeded to cut grass, piling it in the wagons. George told the children to get in and pack it down so more could be put in, but they were getting bit by bugs and he gave it up.

"Forty miles, that's a three day drive with healthy animals an' ours are plumb tuckered," said Jacob. He hunkered down on his heels in the shade of the wagon, scratching his legs. "Damnation! Tamsen, you got more of that salve? My leg're on fire." Tamsen gave Jacob the salve and he smeared it on his legs.

"I think we have enough hay, but some don't have much to carry water in," said George.

"A critter needin' two gallons a day, we cain't carry nearly enough."

"We got no choice, Jake."

Ahead lay a broad salt plain where grew only thorny, stunted bushes. Our direction took us toward a mountain and after a time we began to ascend, nooning by the side of a spring high up on the mountain. After a rest the journey continued, descending the foothills of the mountain to a place where the road began a climb over very steep hills. After much effort the hills were crossed and the group made camp on a ridge on the western side. Ahead, forbidding looking salt flats stretched as far as the eye could see.

In the morning the dry drive began, following the vague wheel-tracks and occasional piece of broken sage that was Hastings' trail. At times the wheels of the wagons sank into soft sand and mud, at other times the hooves of the oxen would break through a hard crust which cut and bruised their feet.

The wagons were strung out with the Reed families in the rear. The desert was a blinding glare, like snowfields in bright sun. Suffocating dust hung above the wagons, caking the nostrils of animals and people, blistering skin, burning eyes. The livestock snorted and sneezed, trying to get the dust out of their nostrils.

Sarah Foster stopped walking and pointed off to the horizon. "Look. I see people coming there."

Mrs. Murphy shaded her eyes with her hand, looking where Sarah was pointing. "Maybe it's Hastings, coming back."

Others stopped to see what the women were gazing at and an excited buzz went through the wagons. But as they proceeded, the image shifted and faded and they realized that it was the desert playing tricks on them. Many times they thought they saw a lake and hastened a little, anxious to get to the water, but the lake would rise or fall, disappearing in the white haze. There was little water remaining in their containers.

On the morning of the third day, the first wagons reached a spring at the base of a mountain known as Pilot Peak. The Donner wagons were still on the desert, the heavier wagons of James Reed yet behind them.

James dismounted from his horse, whistled at the teamsters to get their attention and waved for them to come in. The dogs hurried up, snuffling at James' hands, begging for water. The oxen stamped at the ground, groaning and muttering, their mouths too dry to drool anymore.

"The animals are suffering terrible," said Milt. "They ain't goin' to last much longer."

"I'm going to go ahead and bring back water," said James. "When the oxen give up, let them out of the yokes and drive them ahead as far as they'll go." He walked to where Margaret and the children were sitting on the ground in the scanty shade of the wagon.

"Margaret, I told the men to keep going as long as the oxen will pull, and then to unyoke them and drive them ahead. Stay with the wagons. I'll be back as soon as I can." Margaret slumped down against a wagon wheel, unfastening some of the buttons of her high necked dress and fanning herself. "How much farther is it? We don't have much water, James."

Margaret's usually neat, pinned up hair now straggled around her face and over her shoulders. Her face was white from alkaline dust, her eyes caked with salt from tears. James took his handkerchief and mopped a little dampness from the bottom of a water bucket and wiped her eyes and face with it.

"It can't be far. I'll bring back water."

Mounting Glaucus, James moved off. Margaret touched her fingers to her lips, so dry the skin was cracking open. *Oh God, why did we come on this miserable journey?*

"Can you help her up?" Milt asked Virginia. "We got to get these animals movin'. Miz Reed, we're startin' 'em off again," called Milt. "Best you move away from that wheel."

Margaret scrambled to her feet and then began to walk, Thomas holding on to her skirt.

The Donner family's oxen were still pulling their wagons, but ever so slowly. Elitha was plodding ahead, concentrating on putting one foot ahead of the other. Frances was behind her, staying in Elitha's shadow for shade. She was making Elitha mad because she was stepping on her heels.

Tamsen looked back to see Elitha push Frances. She waited for the girls to come up to her. "Elitha—"

"She started it! She keeps tromping on my heels!" croaked Elitha. She wanted to yell, but just barely moving the lips would split the skin open—again.

"Momma, I'm thirsty," moaned Frances.

Tamsen took a small round pebble out of her pocket and gave it to Frances. "Hold this in your mouth, it may bring out some moisture."

"I want one too," said Eliza, then Georgia.

George heard a horse snort behind him and looked around to see James coming up. James lifted his hand limply in greeting.

"How far back are your wagons?" asked George.

"Not far. I expect my men will have to unyoke and drive them in. Do you have any water?"

"Not a drop."

James plodded on, passing a dead ox. He thought it might be one of Graves'. He came up on Jacob's wagons, leaned over in the saddle to talk to Jacob who was walking alongside the oxen. James's mouth was so dry he could barely move his tongue.

"Do you … have any water?"

Jacob motioned back to the wagon and James saw a water bag hanging on the side. He turned the horse back, took the bag off the hook, hefting it in his hand. There was not much left.

"I been rationing it out," said Betsey, who'd been on the other side of the wagon.

James nodded, took a swallow, holding it in his mouth for a while, then took another swallow and put the bag back. "Elizabeth, I'm going … to water, taking some back. You have an empty water bag? I'll bring some to you."

Betsey found two empty water bags and handed them to James. They both looked to the northwest, shading their eyes against the sun. Far off, floating like an island in a silvery sea, was a dark bump on the horizon.

"We've already come fifty-sixty miles ... wonder how far that peak is, still," said Betsey.

"Too far."

James went on, coming to the Breen wagons. *They probably have water, but I will not ask them,* thought James. He waved and passed on. Glaucus was faltering and James dismounted and walked beside him. After what seemed an eternity, he saw a splash of green at the foot of the mountain that loomed over the desert.

William Eddy saw James coming, the horse with his head down, lifting one foot at a time to move forward, stumbling. Eddy took the saddle and gear off the horse and led him through the reeds to the spring. James sat down next to a wagon and Mr. Graves handed him a water bag.

"It's a hell out there," James gasped.

He gulped the first swallows, then drank more slowly, pouring some over his head, wiping his face with his hand.

"Mr. Graves, I've got to return to my wagons. Can I have the use of one of your horses?"

"How far out are you?"

James shook his head. "I don't know ... fifteen miles. My men will be drivin' the livestock in. I've got to get back to my wagons, my family."

"We'll put your saddle on one'a my horses."

Mr. Graves turned to his oldest boy, William. "Will, put Mr. Reed's saddle on the roan. Where's Snyder?"

"He's still waterin' the stock."

Mr. Graves went to where Eddy had dropped James' gear and untied the water bags.

"Will, never mind, take these and go fill 'em up. I'll saddle the horse."

James got to his feet and followed William to the spring. Glaucus was standing in the water, alternately drinking and shaking off water. James kneeled, dipped water into his hat and then poured it over his head. He took two of the water bags and filled them, William filled the other three.

It was early dark when James left the camp with William Eddy, who carried a bucket of water to revive one of his oxen that had gone down and was left in the desert.

Where it had been hot during the day, now the desert sands began giving up their heat and night chill was coming on. James met his teamsters driving his cattle and horses and then began to meet other wagons. He didn't dismount, but dropped Betsey's water bags where she would find them. At last he saw his three wagons, the white tops looming ghostly in the moonlight.

The dogs ran out to greet him. James found a pan under the wagon and poured some water into it. The dogs pushed and shoved each other to get at the water, whining for more when the last drop had been slurped up. James took his saddle off the horse, gave it a little water, then tied the reins to the back of the wagon. He stretched out under the family wagon, the dogs huddling around.

At dawn James awakened from a brief fitful sleep and crawled out from beneath the wagon. The others began stirring, going off to relieve themselves. All day long under a merciless sun they waited for the return of the teamsters with the oxen. The water was almost gone. Finally, at evening, they set out, everyone on foot, as James had sent Walter ahead with Graves' horse. Little Tommy gave out and James picked him up and carried him.

They hadn't walked long before exhaustion overtook them. James put down a blanket and huddled the whimpering children on it. The cold crept over them, a biting wind adding to their misery. The dogs crawled in with the family. James and Margaret sat with their backs to the wind, trying to shelter the children.

Suddenly, one of the dogs jumped up, barking ferociously. The others dashed into the night, and the startled children sat up. There was a drumming of hooves and a large animal loomed through the darkness, charging directly upon the family. The dogs caused it to swerve and it passed by. It was one of their own steers.

They were energized from the sudden fear and moved on into the night. About daylight, they staggered up to Jacob's wagons. The family was asleep. The Reeds huddled together, shivering in the cold, waiting for the camp to stir.

In the morning Betsey prepared a breakfast of biscuits and gravy for everyone. James immediately set off for the spring, meeting Jacob who had bad news. James' teamsters had lost control of his livestock and they had stampeded off into the desert.

Jacob, with the help of his boys and one of the teamsters, yoked up, taking his family and the Reed family in to the camp at the spring. On the way they met several of the party searching for lost cattle and bringing in wagons that had been left in the desert. When everyone returned, they counted thirty-six head that had been lost, most of them James Reed's.

Margaret, sitting beside Jacob's wagon, saw James and the men bringing their wagon in and walked towards it.

"We'll have only one wagon?" she asked.

"Yes. We could find only one ox and one cow that were ours. Graves and Reed gave me one each. I brought in the family wagon, even though it's heavier, so that you'll be comfortable. It will barely be possible for four animals to pull the wagon—we'll have to cut down to the bare minimum. I divided up most of our provisions with the others."

"Why?"

"So they'll help us carry our goods."

Margaret started to cry. "I can't bear to think of parting with all my things. Can't they let you have more oxen to pull another of our wagons?"

"The others are worried they'll not have what they need. George is leaving one of his wagons, and the German, Keseberg, is leaving one of his."

George went around trying to calm people down. He'd visited all the camps, the last was the Murphy family. George looked at their fire and saw what looked like a fowl of some sort sizzling over the coals. "Smells good, whatever it is."

"William Pike netted a duck and two a' them little mud hens," said Levinah.

"How're y'all doin' for supplies?"

"We're low. A month, month and-a-half, an' that's if we're real, real careful," said Levinah.

"We're through the worst now," said George. "Our concern is keepin' our animals goin'. Mr. Stanton and Mr. McCutchen are goin' to go ahead to Sutter's to purchase provisions. Y'all want a share in that?"

Foster looked at Pike and then at his mother-in-law, back at George. "What supplies will you ask for?"

"Beef an' flour, corn meal, probably."

"What do you suppose we'll have to pay?"

"California prices, whatever it is. We ain't got much choice. We'll send a note sayin' we'll pay in California, which should get the goods. We'll settle up when we get there."

Weary and shaken, the company moved out, following the trace of Hastings' wagons, the trail occasionally marked by the bones of dead cattle and abandoned goods. Spirits lifted now that the company was finally on the road again after the week spent fruitlessly searching for lost cattle. Several in the company were bitter about the delay. They felt they should not be held back by a search for cattle that mostly belonged to James Reed.

Immediately, the weather changed and a snowstorm burst upon them. Instead of desert heat, now bone-chilling cold. But the heat returned—at least in the daytime. At night, they huddled in blankets around their fires, when they could find something to burn.

The line of wagons shortened again. Reed's animals had faltered trying to pull the heavy wagon, so Eddy put his teams to the Reed wagon. Pike abandoned his wagon which was falling apart, taking Eddy's.

The company toiled on, always accompanied by the tortured shriek of the wheels and the curses and shouts of men urging the gaunt animals on. They stopped constantly to hammer wedges into wheels to tighten them.

The country was improving. The mountain ranges tended to run north and south, with meadows up against the eastern wall and good, plentiful water on the western side. After some days of this up and down trek, we saw a higher mountain range floating in the hazy distance, directly in front of the setting sun.

"I expected," said James, "that by now we would have come to a westward river. But it looks like we'll have to cross another range of mountains before we find it. Some call it Mary's River, others call it Ogden's—but there's only one. We'll follow along that river, until it becomes a sink. Then there's a desert to cross."

"Oh, God, I thought we were out of the blamed deserts," cried Mrs. Murphy. She stabbed her finger at James. "It's your fault. You talked us into this ... this cursed wilderness."

James stepped back, stunned. Foster put his arm around Levinah's shoulders, trying to turn her away from James and calm her down, but she kept on. "He's a liar, a liar. Oh, God, why did we listen to him?" Levinah covered her face and began to sob.

Margaret Reed was as shocked as James, but where James

was reticent to speak harshly to a woman, Margaret had no such compunction. She grabbed Levinah's arms and jerked her hands away from her face.

"How dare you call my husband a liar, you Mormon tramp!"

Levinah lost her balance but her son-in-law held her up, "Did you hear her? That snobbish bitch! She called me a tramp."

Levinah's girls came running up. "Mother, calm down!" One to each side they took her back to their wagon.

Margaret turned to find James gaping at her, in shock. She held her hand out to him.

"I fear I'm going to faint …"

James got her back to the wagon before she collapsed completely. "Virginia, go ask Mrs. Donner if she'll come. Ask her to bring her medicines."

Tamsen hurriedly got her things together and rushed to the Reed wagon. She loosened the buttons on Margaret's blouse and swabbed her face and chest with a wet cloth.

"Mother will have a headache and she'll be bedridden for days. It's Mr. Donner's fault!" exclaimed Virginia. "My father told him he didn't want us to travel with those people."

Tamsen looked at Virginia and thought that she'd like to slap her. *Oh, God, this journey is causing us all to lose our sanity.*

Margaret continued to moan. "I never thought a woman could be so debased. How could she talk to me like that?"

"I think you gave as good as you got, Margaret. Can you sit up a little so you can take some medicine?"

"No! No more of your damn tea!" Margaret's face crumpled, tears squeezed out of her tightly closed eyes. "James, tell her to give me some laudanum!"

"This *is* laudanum," said Tamsen.

Margaret's eyes flew open. Raising up on one elbow she took the cup with a shaky hand and downed the liquid. Then she fell back on her pillows. "Oh God, when is this nightmare going to end?" she moaned.

Tamsen rearranged Margaret's pillows and sat down on the opposite bench seat. James stroked back Margaret's hair, noticing for the first time that her dark brown hair now had a lot of gray. Her breathing became more even.

Tamsen leaned close to James. "Hopefully, she won't develop a headache, but if she does and wants to take the teas that I have made for her headaches, I will bring them."

"The laudanum seems to help her more," said James.

"I felt it best to get her calmed down, but I won't give it to her again. I am sympathetic, but she has endured less hardship than any of us. It's time she stops wanting to be molly-coddled and kept in a cocoon of comfort. James, you need all of your energy to help get this company to California. It's time she stopped her nonsense."

The wagons traversed a wide valley and stopped on a rise. The mountain range blocking our path to the west showed no gap, no lowering of the craggy peaks, no pass.

"We could send some men out to scout," said James.

"No, Hastings would have already done that." George put his foot up on a wagon tongue, chin on a fist, thinking over the situation. "I think we should follow Hastings. No tellin' how far this range goes north."

To get around this range of mountains we were forced to take a long detour. We trailed south for three days until at last the road took a turn to the west. We ascended and then descended a gap in the mountains, camping for the night. After supper, James and one of his men went out by horseback to scout the road.

"We followed the road as far as we could to get back before

dark. All we could see is the trail heading north. It follows this river here, straight north."

"I wonder how far ahead the Hastings group is," said George.

"Well," said James, "we know we gained two days on them, from their camping places. After I found them at the Salt Lake, it took me three days to get back—"

"An' it was eighteen days getting through those damned canyons," growled Eddy. "They're three weeks ahead at least. That no-good Hastings—when I get to California I'm going to find him and beat the b'jesus out of him. I'll expose the lying son-of-a-bitch for what he is."

"Eddy, you're just whistlin' Dixie. Fellows like that there Hastings always get away with their doin's. It's the honest man that always seems to catch hell."

Three more days we traveled due north. We were only a mountain range away from where we had camped six days before to the east. The trail led off to the northwest into a canyon and there we camped for the night. The scouts came back to tell us that after this canyon we would be heading west again. The gloom that hovered over the company was relieved a little.

After two days more of travel, the undulating green line of Mary's River was seen. It was a pitiful excuse for a river—shallow, with warm, unpleasant tasting water, but it was lined with willows and had good grass in its meadows.

After fording the river, the company came to a well-beaten trail and realized that it was the main trail to California. Their gratitude was well tempered by the thought that the company was the last of the 1846 emigration. It was still a solace—now the way was marked. The two men that had gone ahead would be coming back any day with supplies, the trail was now known, and the animals were recruiting. Anxiety receded a little.

Patrick Breen took out his fiddle, Dolan clapped and beat out a few steps of an Irish jig on the hard earth beside Mary's River. But the desert had accelerated a collapse that the Wasatch had begun, and it was only a matter of time before what little cohesion they had would be gone. They had no idea that the trouble ahead would be far worse than the trouble behind.

• • •

Day after day, fifteen or so miles of steady, tiring, plodding ahead. The monotony was broken only by a difference of position in the line of wagons and the mundane happenings of daily living. Irritations grew and festered with the strain of bad food, bad water, and failing oxen. No family was probably more affected than that of James Reed. Formerly the wealthiest—three wagons, five hired hands—now reduced to sharing with the Eddys. James was proud and the changed circumstances affected him greatly, grinding on him, tearing at the fabric of sociability.

They began to see Indians, Paiutes. To the emigrants, they looked very poor and sub-human. Their nakedness affronted. They didn't have the good-looks and pageantry of the Sioux. The Paiute stayed off from the company, seemingly shy of white men, but one day some friendly ones ventured into camp. One of them offered some roots and was given biscuits in exchange. Juan Baptiste squatted down with them, using his hand talk, determining that the company was yet two hundred miles from the place where the river flowed into its sink. This news rekindled a nervousness to forge ahead. It was the last of September.

The company traveled now in two sections, the Donner wagons ahead. Then trouble with the Indians began. Two Indians came into camp in a friendly fashion, partaking of the hospitality, even helping put out an accidental fire. The next morning they were gone, and missing was a shirt and two oxen belonging to Franklin Graves. Two nights later, a horse was missing, and several oxen were down, bleeding from arrows.

Nights were getting colder. Pike and Foster ranged out from camp, hoping to find some game. Antelopes were seen, but always too cautious and fast to be taken.

"The Indians are all over," they reported upon returning to camp. "They're skulking in the washes, behind brush. We need to keep a better watch."

"I reckon we do," said George, "but they sneak up and shoot their arrows into the livestock whether we have men out there or not. Billy Graves came up this morning and told me that the rest of the group has lost livestock most every night. He said his father wanted us to hold up, everybody travel together."

"There isn't enough forage for the livestock. We'd be too spread out, trying to find grass for our animals," said Foster.

"Damned if we do, damned if we don't," said George. "We made twenty miles today. If we can do that every day, it'll help."

The next day the forward group came upon an unusually high and long sand-hill. By double-teaming and concerted effort, the wagons were got through, but we made only nine miles before camping. The hill should not have been more of a problem for the group behind, but here the cumulative strain on man and beast came to a head. An altercation that would not have happened in normal circumstances cost John Snyder his life by the hand of James Reed.

The sandy hill was difficult, but two of Graves' wagons made it over by double-teaming. Snyder, driving the third wagon, felt he could get the wagon up and over without assistance. Behind him was the Reed wagon, driven by Milt Elliot.

Milt was becoming impatient because Snyder wasn't moving. He swung his wagon around and started up the hill.

Somehow the teams became tangled. Sharp words passed between the drivers. Then Snyder began whipping his team viciously.

Reed, who had just come up, began arguing with Snyder. Snyder reversed the whip and began hitting James with the heavy whip handle. Three blows landed on his head, opening gashes in his scalp, the last knocking him down. Mrs. Reed, frantic that her husband was being hurt, rushed up, getting between the two men. Scrabbling to his feet, James drew his knife and plunged it into Snyder's chest.

The scene went from unbridled anger to a man dying by the side of the road, air and blood bubbling from his slashed shirt. "Uncle Patrick, I am dead," he gasped. Within minutes it was so.

James, face ashen, threw his knife as far as he could, bent over beside the wagon and vomited. When his trembling subsided he staggered to where Snyder had been carried to the side of the road. The angry Graves men told him to get the hell away. That evening, John Snyder was buried.

Angry sentiments flew about the camp. The Graves family, shocked and grieving, felt Reed should be punished by death. Some of the others argued for it too. But Reed pled self-defense and his men picked up their rifles and stood up for him. Patrick Breen and Dolan had not witnessed the affair, and were loathe to be a party to a verdict of death. It was decided that Reed should be banished from the company; no horse, no gun, no food. Let him perish in the wilderness.

James sat beside Margaret as Virginia daubed at the wounds on his head. He clenched his hands together, trying to hide how badly they were shaking. Milt sat opposite James, turning his hat over and over in his hands.

"They're mad as hell, Mr. Donner. Jim's standin' guard, case some of 'em start over here with a rope. I never seen people so het up for revenge—"

Margaret began moaning and wailing. "Oh, God. Oh, God. Oh, God."

James sighed. "Milt, what I've decided to do is to go willingly. I can't continue in the company with these people feeling the way they do. I'll go on to California, get supplies, meet the group somewhere—perhaps this side of the California Mountains."

"Yeah, I can't see anythin' else you can do. Mebbe they'll cool down by then."

"I've spoken with Breen and Graves. They've promised to look out for the family."

James' brow was creased with worry as he put some things in a pack and went out to saddle up his horse. A group of men approached.

"Reed, you ain't goin' on that horse, you bastard. You just start walking, and I hope you suffer a long time before the vultures pick your bones," yelled Franklin Graves. William and Jay were beside him, the Germans behind.

Milt spoke quietly to James. "Go on, Mr. Reed, just get away, an' I'll bring the horse on out to you later on."

Milt moved in front of James. "You men cool down and give Mr. Reed some space. Go on back to your wagons."

James held his hand up. "Look, I'm leaving of my own free will—not because you're forcing me. I've acted in self-defense, you all know that."

"Reed, it warn't no self-defense, you murdered Snyder."

The sounds of crying and moaning coming from the Reed wagon dampened the ardor in the group confronting James. Their hostility began to melt. Virginia hurried in to Margaret.

James shouldered his pack and a water bag and left the camp, trudging through gray, flinty sand. He walked for two miles or so and then found a hollow in a cut-bank and settled himself against it. He shivered from the cold, pulling his coat closer, tucking his hands inside his pockets. He had time now to go over in his mind what had happened. He found no fault with his actions, but wished fervently that it had never happened.

It was very close to dawn when he heard the clicking of the hooves of horses on the stony ground and stood up. It was Milt and Virginia, bringing him his horse.

Now on horseback, James caught up with the Donner group that was a day ahead of the others. They were stunned to hear what had happened. Tamsen treated the gashes on his head.

"I could not reason with those people—mostly the Graves group and that bunch of Germans. Milt and Virginia brought me my horse and my rifle. The group promised to care for my wife and family, but I have no confidence they will do so with much charity."

Walter Herron, one of James' teamsters who'd been traveling with the Donners, decided to go with James. There were no extra horses, so they would trade off riding Glaucus. Tamsen gave them what she could spare in food and they left the camp.

The river disappeared into its sink. Ahead, another desert. Crossing over a low ridge of sand hills the group encountered heaps of dry and ashy earth, the oxen sinking in many places to their bellies. Lack of food and water took an additional toll. The wagons were lightened again. George and Noah began unloading and rearranging goods in the wagons. Tamsen saw George removing her rocking chair.

"George, it breaks my heart to have to leave my box of books and school supplies. I won't give up my rocking chair."

"Honey, we just got to unload some things, or we're gonna have to leave another wagon."

"George, I would rather give up some of those goods you brought to sell in California—my chair is more important to me than those goods."

"Honey, I'm sorry, but—"

"Oh, George, that chair belonged to my mother. I've rocked all my babies in it. George, please, it's my touchstone, my reminder of all most dear."

George sighed. He looked over Tamsen's head to his gaunt oxen, pawing at the ground. They were hurting for food, desperate for water. "Noah, put the rockin' chair back in the wagon. Take out that box of tools, mebbe I can do without some of them."

We plodded on, each ridge ascended with hope that the other side would be better country, then bitter disappointment to find that there was no green to signal a source of water. Only dry, shimmering hot desert. Everyone was walking to spare the oxen. Fear was a constant companion.

It was becoming increasingly hard for Mr. Hardcoop to walk. He'd been traveling with Mr. Keseberg, but he'd put the man out of his wagon to save his animals. Mr. Hardcoop then went to William Eddy.

"Please, Mr. Eddy, iss hard for me to walk. I haf no shoes, I cannot wear them."

Eddy looked at Mr. Hardcoop's feet. They were so swollen that the skin had burst, leaving weeping splits where dirt and sand had collected. The poor man was hurting terribly.

They were now in a patch of deep sand and the oxen were having trouble. Eddy was pulling on an ox and his wife was pushing another. Margaret Reed and the girls were beside the wagon.

"Mr. Hardcoop," said William, "we're having trouble getting through this sand. I'll see what shape we're in after this stretch. Maybe you can ride then."

Mr. Hardcoop waved in acknowledgement and sank down beside the road. There were no more wagons on the trail.

That evening, Mr. Hardcoop did not come up. Eddy had pangs of remorse, he'd forgotten about the old man. It had been a struggle to get through the sand and his oxen were almost finished. He suggested that someone go back and find Mr. Hardcoop and bring him up. He asked Mr. Breen for the loan of a horse. He would make the effort, but he'd have to have a horse to bring Hardcoop in.

"Mr. Eddy, think about it. What will you do with him after you bring him up? Are you going to put him in your wagon?"

"I don't think I'll have oxen to pull it much longer."

"Yes. You see, even if you do this thing, the man can't walk. So tomorrow there is the same problem. I do not want to loan the horse because it will be a futile effort. The man cannot make it anyway. Do you see what I am saying?"

While most of the people were sympathetic and felt something should be done to help the old man, nobody stepped forward. It was a bitter thing to leave the man behind. But it was now a matter of survival. The country was getting worse; drier, scantier vegetation and heavy sand.

The groups came together at a camping place where they found the bones of one Sallee, a member of Hastings' company who had died of an arrow wound. He'd been dug up by the Indians and stripped of his clothes. Coyotes cleaned the bones. The pall caused by finding the bones of Mr. Sallee was worsened when the next morning the Indians ran off most of Mr. Graves' horses. That night they ran off eighteen oxen and a cow, mostly belonging to Wolfinger and the Donners. Another wagon was abandoned.

They were nearing the sink, the river dwindling to almost nothing, the water more terrible, the grass exceedingly scanty. They reached the sink at midnight, after a long hard drive, one or two oxen failing and left behind.

Keeping a closer guard now, they corralled the livestock all night, but at daybreak they were taken out to grass under guard. Everything was quiet, so the guards came in for breakfast. The

Indians struck, wounding twenty-one head. Most were too badly damaged to go on.

The next evening found the company at a worse spot, the water in fetid pools surrounded by mud. One of Breen's horses became bogged down in the heavy mud and John Breen ran for help, but the horse could not be extricated.

"Yeah, Breen, that's paying you back for not helping Hardcoop," muttered Eddy.

Eddy, with only one ox remaining, was forced to abandon Reed's wagon. The situation for the Eddy family and for Mrs. Reed and the children became desperate. Eddy carried little James, Eleanor tucked baby Margaret in a shawl and put her on her back. They set out across the burning desert with nothing but the clothes they were wearing and a loaf of lump sugar. Eddy's rifle had come apart, but he tucked a few bullets in his pocket, intending to borrow a gun if he chanced on any game.

Margaret bundled up a few things and put them in the Breen wagon. She and the girls set out, leading their one remaining horse with the little boys clinging to its back.

Whips cracked over the heads of the scrawny oxen and the wagons lurched forward. The screech of dry wheels and the rattle of wagons coming apart traveled across the dunes. Ahead lay the last desert. They'd been told it would be forty miles or so now to the Truckee River. It was mid-October.

The land stretched out before them, seemingly endless. In the distance, purple-gray mounds became hills. On the apron of the hills white plumes of steam rose into the air. By afternoon, they were close enough to see hundreds of springs, seething with steam and bitter boiling water. Rumbling noises came from under the ground.

"You reckon this is the place that Mr. Clyman lost his dog?" asked Elitha.

"I remember he said the dog had jumped into boiling springs," Tamsen answered. "Girls, don't get near any of the holes. Stay right here. George, you should take the dogs and show them the danger."

"When I said there was plenty of hell on earth, I didn't know of this place, but it sure qualifies," said George.

"These boilin' springs might be good for washin' clothes," said Betsey. "One of those holes threw up a shirt or some such cloth. Somebody probably put their clothes in, thinkin' the next spout would spit 'em out all cleaned up, but it didn't happen fast enough."

Mr. Wolfinger remained in camp to cache some goods. Two of the German men offered to stay behind to help, and Mrs. Wolfinger walked on ahead with some of the women.

As a point of a mountain was rounded, in the distance could be seen a line of green and here and there a shimmering silver ribbon. At last, the eastward flowing Truckee River.

October 14, 1846
The Truckee River

Grass was abundant, the water clean, cold and pure. They knew this river came down from the California Mountains, and would lead them directly to the pass, the pass they must cross before the snows would begin. They decided to pause here for a day or two to recruit. The mood in the camps that evening was happy.

The mood was broken when Mr. Rinehardt and Mr. Spitzer came up saying that Mr. Wolfinger had been killed by Indians. Three men went back to look for him, found the wagon with the oxen and brought it in.

"We found the oxen grazing along the river unyoked an' the wagon just sittin' there," reported William Graves, "but nary a sign of Mr. Wolfinger an' no sign of Injuns either."

Mrs. Wolfinger was wringing her hands and crying. *"Das Geld! Es ist keine hier. Haben Sie seinen Geld Beutel grefunden?"*

"Mr. Rinehardt, what is she sayin'?"

"I tell her that her husband wass kill by Indians and nossing can be done. She grieves that he won't haf a proper burial."

"Tell her we can't go back to find his body, that we're very sorry for her loss," said George.

"*Señor* Donner, I no understand their talk but I can read the way of the face an' the body an' I tell you that those men they are no good an' they lie. Me, I think they have done something bad. If you will give me the horse I will go back. I will read the signs an' see what they did with the old man."

"Baptiste, we have to leave it alone. I'm sure the man is dead, either way. We can't stop an' fool with this, we've got to move on."

They took Mrs. Wolfinger's wagon to George's camp and tried to console her. George shook his head, making a gesture of helplessness.

"*kein geld*—she's saying their money is gone."

"I asked Mrs. Keseberg if she would talk to her but she would not," said Tamsen. "I asked Mr. Keseberg also. He said he would not be involved. It makes me so angry."

"We'll take it to the authorities in California. What more can we do?"

"We could have a tribunal," said Betsey.

"We have only suspicions, not proof. Those Germans will stick together tight. They're not likely to take it kindly were we to accuse them."

"They're lying," said Mr. Graves. "They said the Indians killed Mr. Wolfinger and burned the wagon. The wagon and oxen aren't harmed. The Indians wouldn't leave the oxen, they've been following us for weeks to get our animals."

"I know it has an ugly look," answered George, "but I don't see that anything can be done about it now. I'd like to get shut of all the problems these people have. It's hard enough to take care of our own. Burger will drive Mrs. Wolfinger's wagon."

It was a terrible shock to the company, this suspicious disappearance of Mr. Wolfinger, but since it involved one of the Germans, they shrugged it off and went back to worrying about themselves. They had plenty to worry about. Several were very low on food.

Wild geese, still not convinced that it was time to fly south, were along the river. William Eddy borrowed a rifle, returning to camp with several of them.

George went around to all the camps. "It should be only a few days to the mountains—way too early for the snows to be deep enough that we can't get through."

"If we don't starve first," said Mrs. Murphy.

"Yeah, we're worried about food, but the men'll be comin' back—should've been back way before now. We need to help out some that's low on food. We'll do our share."

"I got two ox that most likely ain't gonna make it," said Franklin Graves. "I'm thinkin' I should go ahead an' kill them. I'll share the meat if some of you will help me with the work."

"George, when do you think we should move on?" asked Mr. Pike.

"I want to move out tomorrow. Let's get those animals butchered an' the meat dried."

We pressed on through the bottom land of the Truckee River. The valley of the river became narrow and walled in on both sides by high ranges of barren mountains. The wagons wound their way through the canyon, crossing again and again as the river lapped against one steep side and then the other. In places there was no level ground and the wagons were forced to the hillside.

As the sun rose in the sky, warmth would chase away the chill, but as it finished its arc and fell in flames among the hills the cold would come again.

There were numerous tracks of animals and also tracks

of Indians. At one point in the canyon the wagons stopped and they looked to the west where, far-off, could be seen very high mountains.

"Oh, my God, look," said Elitha. "There's snow already on those mountains and that must be the California Mountains."

Talk buzzed down the line of wagons. They were excited to see, at long last, the mountains of California, but to see that they were topped with white struck fear in them. George decided to make camp as they were close to a meadow with exceptionally good grass. The wagons of the Breens and the Murphys continued.

Jacob came up to talk to George. "Mebbe we should go on. It don't make sense, the company splitting up with all the damned Indians around. Their tracks're all over the place."

"The animals have slowed down, they're barely movin'. If we don't give 'em some rest, let 'em graze, they ain't gonna be able to go on. This here's the best grass we've seen so far, no tellin' what it is farther along. I'm itchy too, but we got to think of the animals."

Jacob leaned against the wagon, rubbing his chest. George looked at him for a moment. "Jacob, I've noticed you're havin' trouble gettin' air."

"Yeah, it's harder for me to breathe goin' uphill."

"Can't you ride some?"

"The horse is in worse shape than I am. She sunk her teeth in me when I made to get on. I'll be all right. Sure wish to hell we'd get there. I feel like we never should have left home. All my kids, an' Elizabeth too, are cryin' for home."

"I know, but the worst is over, we're almost there. Buck up, you've always been one to give up early."

The next day we came to another ford in the river and the trail left the river and turned south, heading up a canyon.

"This don't make no sense," said George. "We were

told this here river flows into a big valley right at the foot of the mountains. Noah, ride on up the river. See if there's a road. I'm goin' to ride up this canyon to see what it looks like."

Noah returned first. "I seen why the trail had taken off up the canyon. Up ahead the river narrows down an' goes between some cliff-like places. Where it opens up it's right soft an' marshy. The big valley's past that. I don't think we can get our wagons through there. I hope that canyon's goin' to be easy like. George ain't back yet?"

Jacob pointed. "I see him comin' yonder now."

George dismounted and Jim took his horse. "Well, there's a road, but it's a steady uphill climb for three, four miles. The worst part is that after you get to the top, there's a sharp decline to get down. Noah, does it look like we can follow the river?"

"It don't look likely, Mr. Donner. I think we'll have to take this here canyon."

The wagons creaked and groaned, the oxen murmuring as they were goaded on. The wind came up, slicing through the canyon with sharp edges.

As the wagons moved slowly upward, Jacob was seen sitting, almost laying, by the side of the road. George started to him, looking around for Tamsen, who was already coming up. Solomon stopped the wagons and ran to get Betsey. Tamsen knelt beside Jacob, taking his wrist in her fingers, placing her hand against his chest.

"I cain't … get my breath. Just got weak an' liked to pass out. My palpitator's banging … against my ribs."

"You're very sick, Jacob. George, we need to stop."

"Let me rest ... for a minute. I'll be all right … need to get my breath."

"Let's stop here," said George. Tamsen dosed Jacob with some of her foxglove medicine. After a rest they started up the wagons again and the climb continued.

At the top of the incline Juan Baptiste pointed to the northwest. "The big valley, it is there, and the high mountains. I think those mountains will have much trouble for us."

"I'm lookin' at this decline," said George. "I don't see how wagon's've gone down there, at least in one piece."

George and Baptiste walked partly down the steep slope, their feet sideways, sliding on the soft, loose dirt. The others gathered at the top of the decline and watched. The men climbed back up the slope.

"I reckon we're gonna have to lower 'em down with ropes," said George. "We've got our work cut out for us."

With ropes around a big tree, the wagons were eased down the steep slope. They tied a rope around another tree part way down and the women and older children held on to it, slipping, scooting on their rears, thick dust cascading ahead of them. The small children were tied in shawls and carried on the backs of some of the men making their way down.

At the bottom, the teams were yoked up and started again, making their way through a narrow canyon, in one place so tight between high rocks that the wagon hubs scraped on each side.

They emerged from the canyon in late afternoon, moving down a wide gentle slope. Ahead of them marched a range of high mountains towering over a wide valley edged with brown hills. As the sun sank behind the peaks, color flamed across the tops of the hills on the east side of the valley.

"Such a pretty scene," murmured Tamsen.

Jacob pointed off to the north. "See there, those white tops? It's the rest of the company."

Dawn came blustery and cold. The wagons moved across the valley, fording several creeks, the wheels crunching through ice that coated the shallow ponds. The wind was fierce, flapping and snapping the wagon covers. The valley floor was a sagebrush plain crossed by a few flat streams and sloughs fringed by willows. As we moved to the north side of the valley we saw herds of antelope and deer. In mid-afternoon we came up to the rest of the company.

"Looks like you haven't lost any more stock," said Mr. Breen. "Have you had any more trouble with the savages?"

"No, but they're out there watchin' for a chance," replied George.

Milt took off his hat, twisting it in his hands. "Things ain't good between Miz Reed an' the others an' they don't have any food to speak of. Could I bring her an' the children to stay in your camp?"

"Of course," said Tamsen

"What came of her supplies?" asked George.

"They divided their provisions between several others back in the desert when we had to leave the last wagon. I think most of it's been used up."

"Well, Reed should be comin' back an' the other men too. They'll have supplies. They should have been back by now."

"Yeah, if they made it."

The Donner group had barely made camp when a gunshot was heard. The men grabbed their guns and went off towards the sound, thinking someone had fired at a skulking Indian. But it was tragedy in the camp of Mrs. Murphy. Her son-in-law, William Pike, was killed by an accidental discharge of a gun. John Denton told the others what had happened.

"The blokes, Pike and Foster, were talking of going ahead to get supplies and were sitting around making plans. They noticed the fire was getting low and one chap handed the gun to the other as he got up to get a piece of wood. It went off into his chest."

"Them pepperbox guns is risky," said Jacob.

Mr. Pike was wrapped in a blanket and buried in a shallow grave. After the services, Tamsen and Betsey prepared food and took it to the Murphy camp. After the family had eaten and the dishes were gathered up, Tamsen went to the young widow and sat down beside her, taking Harriet's little one onto her lap. The baby looked at Tamsen with surprised eyes, but after Tamsen cooed at her a little she relaxed and began kicking her little chubby legs and laughing.

Harriet looked sadly at the baby. "I wish I was a child again, never knowin' grief an' sadness."

"It's hard to bear, I know," said Tamsen. "Within a few months I lost my first husband, my little boy, and a little girl that didn't make it full-term." Tamsen's eyes filled with tears.

"What did you do? How did you go on?" Harriet asked.

"I was teaching. Having something that I had to do helped. Then I went back to my birth home. Being with my family was a lot of comfort to me."

Harriet began to cry again. "I can't stand the thought of leaving him here in this wilderness, all alone, nothin' around him but an old blanket."

William came to Harriet, kneeling down at her feet, his head pressed to her knees. "I'm so sorry. I'm sorry."

"I ain't blamin' you, Will. It just happened, that's all. I wish to God we'd never come on this miserable journey."

Except for worrying about food and the depredations of the Indians, the mood of the company had improved considerably with the prospect that there was only one more mountain to cross, only sixty miles to the valley of the Sacramento. But now the death of William Pike depressed their spirits.

"I can't help but think of how our company now cares for our dead," Tamsen said bitterly. "Early in the journey, Mrs. Keyes was laid to rest in a wood coffin with full funeral rites and a carved memorial. Mr. Halloran was given Masonic rites and a coffin, John Snyder was put into the ground with a couple of boards underneath. Now, Mr. Pike, this morning full of life and vigor, is dead and laid to rest in a grave with only a blanket wrapped around him."

"We've had more than our share of trouble," said George.

Jacob pulled up his pant leg and leaned over, scratching a bite on his ankle. "I just wish we could get the damned Indians off of us. Eddy, mebbe you shootin' that one this mornin' will discourage them."

"He got some arrows into the stock before I saw him. I think I killed him. I didn't see him come out of those bushes he rolled into. I didn't want an arrow bad enough to find out. I hope the son-of-a-bitch roasts in hell."

The Breen family left the next morning to begin the ascent of the mountains. With them was their friend Dolan, the Kesebergs, and the Eddys. The following morning the Murphy and Graves families chained up and moved out.

The remaining people, mostly the Donner families, hunched around their fire that evening, wrapped in blankets. The dry leaves in the cottonwood and aspen trees rustled and shook in the wind that rose and fell like swells on a body of water. The canvas on the wagons and tents snapped and whumped, straining against the poles and tethers. One of the horses lifted his ears and knickered, his haunches twitching nervously. George picked up his rifle and stood up. Off in the distance was heard a clattering sound, a sound of hooves moving over rocks. Then a voice broke the stillness.

"Halloo, the camp."

"It's men a'comin, an' horses."

Shapes appeared out of the dusk. It was Mr. Stanton and two of Mr. Sutter's Indians. They were mounted on mules, leading several others heavily laden with packs. The animals snorted and blew, steam rising from their backs. As the men dismounted everyone gathered around, excited, happy. Now there would be food to get the company to California.

Mrs. Reed and her children made their way through the people gathered around and were bitterly disappointed to find it wasn't Mr. Reed. "Mr. Stanton, have you any word of my husband? He was going to Sutter's to obtain supplies."

"Yes, ma'am. We met him four days back. He and Walter were in a poorly state, but they're all right."

"Oh, thank God!" Margaret exclaimed. "Children, did you hear? Papa's all right. He got through."

"They got fresh horses and went on to Sutter's for supplies," said Mr. Stanton. "They should be coming on, but it'll take them some time to get situated."

"We're sure glad to see you, Stanton. Why didn't Mr. McCutchen come back with you?"

"He took sick. I didn't want to wait for him to recover and delay getting back." He turned to George. "I met three groups of the others ahead of you. Is there anyone behind you?"

"No, we're the last."

The mules were impatiently moving their feet, jerking at their halter ropes. One brayed, the sound loud and startling in the thin mountain air. George told some of the men to unload the mules and take them to graze. "Take my rifle and keep a sharp look-out. We can't have any of these mules gettin' shot up with arrows."

"Still having trouble with the savages?" asked Stanton.

"Yeah. They just won't leave us alone. William Eddy killed one of 'em, but it didn't scare 'em none. They're like a bunch of coyotes, skulking on the hill tops and yipping at us."

Mr. Stanton signaled his companions to take coffee and sat down by the fire. "Say, George, what's the story about Reed?" asked Stanton.

"He told us it was a matter of defendin' himself. James did

have some bad head wounds from Snyder's whip handle. It's a troublin' thing. But you remember how it was 'fore you left? We were all kind'a crazed after fightin' our way through those terrible canyons an' crossin' the salt flats. If James can come back with supplies an' animals, it might help cool down some of the company who're still sore."

George told Mr. Stanton about Mr. Hardcoop and Mr. Wolfinger and the accidental death of Mr. Pike.

"Well, it's over now. In a few days all will be behind us. George, what do you plan to do in California?"

"I'm gonna look the place over, find some horse land. I hope to get a good-sized piece. I hear they measure their holdin's in miles 'stead of acres. What's the country like that you went through?"

"It's good-looking country. There's timbered slopes up to these here high mountains. Down farther are gentle hills, good livestock country. I was told it's not good for farming, it doesn't rain in the summer."

"That so?" asked Jacob. "We heard there're orchards, vineyards, an' crops growin' almost wild."

"They say that where there's water you can grow most anything," replied Stanton. "Sutter's growin' some crops. I was told that over west of the valley of the Sacramento there's a range of mountains and on the west side there's beautiful land. That's where there's orchards and vineyards. Missions were built there years ago and they tamed a lot of the Indians, made them kind of slaves. Then the mission people pulled out or were called back to Spain or somewhere. That's where the Pueblo of San Jose is located. Then there's *Yerba Buena,* big bay there, connects to the Pacific, I heard."

"Reed talked favorably of the Pueblo of San Jose," said George. "Mrs. Reed's brother Caden Keyes wrote him of it."

"Mr. Sutter's a true gentleman," continued Mr. Stanton. "He lives like a king in a fiefdom, very civilized. I've heard his holdings are impressive. The fort's not much, just crude buildings made of mud."

"What's goin' on with the Mexican government?"

"Mr. Sutter's fort was taken over by Federal forces and they raised the American flag. I heard that General Taylor's force fought four battles and killed 50,000 Mexicans. It looks like the country's going to be United States territory. You know, the Mexicans have no mind for business, but with all the Americans coming in there'll be money to be made."

"I'm worried about land title, it'll be a mess. I'll feel more comfortable under the flag of the United States."

"Don't you think the government will open it up to settlement like they have in other places?" said Stanton.

"They can't just go in and take land owned by the Mexicans," said George.

"It's been done before," Jacob argued. "Why are they better than the Injuns? The whites just come in an' take the land—"

"Jacob," said Tamsen, "the Mexicans have ruled that country for generations. They have a government and a legal system. They're a civilized society. But I'm sure there are lands that aren't titled, or granted."

"It won't be the good land." Jacob lost interest in the discussion and turned to Mr. Stanton. "What kind of Injuns are those boys? They look different than those we seen so far."

"They're Miwoks. The bigger one's Luis, the other is Salvador. They seem to be stalwart and loyal. I couldn't have come back without these men to guide me and work the mules. Mr. Sutter is most generous."

George shifted around on the stump he was using for a seat, trying to get comfortable. "Mr. Stanton, give us an idea of the country we're facin'. What's that pass like?"

"Actually, George, there's two passes, one at the end of a good-sized lake. The trail goes around the north side of that lake. There's another road to the south, opened by some of the last parties that went over. I suspect that with so many wagons trying to get over at one time, they kind of had a jam-up. The north pass has real steep rock face and the wagons have to be lifted in a couple of places. That takes time. The south way of going is higher, but has a lesser slope."

"Which do you cotton to?"

"The south, since you don't have a lot of men to do that work. I would advise you to hustle along, try to catch up with the others so you can help each other."

"Yeah, we're pretty much tuckered out."

"It's going to take you three days, most likely, to get to that lake, and two days to get to the top of the pass. After you get over the pass, it's still hard going, there's many ridges and canyons before you find the foothills and ease of travel."

"Our animals ain't goin' to make it unless we let 'em recruit. They're in bad shape."

Stanton nodded his head. "It's prudent to rest your animals here. Mr. Sutter assured me there's very little likelihood that the pass would close this early."

In the morning Mr. Stanton prepared to leave.

"Donner, we can travel much faster with the mules than you can with your wagons. We're going on to catch up with the others. We'll take Mrs. Reed and the children."

George shook Mr. Stanton's hand. "I can't thank you enough for everythin' you've done, Stanton. Once our animals are strong enough, we'll come on."

Tamsen and Betsey went to help Mrs. Reed bundle up the things she would be taking with her. "We have goods in the Graves' wagon," said Margaret. "They'll take them on to Sutter's Fort. Mr. Reed will be meeting us on the trail with horses."

Mrs. Reed and Tommy were placed on one mule, Patty and James each behind one of the Indians and Virginia with Mr. Stanton. We watched them make their way to the river and turn west. A moist wind whipped down the side of the mountain and dark clouds hid the high spine of the mountain range. Misty veils were flowing down the clefts into the valley below.

Tamsen gathered her shawl tightly around her shoulders. "It makes me nervous to think we're the last people on this trail."

• • •

After leaving the rest of the group camped in the valley, the Breen family followed the river west. The ground was covered with coarse and sharp-edged gravel that cut and bruised the feet of the animals, adding greatly to their distress.

To the left rose tall mountains, to the right across the river was a flat-topped hill. Ahead loomed the river canyon. It was a magnificent sight—the tumbling and sparkling water, the towering mountains with mists hanging on the slopes like thick white spider webs.

The wagons crossed and re-crossed the river, lurching through gullies and side-slipping across slopes, the oxen stumbling and complaining as they pulled the wagons on. The river rushed past, cascading over rough areas and splitting around great boulders as the sides of the canyon began to narrow. They were awed by huge trees that dotted the river canyon and stopped to measure one with their arms.

"At least eighteen feet around. It would be hard to cut that tree down," said Dolan.

About mid-day they left the river, climbing out of the

canyon to flat land at the base of mountains to the north and west. The sky turned gray and threatening, and soon it began to rain. They stopped to rest the oxen a little, then pressed on, entering a very narrow, winding canyon.

"Ahh," said Mrs. Breen, "Patrick, do you smell the pine trees? Refreshin' it is."

"Yes. If it wasn't that I was gaspin' for air in this high place, I could breathe it in better."

Almost immediately after entering the canyon, the trail left the gully of the dry stream bed, the wagons creaking and groaning as they started up a steep hill. The Eddys were struggling to climb and carry their children. Mrs. Eddy took the baby off her back and eased down on a fallen log. She gazed up the slope.

"William, I've got to stop. I don't have the strength to go up that hill."

Eddy put James down and sat beside his wife. The Keseberg wagon passed them, grinding its way ahead, the wheels crushing through stiff grass, fallen limbs and twigs. Mr. Keseberg nodded stiffly and turned his attention back to his animals. Mrs. Keseberg looked at them sympathetically but said nothing.

Margaret Breen looked back from the top of the hill. She called to her husband, pointing to the Eddy family at the bottom.

"Let's put the little ones in our wagon."

Breen stood gazing at the Eddys, scratching his chin.

"I'll put them in my wagon," said Dolan. Tying a rope to the back of his wagon he eased down the hill, playing out the rope. Dolan picked up James, William carried the baby and they pulled themselves up the hill to the wagons. They stood for a moment looking back down the mountain. In the distance they could see the valley they had left that morning.

"That would be a good place to settle. Good horse and cattle country," said William.

"And Indians that will kill us and take our cattle. If we had any," said Eleanor bitterly.

"Won't always be like that. White men will settle, get rid of the Indians."

"William, you promised me California," said Eleanor.

He put his arm around her. "And I'm keeping my promise, my love."

William walked up front with Dolan, Eleanor stayed to the rear of the wagon, speaking softly to her children peeking out over the wagon gate.

The wagons moved slowly up the mountain, sometimes in a ravine, sometimes on the ridges high above the canyon, only to jolt back down to avoid the deep crevices and rocks. They had to stop often to rest.

It was coming on to dusk when they reached the summit and gazed down into a deep valley. In front of them was a steep pitch, already grooved deeply by the locked wheels of wagons. The first wagon was eased to the edge of the pitch and some of the oxen were unhitched from the wagons and used as a counter-pull.

The next day found them struggling over a second summit, but after that it became easier traveling through country that was more open and rolling. At times they caught glimpses of the high mountains and saw the snow on top. Their throats tightened in fear, and they lashed the animals harder.

October 30, 1846
Trapped

It was October 30 when the advance wagons reached the valley at the foot of the pass. There was an inch of snow on the ground and it was starting to snow again. A deserted cabin was passed. The group decided to follow the road that went to the south of a large lake. Worried they might not make it over, they turned back and waited for the others to come up, which they did by the next day. All except the Donner families and those with them.

With Stanton and the Indians as guides, they tackled the pass again, using the livestock to trample the snow down for the wagons, but had to give it up. The snow was deep and getting deeper. They abandoned the wagons, packed some goods on the mules and the backs of oxen. The mules were accustomed to this activity, but the oxen were not. They bucked until the packs came off, or rubbed the packs off against trees and rocks. It took time and effort to get them moving and time was running out.

They clawed their way upward, over craggy rock face and slippery rounded granite. Just below the summit they stopped to rest. It was snowing, they couldn't see where to go. Stanton, with one of the Indians, went ahead, trying to figure out if they were over or short of the summit. They found the summit and went back to urge the others on.

Someone had set a tree on fire and the exhausted people had collapsed beside it, too weary to go on. Stanton argued, but to no avail. They huddled by the fire and in the wagons, awaiting the dawn. It snowed all night and by morning it was too deep to get through, too soft to walk on. They struggled back to the east end of the lake, wet, frozen through, dispirited. They were trapped.

Patrick Breen claimed the abandoned cabin and moved his family in. It was perhaps twelve feet by fourteen feet, no windows. The roof had been covered with lapped pine boughs but the branches had long since lost the needles that shed rain and snow. A hide-covered door frame hung by one strap. There was a fireplace and a little dry wood.

They cleaned the accumulation of pine limbs and needles off the packed dirt floor and unloaded their wagons, draping hides and canvas over the boxes and trunks. The rest of the group, minus the Donner families and those with them, crawled under or in the few wagons that hadn't been left on the mountain.

The next morning dawned cold and blustery. Elizabeth Graves heard stirring around. She lifted up the wagon canvas and saw her husband hunched against the biting wind, talking to Stanton and the two Indians.

"Franklin, the children's all a'cryin' from the cold. You got to get a fire goin'," she yelled.

Franklin turned towards her. "I'm a'workin' on it. Just stay in there, wait."

Eleanor pushed past her mother and jumped down from the wagon. "I've got to pee or I'll burst."

"I need to get out too," called Lovina.

"Well, go then."

Lovina picked her way between the little ones, stepping on one of them. The injured one began howling.

"Oh, for godsakes!" cried Elizabeth. "Lovina, go on, get out!" Now the children were all crying, their faces screwed up, lips trembling.

"All a' you, hush up, now!" yelled their mother.

"She stepped on my hand!" screamed Jonathan.

"She didn't mean it. She's sorry. Here, come here. Let mother look at it."

Elizabeth took Jonathan's hand and rubbed it, then hugged him. "You ain't hurt." She pulled a heavy shawl around her shoulders. "Father's makin' a fire. I got to go rustle up the breakfast makin's. Just keep bundled up. Nancy, you tend the baby."

As Elizabeth got down from the wagon, Nancy held the baby out to her. "Ma! She pooped. An' it's all over everything!"

"Nancy, will you jes' keep her for a minute? It's not the end of the world. I got other stuff to do."

Eddy, Foster and Mrs. Murphy had come up. Franklin sent William and the two girls to scare up some dry wood.

"Y'all look under downed logs, there's usually small dry stuff under there. If we can get it goin' good, some of the wetter stuff will burn. Foster, you people got an ax?"

"Yeah, a dull one. Do you have a sharpening stone?"

Mr. Graves turned to William. "Will, see if you can find my stone—give it to Foster. We need to cut down a medium sized tree—say six inches across. Then we'll cut it up in four footers, and we'll lay that down to build the fire on."

Levinah came over to Mrs. Graves. "The Breens got a fire goin'. I took my little ones in the cabin an' my kettle with some mush. Why don't you take yer kids in there?"

"That's an idea. Mrs. Murphy, let me give you my kettle." Elizabeth was taking the gate down on the other wagon while she talked. She took her kettle out of a box and handed it to Mrs. Murphy, who started towards the Breen cabin. The others were leaving their sleeping places. While they waited for the women to fix coffee and some breakfast they talked about their situation.

"We surely have our tails in a crack now," said Milt.

"The first thing is, we got to get some shelter made," said Franklin. "Mebbe this'll melt off, or harden up, but to me it looks like we're gonna be here 'til spring."

"Breen thinks so. He's already plannin' to start butchering his animals," said Stanton.

"We'll need more than one cabin," said Franklin. "I been thinking it over an' I got a spot picked out. There's more grass than here. It's over yonder." He pointed. "I'll build a double cabin. My family in one side, an' Miz Reed and her people in the other." He looked around the group. "An' Miz McCutchen."

Franklin gazed off to an open space between the trees and the spot he'd picked to build his cabin. The snow was coming down, a white gauze dimming out the sun.

"I was hopin' it'd stay clear, but as usual, everything is against us," said Franklin. "We'd better get started. Miz Murphy, you best pick out a place. We'll commence cuttin' trees. It's gonna take awhile to get enough. I'm goin' to move my wagons yonder to where I'm goin' to build. Y'all pick a place for your cabin an' when we get enough trees downed we'll come an' get your's cut. We need straight ones, 'bout twelve inches across. Twelve-footers, I think. We'll commence cuttin', then I'll figure how many we'll need."

"Mr. Graves, I'm worried about the Donners," said Stanton. "They should have caught up by now. I'm going to go back and see what's happened. We can't help much here until trees are cut."

"Yeah, you go ahead. I was startin' to worry too."

"What about my family?" asked Mr. Keseberg. "What am

I to do? I cannot work with my foot hurt like it is."

"Why don't you go talk with Breen?" Franklin pointed. They could see Patrick Breen and Dolan dragging hides up on the roof of their cabin. Keseberg frowned, started to say something, shrugged. With the aid of a stick, he limped towards the Breen cabin.

Mr. Breen wasn't happy to see Mr. Keseberg coming up, but he spoke to him pleasantly. "Good mornin' to you, Mr. Keseberg."

"I need shelter for my family. The others said I should talk to you."

Patrick came down the ladder he'd made from cutting wedges out of a log. He took off his cap and shook off the snow.

Keseberg pointed at his bandaged foot. "You see I cannot work to cut trees. Can we stay in with you?"

Patrick looked at Mr. Keseberg's foot. He scratched his chin, thinking. *I dinna want this man in my shanty. I feel sorry for his wife, sure ... an' the wee ones ...*

Dolan had heard them talking and came over. "Patrick, we can cut some trees, lean them agin' the shanty, make a lean-to for Mr. Keseberg an' his family."

Patrick nodded his head. "Mr. Keseberg, do you have hides to make a cover?"

"Yes, I think so."

"Bring your wagon. Your wife an' children can stay in the shanty with Mrs. Breen until we can make something. When we finish this work here," he motioned towards the roof, "we'll cut some trees."

Patrick Breen got some of the men to help cut down trees and made a kind of shed against a wall of his cabin and Keseberg began to move his things inside. He found Mr. Spitzer sitting next to the fire when he returned.

"You didn't help—now you expect to stay here?" Keseberg growled at the man.

"I have no place to go," Spitzer answered.

Keseberg looked at his wife, who shrugged. "We need wood for the fire, Lewis. Perhaps Mr. Spitzer can help, it is hard for you to walk."

"*Ja*! I will get the wood. Thank you. Thank you."

The site that Franklin chose for his double cabin was on the stream flowing east out of the lake, a couple of hundred yards from the Breen cabin. The Murphy group found a huge rock about a quarter mile south and decided to build their cabin against it.

The cabins were crude. The walls were of unpeeled logs, high enough that a man could stand up. The roofs were flat, covered with hides laid over green poles spanning the walls. No windows, only hide covered branches for doors.

Mr. Graves built a fireplace at each end of the double cabin. The rock wall of the Murphy cabin served as their fireplace, the smoke drafting up the rock and seeping out through the crack between rock and roof. But at least they were out of the weather.

They got as close to the fire as they could, drawing comfort from the curling and dancing flames, but little warmth. The wind rattled the roof coverings and came between the logs, sending snow inside to drift against the trunks and boxes, covering the blankets on the make-shift beds.

Mrs. Murphy shivered, pulling her shawl tighter around her shoulders. "We need to close up some of those places between the logs."

"I'm more worried about food. What Mr. Stanton brought is almost gone," said Sarah.

"Miz Reed got two ox from Breen, two from Graves. William, go over there—to Mr. Breen—see if he can spare us an ox. Two would be better."

"Miz Reed had to sign a note to pay two-for-one in California for what she got."

"Just get the meat, William, whatever you have to promise, we'll take care of it."

"I've seen no game at all," said Eddy. "We should have stopped to hunt more. When we started up the mountains there were deer. But now with the snow, they're gone. I'm going out, see if I can find something."

The next day brought damp wind from the north and heavy gray clouds. Mid-morning it began to snow heavily.

The Graves family was outside butchering an ox they'd killed that morning when they heard faint shouting and saw shapes coming through the blowing snow. It was Charles Stanton and the Indians. Stanton reported that George Donner had broken an axle on his family wagon on a steep grade and they'd had to stop to make a new one.

"George's hand was hurt," Stanton said. "They were working to make the axle and a chisel got him right across the back of the hand. They should be coming up soon."

Stanton looked at the cabin. "Tidy job, Mr. Graves."

"We need more coverin's to put on the roof. We'll throw this hide up there soon as we get through. It's tidy, all right, but right crowded."

Mr. Stanton gazed at the cabin for a moment wondering how it was going to work—Indians in with the white people. *Maybe they'll have to make a shelter for themselves...but it's so cold.*

The Indians were almost completely naked, only a skin partially covering their shoulders and back, a cloth covering their privates. Stanton had given Luis one of his blankets and begged another for Salvador from Mrs. Graves.

Stanton stamped his feet, waved his arms back and forth.

Damn, it's cold. "Mr. Graves, we need to get the mules taken care of. We killed two deer back there, we need to get the meat off, let the mules graze."

"There ain't no grass here to speak of." Franklin pointed to a small meadow about fifty yards away. "There's some grass yonder, it's been chewed over pretty good. Your other mules are down there with my stock. Mary, you girls help Mr. Stanton with that meat. We got to get this done, it's comin' on to storm."

• • •

Back on the trail, the Donner families had a terrible dilemma. Their oxen, now just skin and bones, were struggling to pull the wagons through the heavy wet snow. They didn't really know how much farther it was to where the others were, but they felt they were close.

They were in the middle of a sage-covered flat that had no wood, water or forage, no trees to halt the bitter winter wind. George sent Noah and Juan Baptiste ahead to find a campsite. They returned telling of a place up against a ridge on the west side of the trail.

Noah had to shout against the wind to make himself heard. He pointed to the southwest. "It's about three miles. It's off the road a piece, but there's no place close to the road that offers wood or grass."

George nodded. *If we can make three miles.*

The site was a good one—a clear flowing stream, a meadow covered with grass and an abundant supply of dead-fall wood. They commenced to cut down trees with the intention of building a cabin, but a storm came on during the night, burying them in a foot of heavy wet snow.

"The snow's broke in the bows on one of our wagons," said George. "If'n we don't get it cleared off, it'll break in the others. We've got to get some shelter made to keep us out of the weather 'til we can build somethin' better, or if the snow melts off, go on to where the others are."

They scraped away snow, setting up a sleeping tent beside a huge tree, leaning tall poles against it, partially enclosing the tent. It was a semi-circular affair, resembling half of an Indian lodge. Limbs were woven over and under the poles making a form of lattice and then covered with hides, ground sheets, quilts and what-all—not satisfactory but it was all they had.

Jacob went across the stream from George, backing two of his tents up to a massive downed tree. Then a framework was built over the tents with a combination of willow brush, pine boughs and hides. The single men made a teepee like shelter for themselves.

The storms raged for eight days. The people huddled inside

the huts and cabins, listening to the fury of the wind as it came booming down from the mountains, thrashing and bending the trees, tearing at the flimsy shelters.

When the skies cleared, there was deep snow around the shelters. Their situation was dire, worsening every day as the scanty food supplies diminished. In mid-November, a group of thirteen men and two women made an attempt to get over the mountain but had to turn back.

When the storms withdrew they would look at the snowy crest and tell each other that any day, Reed, or McCutchen, or someone from the fort would come, bring food, help them get over the mountains. But even as they talked of it, they knew that if they could not get out it was unlikely that anyone could get in.

William Eddy, with fear guiding his hand, managed to kill some game: a squirrel, three ducks, an owl, a wolf. The wolf was given to the dogs, at that point, the people were still a little choosy—and then he managed to kill a bear. Eddy was driven by desperation, but it took courage, tackling an eight-hundred pound grizzly with a one-shot muzzle loader gun. He placed a bullet in his mouth, the more quickly to reload.

He'd spotted the bear snuffling amongst the twigs and bushes sticking out of the snow. He aimed carefully and fired. The wounded bear found the smoke from the gun and charged Eddy, who was frantically trying to reload. He backed around a tree, the bear swiping at him, horrible deep roars coming from foaming jaws. He got another shot off into the bear's shoulder. Not being able to reload, Eddy clubbed at the bear with the rifle, and finally it collapsed on the bloody snow. Eddy went back to get help and they hauled the bear back to the cabins. Now there was food in the Murphy cabin—they would survive until help would come. They thought that surely it would be soon.

• • •

In the afternoon of one particularly cold, windy and snowy day, Patrick Breen eased to his feet, massaging his back.

"Patrick, have you the trouble again?" asked Margaret.

"The gravels, I think. Margaret, I seem to remember we had some letter paper?"

"In the black trunk."

"I need more than one ... do you have eight?"

Patrick sat down, placing a board across his knees. He cut and sewed the paper into a little book of thirty-two pages. He explained to the children, now gathered around, that it would be a journal, a record.

"A record of what?" asked Patrick Jr.

Patrick Sr. creased the paper tightly along the stitching with his fingers. "Oh, what has happened, what the day brings, I guess. I can't really say as to that ..."

That evening he got out his pen and bottle of ink, and carefully wrote the first page of a diary.

Friday Nov. 20th 1846 came to this place on the 31st of last month that it snowed we went on to the pass the snow so deep we were unable to find the road, when within 3 miles of the summit then turned back to this shanty on the Lake, Stanton came one day after we arrived here we again took our teams & wagons & made another unsuccessful attempt to cross in company with Stanton we returned to the shanty it continueing to snow all the time we were here we now have killed most part of our cattle having to stay here until next spring & live on poor beef without bread or salt it snowed during the space of eight days with little intermission, after our arrival here, the remainder of time up to this day was clear & pleasant frezeing at night the snow nearly gone from the valleys.

Juan Baptiste plodded his way through drifts of snow, icy pools of water and gooey mud, thinking that it was a good thing that the *Señor* Donner had another pair of boots for him. He reached inside his shirt, taking out the folded letter that Tamsen had written. It was to be given to Mr. Eddy or Mr. Breen, Tamsen wasn't sure who could read and write. He tucked the letter back into his shirt and pulled the heavy Indian blanket tighter around his shoulders.

"Baptiste, are you sure you know where you're goin'?" asked Milt. "We didn't come this way. We come over that ridge, through the canyon."

"This way is better, I think."

Milt and two others had gone to the Donner camps from the lake camps a week earlier and they were heading back now with Juan Baptiste and several of the single men who'd been at the Donner camps.

Baptiste had a good sense of direction and knew that the trail had been heading south, and that their camp was on the west side of the trail. From the camp they couldn't go directly south without going over a high ridge, so he followed around the foot of the ridge. When they got to the camps they found Mr. Graves, William, and Baylis chopping wood in front of the cabin. Mr. Graves put down the axe he was sharpening and approached them.

"Where are they?"

Milt pointed to the north. "You see this mountain? On the other side, but a distance more to the east. Mebbe six miles, eight miles, altogether."

"It is a good place, but the shelters, no good," said Baptist. He looked at the cabin. "Your house here, it is much better." Baptiste took the letter from his shirt. "The *Señora* Donner, she send this letter."

Mr. Graves took the letter, looked at it. "I ain't much for readin'. Let's take it in to Miz Reed."

Margaret was sitting with her children by the fire. She took the letter and began reading it.

"She says they're all right. George hurt his hand and is suffering from it. They want to know if we're making plans to try to get over the mountain, we're to send Baptiste back with word."

Mr. Graves went outside to Baptiste, squatting down by the cabin with Milt and Baylis. "The group's leavin' tomorrow." He raised his eyebrows, looking at Milt. "You got what we needed from Donner?"

"We got most of it," said Milt, "but they didn't have provisions to spare 'cept tobacco, some salt an' coffee."

Graves looked at Baptiste. "We been waitin' fer the weather to break, looks like it's clearin' now. But we can't wait for you to go back and tell them. By the time they could get ready it might start stormin' again."

"Then what I do?"

"I don't know what to tell you. You can go back. They can start out on their own, like we are."

"No, I think I go, see if you get over. Then I go back."

"You got some food? We don't have any we can spare."

"I have only a little." Baptiste pointed to the dead ox that was hanging from a tree. "You no can give me some meat?"

"You ain't our responsibility."

"The *Señor* Breen? He will have some to give to me?"

"Haw! He ain't sharin' with nobody, less'n you pays for it. Some of the others done already been askin'. Stanton's over there now, trying to get some meat. Anyway, there's fifteen or so goin'. We're headin' out first light, tomorrow mornin'."

They didn't make it over. Patrick Breen recorded the return of the group.

Monday 23rd Same weather wind W the Expedition across the mountains returned after an unsuccessful attempt.

The failed escape left the group cold, wet and discouraged, but they kept planning to make another attempt. On the evening of the 25th of November it began snowing and on the 29th Breen recorded three feet of snow on the ground.

"If we can't get out, how the hell you think they're gonna get in?" argued Franklin Graves to a gathering of people in the cabin. "If it don't snow no more, if the snow up there freezes hard, maybe it'll be possible. Right now, I guess we wait, see how it goes. We got to be right careful with our stores, we ain't got enough to last 'til spring."

Franklin and Elizabeth took stock of what they had left to feed twelve adults and children.

"Franklin, we cain't give any more oxen away."

"I didn't give any away, I sold 'em. At two-for-one California."

"Whatever, give 'er sell, we got to keep what we have fer our own."

"We got Miz Reed and that whole bunch over in the other side, they ain't got nothin' to speak of. There's eight of them and Stanton and the two Injuns—what're we gonna tell 'em when they come over here beggin'?"

"Miz Reed got four ox, two from you, two from Breen, they'll just have to make do. They ain't our worry—well, we can feel sorry—but we just got to think of ourselves."

"We sort of told Reed we'd look out for 'em—"

"Franklin! We got to take care of our own. We ain't got enough for ourselves. You want us to die to save some of them?"

At the Breen cabin, Patrick and Dolan had worked all morning to kill and butcher the last of their oxen. Dolan asked

Patrick about two animals that they hadn't taken down.

"I told Foster he could have them," said Patrick. "They have little to eat, those people."

"Ah, and I see him comin' now."

Patrick stopped his work and greeted Foster. "You have the security? The watch?" he asked.

William handed him the gold watch and Patrick looked it over. "You understand, it is two-for-one in California?"

"You've been pretty clear about it, Breen. You paid maybe twenty dollars for the two of them."

"It does not matter what I paid for them, Mr. Foster. What matters is what the animals would bring in California. I don't really want to give them to you—"

"You don't seem to be giving them to us, sir."

"Well, we are clear on the terms then?"

"Yes.

Patrick was bothered by the conversation. He mumbled to himself as he cleaned up one of the hides. *I should not have let them have the oxen. If we cannot get out before spring we won't have enough to keep ourselves. I cannot let any more of our meat go.* He sighed heavily.

Dolan looked at him. "Aye, it is a difficult thing."

• • •

At the Donner camp, the crunch of boots on the snow was heard long before Baptiste entered the hut. They looked up, listening.

"It's Baptiste," said George. "He's going to be frozen."

A storm had come in the evening before and now rain intermingled with sleet. A blast of wind, ice and rain entered the hut as Baptiste pushed open the hide door. He stomped several times, trying to dislodge the thick coating of snow and ice on his boots, then peeled off the blanket wrapped around his shoulders. The blanket had a heavy coating of frozen ice, and he stood it up by the door, still in the shape of his body.

"Is it cold out there, Baptiste?" George asked, chuckling.

"Oh, no, *Señor*, is like a day of the s..summer."

"Come on over here, son, get close to the fire. Get those wet boots off. Did you come back by yourself?" asked George.

"No, Smith he come back, the others, they stay. He is slow, I no wait for him."

Tamsen pointed to her rocking chair. "Baptiste, sit down, I'll get you some coffee. Please, tell us about the other camps. Are they going to try to get over?"

"It was three days," Baptiste's teeth clicked together as he shivered. "S..some of the people, they try to go over, but the snow *es mucho*." Baptiste held one hand up high.

"Still deep?" asked George.

"*Si, mucho* deep. I am afraid. I think we no get out of this place. Smith, he think it too."

They became quiet. The fire crackled and sizzled, now and then a spitting hiss as a drop of water hit the fire.

"The people that want to go … they say they will try again," said Baptiste. He pulled a paper from inside his shirt. "They send a letter."

Tamsen took the paper. "I can't see to read it." Taking a little stick, she held it to the fire until it glowed red, then put it to the wick on a lantern. The flame guttered and then held steady, making a warm glow in the gloomy hut.

She held the letter to the light. "It was written by Mr. Eddy. He says that some of them will try again."

"*Señor* Graves, he talk of making the things for feet to walk in the snow. I will make some too. I learn this from a man who travel in the mountains," said Baptiste.

"George, I wonder if we could make …" Tamsen furrowed her brow, thinking. "Could we make some sleds, you know, that we could pull on the snow to carry some things, and the children?"

"What would we make them out of?"

"Well, we've got hides. You remember those boats, the bull boats that were on the Platte—"

Tamsen took her journal and made a sketch.

"See? Something like this, Baptiste?"

Baptiste was excited. "*Si, si*! I can do this thing."

Everybody straightened up a little, trying to see the drawing, even Mrs. Wolfinger. She didn't understand everything but was picking up on the excitement.

That night Tamsen was too restless to sleep. She rocked in her chair, staring into the fire, where only a few red streaks showed under a gray mantle of ash. She got up, adding a few sticks of wood, poking up the ashes to get the wood burning. She shook tea leaves into the kettle and moved it over the flame. Then she sat down again, pulling her shawl tightly around her body.

Elitha got up from the bed she shared with Leanna and came to the fire, wrapping her blanket around herself.

"It's so damn cold in here, it's hard to sleep."

"Elitha, please. Curse words—"

"Oh, don't lecture. I don't care about being a lady. What does it matter? This horrible place, we're cold all the time, water dripping on us day and night, all crammed together. The hogs back home live better than we do." She began to cry. "I'm just so miserable."

"And you're the only one who's miserable?"

"No."

Tamsen poured tea into cups, handing one to Elitha.

"We may be able to leave soon, but if not, we must think of

when we can leave. We can't allow ourselves to wallow in despair. Think of things you can do to get your mind off the misery. I practically have to beat you to get you out of bed and moving around, but activity does help."

"I know. I know. But what's the use? We'll probably all die anyway."

"Honey, this will all pass. We'll get to California and have a wonderful life. We just have to grin and bear it for a while longer."

Elitha took the hem of her night dress and wiped at her tears. "I've started my monthly. Where did you put the cloths?"

"They're in the brown trunk, I'll get them for you."

Tamsen went to the trunk, returning with several strips of cloth and some cottony stuff.

"It was so hard to wash the things when we had no fire, I burned the old ones. Wrap some of this cattail cotton inside the cloth. It absorbs well."

Elitha returned to bed. Tamsen put some more wood on the fire and sat down again. She sipped her tea, rocking slowly, soothed by the motion. *Surely we'll be able to get out before our food is gone. But what if we can't?*

The snow continued, day after day. Patrick Breen wrote in his journal.

December 1st Tuesday Still snowing   wind W snow about 5-1/2 feet or 6 deep   difficult to get wood   no going from the house completely housed up   looks as likely for snow as when it commenced, our cattle all killed but three or four [of] them, the horses and Stantons mules gone & cattle suppose lost in the Snow   no hopes of finding them alive. Saturday 5th Fine clear day beautiful sunshine thawing a little looks delightful after the long snow storm.

With the weather clearing, Franklin Graves and Charles Stanton began making snowshoes for another attempt to get over the mountain. On the ninth it began snowing again. Milt Elliot and Noah James hurried over the ridge to see if they could get through to the Donner camps.

They were all outside when George saw them approaching. "Looks like company comin'. Can't see who it is."

Baptist quickly shimmied up a tree. "*Es* Noah an' Milt."

When the men came into camp Noah took George's outstretched hand. "Good to see you, Mr. Donner."

He nodded at Tamsen. "Missus," then waved at Baptiste. "Hey, Baptiste."

A sudden gust of wind picked up powdery snow on the tops of the drifts and blew it stingingly against them. They turned and looked at the sky.

"Those are some mean looking clouds yonder. Looks like we're in for another storm," said George. "Let's get inside. I'm anxious to hear what's goin' on at the other camps."

The visitors settled themselves on their heels, leaning against the poles that had been driven in the ground to make bed posts. The children and Mrs. Wolfinger sat on the beds, George sat down in Tamsen's rocking chair. Tamsen dipped coffee from the kettle into cups.

"Milford," said Tamsen, "I'm going to fix you men some food and then I'll treat your eyes."

Milt had a bad cough and both men's eyes were red and swollen from snow-glare.

"Appreciate it, ma'am. They're botherin' us terrible."

George passed out tobacco. Frances asked about the other children in the lake camps.

"They's doin' all right, considerin'. Virginia an' Patty told me to tell you all hello an' they wanted to know if you had any books you could send. They left everythin' of theirs back in the desert. It gets powerful borin' with nothin' to do but sit an' stare at the fire. There was some readin' stuff left in the cabin that the Breens took. We done read it all a hundred times. Mr. Graves is making snowshoes an' getting' ready to try to get over again. There's about twenty that'll go. We'll go too if we can get back before they leave."

"How's he makin' the snowshoes?" asked George.

"He uses ox bows, cuts 'em in half an' weaves strips of hide back and forth. They're right clumsy, but better'n nothin' I guess."

"My snowshoes, they are much better," said Baptiste.

"I like yours," said Noah, picking up one of the snowshoes and turning it over in his hands. "How'd you make it?"

"It is the Indian way. The willow, it is strong and limber, it no break. I put the willow to the fire for a time an' I peel it an' bend to the shape, you see, an' weave the willow back and forth. Like you make a basket."

"Yeah, better, not as heavy."

Milt began telling of the happenings at the lake camps.

"They've recovered most of the dead animals by now, but it's poor meat an' we ain't got any salt. Miz Donner, do you have any you could share?"

"Yes, I have a little."

"I brung a note from Mr. Stanton. He wants to buy some goods. We're to carry them back with us." Milt pulled a paper from his pocket and handed it to George. "He wrote a list. Tobacco is one thing."

"We have plenty of tea, coffee and tobacco," said George. "Now our cattle's buried under the snow or we could give you some meat. We been searchin' for 'em, this new storm's goin' to make that harder."

"Yeah, 'spect so." Milt rocked on his heels, scrunched around, tried to get more comfortable.

"What's the snow level over there now?" asked George.

"Six feet, mebbe." answered Milt, coughing. "Seems like it's not as deep … over here." His coughing grew worse and he took a swallow of coffee, but almost choked on it.

Tamsen went to a shelf and took from it a bottle of dark looking liquid and poured some into a medicine cup.

"Try this, Milt, it might help."

Milt looked at the cup, shrugged his shoulders and downed the liquid.

"She makes us take that stuff all the time. It tastes awful!" exclaimed Leanna.

Milt wiped his mouth, grimacing. "I guess I've tasted worse, but I don't remember when."

When Milt's coughing subsided he continued.

"Eddy killed a good-sized she bear. He pret' near came to an early end 'cause he wounded it, but couldn't reload 'fore it charged him. It chased him around a tree for a spell 'fore it gave out. Scared the bejeezus out of him. That meat helped but with so many it won't go that far."

"Baptiste goes out to hunt when he can, but he hasn't seen anythin'. With the snow so deep we just don't have the strength to go far off."

"How's Jacob an' Miz Elizabeth?" asked Noah.

"We're very worried about Jacob," said Tamsen. "It seems like he's just given up. I fear that …" Tamsen's words trailed off. She looked at George. "We need to go see about Jacob."

George nodded. "Yeah. The single men don't do much movin' around either, just Baptiste here, an' Denton." George sighed, took the stick he was chewing and threw it in the fire. "I can't do much with this hand of mine the way it is."

"What're you doin' for it?" asked Noah.

"Aw, Tamsen pesters me with all the treatments she can think of."

"There's some back to our camp that's in bad shape," said Noah. "Spitzer, he can't even walk now, he's so weak."

"Breen took him in, he's improved a little," said Milt. "Baylis, he's 'bout gone."

• • •

Milt and Noah didn't make it back to the lake camps before a group of seventeen people, led by Charles Stanton and the Indians, left the cabins to go over the mountains. The men and boys: Charles Stanton and the two Indians, William Eddy, William Foster, Jay Fosdick, Antonio, Charlie Burger, Patrick Dolan, Lemuel and William Murphy.

There were five women; Mary Ann Graves, Sarah Fosdick, Harriet Pike, Sarah Foster and Amanda McCutchen. Charley Burger and William Murphy turned back the first day, the others pushed on.

It was difficult going. The crude snowshoes sank down into the soft snow and it was terribly tiring to lift them out with every step. They made the top of the pass late in the afternoon of the second day.

The snow was twelve feet deep, too deep to clear away for a fire, so they laid down logs of green wood, building a fire of dry wood on top. Hunched around the fire, they nibbled on their dried beef, then rolled up in blankets and tried to get some sleep.

The next day was easier, downhill. But the exertion and lack of sufficient food was beginning to tell. Crossing a treeless expanse, the glare of the white surface brought on snow-blindness. Stanton was the worse affected, the weakest too, and he gradually fell behind. A brutal cold wind and snow flurries added to their misery. They made camp. Stanton came in an hour or so later.

The fourth day repeated the third. Fierce squalls of snow battered them, the wind pushing against them like a wall, seeming to come from everywhere at once, slamming at back and front and sides, so there wasn't a way to turn the head to shelter the face. It was so cold that their feet started freezing. Stanton still lagged.

The morning of their sixth day dawned. Eddy dug into his pack hoping to lighten it a little. To his amazement he found a piece of bear meat and with it a note written by his wife, Eleanor. The note urged him to save the meat for the last extremity; she felt that it might save his life. He looked around at the others and tucked the meat back into his pack.

Fatigue, snow-blindness, and starvation had worn Stanton down. As the others were setting out, he remained by the campfire smoking his pipe. Mary Graves asked if he was coming.

"Yes," he said, "I am coming soon."

They trekked on, but now the Indians were unsure of the trail. The group began following canyons southward, completely losing their way. Stanton never came up.

There was no food remaining except for that little piece of meat tucked away in Eddy's pack. They climbed to the top of a ridge to survey the country. To the north, forbidding mountains, to the west a high ridge. It seemed best to keep south. After two days of starvation, a storm burst upon them. They huddled together, despairing. All the men, except Eddy, favored turning back. All the women were determined to go ahead.

All that showed above the whiteness were a few huge rocks and the tops of tall trees. They began to discuss the thing that they all—except the two Indians—were thinking. Then Patrick Dolan voiced it. Should one die, to furnish food for the others? Now, it had been said, and it hung there, between them. They couldn't look at each other.

They talked about drawing lots, but they knew they could not deliberately take a life. They would struggle on until someone died. When it was almost dark they stopped. It was hard to get a fire built. The flames danced and bent in the increasingly heavy wind. They lay in their blankets around the fire, watching to see who might die. The storm increased in fury, hurling sleet and snow against them. They were numb in body, numb in mind. As the night deepened, their supply of wood was exhausted. Someone got up to chop more, and the head of the axe broke off and flipped away. They couldn't find it.

They hadn't noticed, but the fire had seeped below the green logs—perhaps they weren't as thick as they should have been—melting the snow into watery ice. The fire gradually sank into a pit, and went out. They could not get it started again, nor build another one without the axe.

Eddy seemed to have more presence of mind than the others. He got them together in a circle under blankets and soon they were totally covered with several inches of insulating snow, safe from the wind. The combined heat of their bodies kept them from freezing, only their toes and fingers suffered from frost-bite.

Antonio died. Then Franklin Graves. In his last moments, he begged his daughters to use his body for food. Through the night the storm roared on, never slackening for the dawning of Christmas Day. Patrick Dolan became deranged, leaving the blankets. Eddy struggled and argued with him. Finally Dolan settled down, slipped into sleep, and towards dusk he died.

Throughout Christmas night the storm still raged, but most of them, four days without food in excruciating conditions, were only half alive. Lemuel Murphy, raging in dementia, had to be held beneath the blankets.

Dawn broke. In desperation to start a fire, Eddy used gunpowder for tinder, accidentally blowing up the powder horn, burning himself on the face and hands. Two of the women were close enough to suffer burns also.

Later, Eddy crawled out from under the blankets a second time, desperate to start a fire, but the wood was too wet. Harriet Pike came up with a little dry cotton from the lining of her cloak. Eddy knelt down and gingerly, prayerfully, struck sparks into it with a flint. A black spot showed a little smoke, a tiny flame flickered. Eddy gingerly fed the flame until he had enough to start a dead tree on fire. The flames shot up. They crawled and groped their way over the snow to bask in the warmth.

Now, the will to live overcame the taboo. Averting their faces from each other and weeping, they began to eat of the dead. The two Indians refused the food, going off a distance.

Lemuel sank into a stupor and died. They remained there for three days, resting and gaining strength. They stripped the flesh from the bodies, ate; dried the rest to carry with them. They began to walk once more. They had no idea where they were. They knew they must head west, but the topography was against them, most of the ridges running north and south. They would slip and slide down one slope, only to have to climb up the next.

Their foot coverings had long since fallen apart and their feet were sore and bloody from exposure and the cutting edges of snow, ice and rock. It became painful to walk. Since losing the hatchet, they had to find dead trees to build a fire.

They were into lower country where the snow was not as deep, but that didn't make a lot of difference if the ground was still covered. They worked their way laboriously across the rough country. The smaller streams were covered by ice and snow which formed snow-bridges over the stream. Now and again as they crossed a snow-bridge they would look down through an opening and see water rushing below.

They came on to a high ridge, on each side deep canyons. They had no choice but to go forward along the narrow crest. From this vantage point they viewed distant dark ridges which had no snow. Even more distant they saw a broad green plain. It was the valley of the Sacramento.

As they gathered on the top of the ridge hope flashed through them, buoyed their spirits, made it all seem possible now. They might not die on the wind-swept snowy peaks of the California Mountains. The exultation was brief. As they made their way ahead they saw that the ridge they were following came to an end and the gorge to their right turned sharply in front of them. Now, directly between them and the valley was a great steep-sided canyon, two thousand feet deep. They camped on the brink, worn out, apprehensive that the gorge might be their final defeat.

• • •

ack in the mountain camps, each day brought more and more desperation. On December 17th Patrick Breen recorded that Baylis Williams died on the 15th. When he took up his pen on December 20th, his journal included prayer.

> *Sund. 20th Night clear froze a little now clear & pleasant wind N.W. thawing a little Mrs. Reid here, no account of Milt. yet Dutch Charley started for Donnghs turned back not able to proceed tough times, but not discouraged our hopes are in God. Amen.*

> *Mon. 21 Milt got back last nght from Donos camp sad news. Jake Donno Sam Shoemaker Rinehart, & Smith are dead the rest of them in a low situation snowed all night with a strong S-W wind today cloudy wind continues but not snowing thawing sun shining dimly. In hopes it will clear off.*

Tues. 22nd   Snowd. All last night   Continued to snow all day with some few intermissions   had a severe fit of the gravel yesterday I am well to day, praise be to the God of Heaven.

Wend. 23rd   Snowed. A little last night   clear to day & thawing a little. Milt took some of his meat to day all well at their camp began this day to read the Thirty days prayer, may Almighty God grant the request of an unworthy sinner that I am. Amen.

That evening, Patrick began the prayer rituals that would help the Breen family, and later on, Margaret Reed and her children, through the terrible ordeal.

"Ever glorious and blessed Mary, Queen of Virgins, Mother of Mercy, hope and comfort of dejected and desolate souls …"

December, 1846 - February, 1847
Ordeal of Hunger

It was snowing again as Christmas Day dawned. In the Donner camps there was meat, Juan Baptiste had managed to kill a bear cub. Tamsen made dolls for the little girls and Baptiste made small snowshoes for the boys. After the children had their gifts, everyone gathered around the fire and George told the story of the birth of Jesus.

At the lake camps, there was brief joy in the Reed cabin. Milt had gone to the Breen cabin two days before and brought back the last of the meat that Patrick Dolan had left for the Reed family.

Margaret told her children that they would have a special meal for Christmas. The children eagerly watched as their mother took out the food that she'd hoarded for this day. Into the simmering pot of beef went some beans, a little rice, a strip of tripe and a few dried apple pieces. The children hovered near the kettle, breathing in the delicious aroma, jostling to be the one to stir the precious food. At last Margaret began to dish up the meal.

"Children, on this day, you may eat all you want."

In the Breen cabin, the family gathered at the fireplace, the little children taking turns holding up a burning pine stick so that Patrick could see to read the Christmas prayers. They nibbled on a scanty meal of stewed beef. Patrick was ill, hunched over from the pain of kidney stones.

"O Virgin Mary, Mother of God, you revealed your Immaculate Conception to the humble. We beseech you to gain for us who pray to you the blessings and graces we need ..."

Friday 25th began to snow yesterday about 12 oclock snowed. All night & snows yet rapidly   wind about E by N great difficulty in getting wood   John & Edwd. has to get I am not able   offerd our prayers to God this Christmas morning   the prospect is appalling but hope in God Amen

Patrick stared at the journal entry, tried to straighten his back, grimacing as pain shot through him. He'd suffered from the gravels many times, but this was the worse. Patrick was optimistic that faith and prayer—and a diligent husbanding of their stores—would bring them through. They would have to start eating hides to stretch their supply of meat. Every night they knelt before the fire to pray.

"Lord Jesus Christ, listen to our prayers that you may grant what we ask. Hear our prayers and listen to our voices, for we are in need. O Mary, grant us the grace to accept our burdens and carry out our responsibilities in the true spirit of devotion to you and our Lord Jesus Christ, Amen."

Now, most of the people had only hides to eat. They prepared the hides by scraping off the hair, cutting them into pieces and boiling for hours. A scummy foam would form, then the boilings would become a jellied glue-like substance. Some of the people could tolerate it more than others. Desperate to find something more palatable, they took animal bones that had every vestige of meat scraped away, boiling them again and again until they could pound the bones into a mush. They withered, became weak, cursed their fate. A new year dawned and death came calling.

[Breen Journal]
Wedsd. 30th   Fine clear morning   froze hard last night Charley [Burger] died last night about 10 o clock   had with him in money $1.50 two good loking silver watches one razor 3 boxes caps   Keysburg took them into his possession   Spitzer took his coat & waistcoat Keysburg all his other little effects   gold pin one shirt and tools for shaveing.

Thursday 31st   Last of the year, may we with Gods help spend the comeing year better than the past which we pur-pose to do if Almighty God will deliver us from our present dredful situation which is our prayer if the will of God sees it fiting for us Amen   morning fair   now cloudy   wind E by S for three days past   freezeing hard every night looks like another snow storm   Snow storms are dredful to us   snow very deep   crust on the snow

Jany. 1st 1847 we pray the God of mercy to deliver us from our present calamity if it be his Holy will Amen.   Com-menced snowing last night   does not snow fast   wind S.E. sun peeps out at times   provisions getting scant   dug up a hide from under the snow yesterday for Milt   did not take it yet.

Mond. 4th Fine morning looks like spring thawing now about 12 o clock wind S.E. Mrs. Reid Milt. Virginia & Eliza started about ½ hour ago with prospect of crossing the mountain may God of Mercy help them left ther children here Tom's with us Pat with Keysburg & Jas with Graveses's folks, it was difficult for Mrs. Reid to get away from the children.

Weds. 6th Fine day clear not a cloud froze very hard last night wind S.E. Eliza came back from the mountain yesterday evening not able to proceed, today went to the Graves, the others kept ahead.

Friday 8th Fine morning wind E froze hard last night very cold this morning Mrs. Reid & company came back this morning could not find their way on the other side of the mountain they have nothing but hides to live on Martha is to stay here Milt. & Eliza going to Donos. Mrs. Reid & the 2 boys going to their own shanty & Virginia prospects dull may God relieve us all from this difficulty if it is his Holy will Amen.

Now most of the hides from Mrs. Reed's side of the cabin had been removed from the roof to use for food. Without shelter, they went from place to place. Patrick recorded on the 9th that Mrs. Reed and Virginia were in the Breen cabin (Virginia's toes somewhat frozen) and then on the 11th he wrote that Mrs. Reed was with Keseberg, but soon the entire Reed family had been taken into the Breen cabin.

Patrick and Margaret continued to hoard their meat, eating hides, saving the little they had left for the last extremity. The Reed family survived on hides and boiled bones, but a few times, when Margaret Breen realized that Virginia was close to dying, she gave her a little meat.

The Keseberg family moved into the Murphy cabin. Young William Murphy removed the hides from the Keseberg lean-to and took them to the Murphy cabin. It would be all they had to eat.

By the end of January two more were dead. The Keseberg baby, Lewis Jr., and Landrum Murphy.

Day by day, they grew weaker. Day by day, they talked and prayed for rescue. When the clouds would lift their eyes would search the mountain for specks moving across the white expanse.

When the storms receded, those without resources went from cabin to cabin, asking for food. Juan Baptiste had come from the Donner camps and he, John Denton and Eliza, the Reed hired girl, mushed through the deep snow to the Breen cabin.

"Miz Reed, Miz Graves won't give us nothin', won't even let us take the hides of'n the cabin. Don't you have anythin'? We're starving. Milt's weak, he cain't move aroun' much, his toes still froze from when we tried to get over."

"We're eating hides, Eliza. We have nothing else."

"I can't eat that stuff, I cain't stomach it."

"I'm sorry, Eliza. It's all we have. You can live on hides, or you can die, it's your choice."

Margaret pulled a shawl around her shoulders, following them as they left the cabin.

"The Breen's got meat, they must be givin' you some," cried Eliza.

"I wish that were true!" Margaret exclaimed. "My children are starving. I have nothing to give them. Oh, Eliza, if I had it to give, I would."

"Why cain't they just share some of it?" wailed Eliza.

Margaret moved her hands in a gesture of helplessness,

and didn't answer. Eliza turned away, her shoulders drooping in discouragement. Baptiste started down the path to the Murphy cabin.

"Miz Murphy, she's got nothin'. I been over there already," said Eliza.

Baptiste shrugged his shoulders, and the three began the trek back to the Graves camp. When they got there, Baptiste gathered up his pack. "I go back. The *Señora* Donner, she tell me to come back *pronto*. I am the only man to do the work."

"We heard you killed a bear. Is there any of that meat left?" asked Denton.

"I kill the bear. A young one." Baptiste measured a height with his hand. "no big." He shrugged his shoulders. "*Quizas* there is some of the bear that remain. I go now."

Milt was staring morosely into a fire that was only one or two flames licking weakly from a thin burned out section of a pine limb. Part of the roof of the cabin was open to the sky and the edges of the remaining hides flapped and curled in the wind.

He looked up when Eliza and Denton entered the cabin. He could see they were empty-handed. His shoulders sagged, and he muttered an oath. He turned his attention back to the pitiful fire.

Denton had managed to pull a half-dead limb off a pine tree when they were out, and he began breaking it up, carefully feeding small pieces into the fire. Milt lifted up, scooting the box he was using as a seat over a little. "The fire's puny, take care you don't put it out."

"Yeah."

Eliza pulled a stool close to the fireplace and sat down.

"Miz Reed don't got nothin' but hides an' she's needin' the rest of 'em off the cabin. I guess we got to go stay in with Miz Graves or get covered with snow here. Miz Graves still got some meat, but she ain't gonna share any of it. She says she got to keep her own family alive an' we can go to hell for all she cares."

"She said that?"

"No, but she's thinkin' it."

The worry of feeding and caring for her seven children and Amanda McCutchen was driving Mrs. Graves almost crazy. Her seventeen year old, William, and the two girls, Eleanor and Lovina, were sent out each day to get wood, but some days the hide they used to carry the wood might have only a twig or two in it. All of the low wood around was deep in the snow. Having to stand in soft snow made it hard for William to get leverage to swing an axe on a branch, much less a tree of any size.

The strain caused the normally agreeable Mrs. Graves to grow depressed and irritable. When Mrs. Reed came to get hides off the roof of the cabin, Mrs. Graves lit into her.

"You ain't takin' no hides from here, you ain't takin' no goods neither, 'til you give me what you owe fer the animals. I wish Franklin hadn't given them to you."

"Mrs. Graves, you know that Mr. Graves let us have those oxen to be paid in California. My husband will—"

"Yer husband! That murderer! Why would I think he would pay us? An' why ain't he comin' back? Said he'd come back with provisions—where is he? He don't care 'bout you nor any of us."

"He'll be here, any day now. He wouldn't leave us here without trying with all his body and soul—Mrs. Graves, I need those hides, we have nothing else."

"Get out of here, get out of my sight. Take yer damned hides. It's takin' food out'a the mouths of my babies."

Milt and John Denton pulled the last of the hides off the Reed's half of the cabin and took them to the Breen cabin.

"Miz Reed," said Milt, "I'm goin' over to the Donner's camp an' Eliza's goin' too. Mebbe they have some food."

Margaret looked at Milt in sorrow. "Milt, I wish—"

"It ain't yer fault, Miz Reed."

Milt's face was gaunt, haunted, his eyes looking out of dark hollows under his brow. His mouth twisted bitterly. "It ain't nobody's fault."

"You can make it? With your feet so bad?"

"There're some better."

Margaret looked at Denton. "You're going too? To the Donners?"

"No. I'm thinkin', maybe I'll head over the mountain, first good day …"

"I don't think it's possible, John."

"Yeah. Well, anyway, Mr. Reed will be bringing supplies. He should … be getting' back."

Milt and Denton began walking back to the now denuded Reed cabin. "Look, Milt, if you can, bring back some food. Tell George it's for me."

"Yeah. I'll do 'er. Maybe they'll have somethin' besides hides. Mebbe there'll be some game over there, mebbe Baptiste's been able to hunt."

Eliza and Milt set out for the Donner camps, trying to find places where the snow was hard enough to walk on, but most of the time they sank down several inches. The wind came up, pelting them with ice crystals. The mountains and meadows were beautiful, the dark green trees standing out in bold relief against the glistening white snow. They had no eye for the beauty of the scene. To them it was forbidding, ugly, oppressive.

As they walked, the sky became gray, the wind fiercer. When at last they spotted the Donner huts, they quickened their steps, anxious to get out of the wind and cold. The Donners were glad to see them—it was good to have company, to hear the news from the other camps. Any change in the daily routine relieved their terrible boredom.

"Oh, Miz Donner," said Eliza, "it be the worse kind of fate we have. Miz Reed, Virginia, Milt an' me, we tried to get over agin' a few days ago an' we like to froze to death. We couldn't find our way an' had to come back." Eliza spoke in a strange flat voice that was hard to understand because she was almost completely deaf since childhood.

"Baylis died the middle of December. Went into a delirium like an' was gone. Now I have nobody."

"We heard of it, Eliza, we're sorry," said Tamsen.

"Charlie Burger died a week or two back," said Milt. "Several are in a bad way, too weak to get around. Breen's been sufferin' from the gravels. His boys get wood an' help the others with the buryin' an' such." Milt shook his head, sighing.

"We've got only hides to eat," said Eliza. "I jes' cain't eat that gluey stuff, I throws it up. Breen's still got some meat, an' the Graves boy dug a horse out of the snow a day or two ago, but neither is sharin' any of it. Do you all have any food at all?"

"We have a little bear meat. I still have some cattail roots. They make a tolerable stew with a little meat."

"I seem to remember you diggin' up all those roots when we was camped in that grass valley," said Milt. "Seems like a hundred years ago."

"We have to look out for Jacob's family too," said Tamsen. "We must be very careful with what food we have."

Tamsen handed Eliza a cup of tea. "The tea is soothing to one's nerves and will help you forget about food. It has a little sustenance too."

If Eliza could see a person's mouth when talking, she understood most of what they said. "Thank you kindly, Miz Donner, but there ain't nothin' that's goin' to keep me from thinkin' about food. Some of yer coffee'll taste good to me too."

"I'll have some coffee, ma'am," said Milt.

"The coffee helps get us through the day," said George. "That'n tobacco. Smokin' is just about the only comforting thing I got left." He handed Milt his tobacco sack.

"Thank you kindly." Milt filled his pipe and got it going. The smell of the tobacco was sharp and good. Milt took his knife out of his pocket, picked up one of the firewood sticks and began whittling on it with the knife.

"Keeps my hands busy. I'll make some fire startin's for you, Miz Donner."

They were quiet for awhile, watching Milt as he stripped yellow-white pieces of wood onto the dirt floor of the hut. He cleared his throat.

"I feel bad that I can't do nothin' to help Miz Reed and the children. It's my fault that Mr. Reed had to leave them. If I hadn't got to arguin' with Snyder, if I'd just waited instead of tryin' to drive the wagon past—" Milt's face twisted in anguish. "It's a hard burden to bear, thinkin' I was responsible."

Tamsen leaned towards him. "Milt, it was not your fault. You were not responsible for Snyder's anger—he was. You were not responsible for James drawing a knife and plunging it into the man—James was."

Milt nodded his head. "Yeah, my pap always used to tell me that fightin's somethin' you do when you've tried everythin' else an' I think I've followed that … but it eats at me."

"You see," said Tamsen, "the whole matter could have been just a small annoyance, but something in James triggered a murderous impulse. He should have had the control to step back. If he had backed off and left Snyder alone, it would not have happened. You followed the correct path by stepping aside. He did not. You cannot blame yourself."

"Tamsen," said George, "Snyder didn't have to start hittin'

on James with the whip handle. He could've backed off."

"Yes, he was to blame for that," agreed Tamsen. "Oh, it was all so stupid!"

Milt puffed on his pipe for while, then spoke again. "We've gone through the four ox Miz Reed bought from Breen an' Graves. The company agreed to look out for the family, but now none of 'em will help her, leastways they won't part with any food."

"That Miz Graves is mean as a stewed witch," said Eliza. "Miz Reed came to get the hides off'n her cabin an' Miz Graves told her she had to pay for the two oxen before she could have her goods."

"Hard times can make a person say things they don't really mean," said George.

"Mrs. Graves struck me as being nice," said Tamsen.

"You ain't had to live rubbin' elbows with her like we have. Miz Reed, she ain't accustomed to have to make do and not get her way. An' you know, it's strange, but Miz Reed, so weak an' frail like with those terr'ble headaches, you know, she don't have 'em no more, leastways that I notice."

"That's right," said Milt, "she don't. I reckon God just up an' cured her, 'cause she has to look out fer the children an' all by herself."

"I no think *Dios,* he cure her," said Baptiste. "I think she no have the husband to feel sorry for her, so it no good to have the headache."

"Well, let's give her the benefit of doubt." said George. He turned to Milt. "We've still not found all of our oxen. We keep hopin' for a real good thaw so's some of 'em will start showin'. They were poor, mostly skin and bones, but if we could find 'em we could share some with you. I can't do a gol-durn thing, I'm weak as a kitten. If it wasn't for Baptiste, we'd have a mighty hard time."

"Mebbe I can help Baptiste look for 'em." said Milt. He stared into the fire for a moment, then looked at George, speaking quietly. "Some of 'em's talkin' about usin' the dead for food. They ain't come to it yet." He paused and cleared his throat. "I dunno, I think I'd rather pass on from starvation than have to ..." His voice trailed away and he stared into the fire, then began whittling on his stick again.

"Things are that bad, then?" asked George.

"With some of 'em, it is. Graves still has some meat, an' Breen, but the rest of us is livin' on hides. I got the last of Miz Reed's meat from Breen two days before Christmas, and we've eaten all the dogs that were still with us."

"The only dog we still had disappeared a few days after Christmas. He wouldn't have made much of a meal anyway. Sure wish it would thaw. If we could find an ox or two you could take some back, help the people out. They must be desperate to be talkin' like that."

Baptiste got up from where he was sitting on the floor and began to work on the fire, poking and gathering the coals. The damp wood sizzled in defiance as he added more sticks.

"You know the *Señor* Kit Carson? He tell me that one time he eat the man meat. He was in the camp of the Crow Indians an' he did not know this. They make the fool with him. He say the meat was *chungo ... que is el Inglés*? Uh, rope. It was like rope."

Baptiste shrugged. "Maybe it was an old one. He say the color was strange. I do not know if he tell the truth. Maybe he tell a lie."

"Oh, please! You're making me sick," cried Elitha.

Baptiste looked down at his feet, crestfallen. "I only say what someone tell me."

"Some will do it to live," said Tamsen. "I cannot say what we would do. I hope we never have to make a choice."

"I would rather die!" exclaimed Elitha.

"You ate the mouse, is it different?" asked Baptiste.

George frowned and raised his hand, signaling Baptiste not to say anything more.

Everyone became silent, the only sound for a few moments the fire murmuring at the wood and the scratch, scratch of a branch against the frozen hides on the top of the hut. Then, the keening howl of a wolf on the ridge to the west of the camps.

"Die Wölfe, ich hasswe das gerauch! Es macht mich Wahnsinnig!" exclaimed Mrs. Wolfinger.

"Yeah, they bother me too, *Frau* Wolfinger," said George.

"The wolves came right up to our hut when we were dressing out the bear Baptiste killed," said Tamsen. "Baptiste, I want you to shoot them."

"Yeah," said Milt, "they're all over where we are, howling their fool heads off all night, but just go outside with a gun and they're nowhere to be seen."

"Tomorrow I will hide myself an' wait for them. For dinner, *los lobos* will have the ball of lead."

Tamsen stood, shaking out her apron. "Elitha, take the girls with you, go over to Betsey's and ask her to bring everyone over. I'm going to make some supper."

After the girls had gone, Tamsen told Milt and Elitha of her concern for Elizabeth and her children.

"Betsey's oldest boy, Solomon, took off, wandered in circles, finally came back, but he's kind of demented. Baptiste's been staying there to help her, but if relief doesn't come soon, I fear she won't make it."

"Those folks that went out a month ago, they should be back by now," said Milt. "Mr. Reed, he's gonna be worried sick about his family. I don't understand why he ain't back yet."

Tamsen had unpacked her good dishes, putting them on a

shelf made from a box. Now, she took the plates and cups from the shelves, wiping them off as she set them out. Her mind went to her warm, cozy kitchen back in Illinois, when she'd packed the dishes for the journey. She'd put corn meal in the bottom of a barrel, then some of the dishes, carefully making sure each was surrounded by the cornmeal, adding more meal and dishes until all were safely tucked inside. The cornmeal had been used up weeks ago. *Oh, why did we leave our home? Why were we so foolish?*

For supper Tamsen gave each person a cup of stew made from cattail roots, dried mushrooms and scraps of bear meat, adding a small piece of pine-tree bread and a square of tallow.

"What is this stuff?" asked Eliza, pointing to the bread.

"It's from the inner bark of the pine tree, the cambrium. Tell your people over there about this. It's not easy to obtain and you can only get a small amount from each tree. It has sustenance, it can help keep one from starving if you can get enough of it."

"It don't taste bad, kinda sweet," said Milt.

"I used the last bit of my molasses in these, which makes it better. If you have any fat to mix in, that helps."

"I hanker for salt powerful bad," said Milt. "We used up what you gave us the first time we were here."

Tamsen looked at Milt, sorrow in her eyes. "I have only a little left. I have been using it very sparingly. I know that the body needs salt, the complete lack of it causes weakness. We will share what food we have with you for a few days, but we won't be able to feed you longer. Surely the Graves or the Breen family will give you something."

Eliza began to cry. "The Breens have plenty of meat, but they won't share."

"They did give a piece to Miz Murphy for Landrum. It was too late." Milt shook his head.

"Miz Breen gives a little to Virginia, now and again," said

Eliza. "Leastways that's what Miz Reed tol' me, but that don't help us none." Eliza snuffled for a while, poking at the fire with a stick, raising sparks that blew upward in the dark.

"It looked like Virginia was goin' to die. Miz Breen felt she had to help her," said Milt.

"Listen," said George, "I think the wind's changed. It's comin' from the northwest. Likely it's goin' to storm again."

"I don't hate anything in this world as much as I hate snow," said Betsey, "less'n it's the damned wind."

Milt got up and pulled open the door. A blast of cold, moist air showered the inside of the hut with tiny sharp particles of ice. He pushed the door shut. "Yep. It's already startin'."

"Well," said Eliza happily. "We cain't leave until it stops snowing anyways."

The days dragged on. The inmates of the mountain prison were dejected and sick, several close to death. They prayed for the storms to end, the snow to melt, for help to come from California. It was the same conversation in every cabin and hut.

"Reed should have been back long ago. The snowshoe party left middle of December. Even if they'd made only six miles a day, it's long past time for a return party. Something must have happened to them. Oh, God, maybe none of them made it. Maybe no one will ever come."

• • •

On the east side of the mountains, the snowshoe party began the descent down the steep canyon. By that time their snowshoes had fallen apart and they were toasting and eating the leather thongs. They stepped crosswise to the slope, but many times their feet would slip and they'd skid across the hard, icy surface, tumbling until stopped by a stray bush or rock. It was two thousand feet almost straight down.

After crossing the ice-choked stream in the bottom of the canyon, they rested, looking up at the other side of the canyon, wondering how they could find the strength to climb it. Eddy got them up, helping one and then another to their feet. Harriet Fosdick bent over her husband, urging him to get up.

He shook his head. "I don't think I can make it."

"Jay, we're close, pretty soon we'll be out of the snow, it's just a little farther."

Eddy came over and between them they got Jay to his feet. Slowly, painfully, they began to climb. They worked their way up, digging their feet into the snow and mud, going across the slope for a distance, then turning back, moving upward, grabbing onto a bush or a root, sometimes a rock sticking out of the slope. It was evening when at last they crawled over the edge of the precipice.

That night they ate the last of the dried flesh, in the morning they started out again. The snow depth had lessened with the lower elevation, the surface was firmer and it became easier to walk. Oaks began to mingle with pine and cedar.

Their shoes had disintegrated and their feet were raw and bleeding. Strips were torn from their blankets to wrap around their feet. They pressed doggedly on, hardly aware of their surroundings. Fosdick dropped behind, his wife bending over him. The others paused, looked at him, turned and went on. With the help of his wife, he came up that evening.

Now out of food, someone still had a few pieces of a shoe and some rawhide strips. They divided them up. A charred string and a two inch square of leather—supper. They began casting eyes upon the two Indians who soon became uncomfortable, disappearing during the night.

They made only two miles the next day, Foster holding them back. They camped that night on bare ground, under an oak tree. Foster collapsed, he was dying.

In the morning, Eddy and Mary Ann Graves set out, the others following at their own slow, painful pace. The Fosters dragged along in the rear. Eddy and Mary Ann noticed a place where a deer had lain and hope and elation surged through them.

They proceeded warily. At the bottom of a downslope they spotted the deer at the edge of a snowdrift. When within shooting distance Eddy summoned the strength to hold the rifle and fired.

Those behind heard the shot and struggled ahead a little faster. They found Eddy and Mary Ann roasting the meat of the deer. The Fosdicks were still up on the plateau. Jay could not go on. Later that night, he died in his wife's arms. Sarah wrapped his body in their only blanket, sitting beside him all night hoping that she would die too. At dawning, she hadn't.

Easing herself up, she staggered on. She found the others, coming back. Sarah begged that they not use her husband's body, but by then they were hardened to the use of human flesh and it was not to be wasted. The food helped, but still they were in a pitiful condition. They had suffered the extremes of fatigue, freezing, and mental strain, and twice had spent a period of several days without food.

On they went. They found sticks to support themselves, as they were constantly stumbling, tripping over things, their legs collapsing under them. Another canyon, a descent, a steep climb. On and on. The food was gone. More starvation.

They were all somewhat demented, Foster more so. They talked of killing one of them in order that the rest might live, but were kept from it by finding the two Indians, almost, but not quite, dead. Salvador lay on the ground, a little way off Luis, too, was helpless.

Convinced that the Indians would live only a few minutes or a few hours, Foster raised his rifle; fired twice. Now they had food for a few days.

A storm descended upon them, adding piercing cold to their misery. They were now in grassy, thinly wooded hills. They came across tracks and a trail. Following on, they staggered into an Indian village. They were given acorn flour to eat and helped from village to village, finally reaching the settlements near Sutter's fort.

It was mid-January. After thirty-three days at the extremes of human endurance, five men and two women survived of the fifteen that had left the mountain camps. The alarm went out. People were dying in the mountains.

When the members of the snowshoe party were brought to Johnson's Ranch in mid-January, John Rhodes, a recent arrival in California, volunteered to take news of their arrival to Sutter's Fort. The fort had been taken over by federal forces and was now Fort Sacramento, with Army Lieutenant Edward V. Kern in charge.

Mid-January, 1847
Rescue

THE CALIFORNIA STAR, YERBA BUENA,
January 16, 1847

It is probably not generally known to the people, that there is now in the California mountains in a most distressing situation, a party of emigrants from the United States, who were prevented from crossing the mountains by an early heavy fall of snow. They were almost entirely out of provisions, when they reached the foot of the mountain, and but for the timely succor afforded them by Capt. J.A. Sutter, one of the most humane and liberal men in California, they must have all perished in a few days. James Reed, after a failed attempt to reach the party in November, had been promoting relief efforts and was in Yerba Buena when the news of the snowshoe party reached him on February 5th. Hull took command of the relief, appointing Midshipman Selim Woodworth to take charge. James Reed was appointed his assistant.

Kern, even before notifying and getting authority to do so, had begun rounding up volunteers, offering three dollars a day, considered very high wages. The first men to enlist were Aguila Glover, Riley Septimus Moutrey, and Joe Sels. Provisions and horses were provided by Sutter and John Sinclair, and several more men were recruited. They included Adolph Bruheim, Edward Coffeemire, and Daniel Rhoads.

The party arrived at Johnson's ranch and set to work slaughtering cattle and bagging flour. There, John Rhoads, Reason Tucker, William Ritchie, and Jotham Curtis were added to the pay-roll. Before the relief party moved out they were joined by George Tucker, Joe Verrot and Billy Coons. William Eddy, after less than three weeks of recuperation, was there.

The strategy was to set up provision points along the route. At Mule Springs, about thirty miles away, the snow was three feet deep. Eddy and Joe Verrot were assigned to bring the weakened animals back to Johnson's for replacement with fresh stock. Young George Tucker and Billy Coons were to stay to guard provisions. The remaining ten men continued into snow over five feet deep. They stopped to fashion snowshoes from pine boughs and rawhide strips. After a few days of the heavy work, Ritchie, Curtis, and Bruheim dropped out and the seven others continued. This was the first relief party to leave for the mountains, the second would be under the leadership of James Reed.

• • •

Back at the camps, the people who were still alive huddled in the dank, dark shelters, only the flickering fires making a little orange-yellow glow against the gloom. Now almost all their time was spent in bed, covered with smelly, putrid blankets and quilts that hadn't seen a washing or airing in weeks. The cabins reeked with the smell of human waste, sickness, filth. They were unbathed—most too weak, others husbanding their strength to gather firewood. The death toll mounted. Sometimes the dead bodies lay for days before they could get enough people together to take the bodies out. The snow was higher than the roofs of the cabins. They shoveled out inclines and made steps of snow in front of their doors to get into and out of the cabins. Patrick Breen had little to record that was hopeful.

[February 1847]
Frid. 5th Peggy very uneasy for fear we shall all perish with hunger   we have but a little meat left & only part of 3 hides   has to support Mrs. Reid   she has nothing left but one hide & it is on Graves shanty   Milt is living there & likely will keep that hide   Eddy's child died last night.

Patrick sent John to the Murphy cabin to bury Landrum Murphy. He made a grave in the snow and he and Mrs. Murphy laid Landrum in it. They packed the snow down hard, hoping the wolves which howled around the cabins at night would not be able to dig the body up.

John took wood into the cabin and built up the fire. Before leaving he leaned over Eleanor's bed to see how she was. She took his hand.

"I don't think I will last another day. Would … would you ask your father to pray for me and my little ones?"

Now Patrick led his family, and Margaret Reed and her children, in prayer morning and evening.

"O Blessed Mother, grant us the gift of faith and courage to face our trials. Please intercede with Him that through His divine love he may hear and answer our petitions …"

Mond. 8th Fine clear morning wind S.W. froze hard last Spitzer died last night about 3 o clock we will bury him in the snow Mrs. Eddy died on the night of the 7th. Beautiful morning wind W froze hard last night, to day thawing in the sun Milt Elliot died last night at Murphys shanty about 9 0 clock P.M. Mrs. Reid went there this morning to see after his effects

J Denton trying to borrow meat for Graves had none to give they have nothing but hides all are entirely out of meat but a little we have our hides are nearly all eat up but with Gods help spring will soon smile upon us.

The people in the Breen cabin were the first to hear the shouted halloos of the rescuers. At first, the seven men saw only the fields and drifts of snow as their snowshoes rasped and glided over the frozen lake. William Eddy had told them they would find the cabins in the trees at the east end of the lake.

"Halloo! Halloo!" They looked at each other in puzzlement. "They must all be dead, covered up in the snow." Then, they saw wisps of smoke coming out of the snow, and found the steps to the door of a cabin. "Anybody here?"

Haggard, hollowed eyed, mere skeletons now, the people came out into the glaring sunlight, squeezing their eyes to slits, trying to shade their faces from the brightness.

"Are you men from California, or are you from heaven?" quavered one of the women.

The rescuers were shocked, didn't quite know what to say to these poor, wretched people. But soon they opened their packs and began to hand out food in quantities that would be safe for the famished stomachs. Too much at once could kill them. That was hard for the starvelings to understand.

The next morning three of the men, Tucker, Moultry, and John Rhodes, set out for the Donner camps.

• • •

Señora! Veo a los hombres! Señora Tamsen, there are men coming. It is men from California. Three men are coming!"

Baptiste was yelling and jumping up and down. Tamsen and the girls were outside when they heard him shouting. They ran up the snow steps and started towards the men, yelling, floundering in the snow. Tamsen waved her shawl.

Baptiste shouted. "We are here. Men, men—"

"Oh, God, do they see us? Do they see us?"

"*Si, Señora.* They come."

It seemed hours before the men came close. Walking in the lead was a man who, with all his winter clothing on, looked to be about as broad as he was tall, his face red and chapped, his lips cracked and sore from exposure.

"Miz Donner? I'm John Rhodes. We sure been worried about you people, and it seems, rightly so."

"Yes, I'm Mrs. George Donner. We are very glad to see you. You weren't able to bring mules or horses?"

"No, ma'am. No way could mules, or any livestock, get over the snow. We brought what food we could carry in. Most of it we cached back along the trail to use on the way out."

"Well, we're very glad to have what you have brought. Please come in and talk to my husband. He's suffering from weakness caused by an injury to his hand."

Mr. Rhodes pointed to the other men. "This is Sep Moultrie an' the man coming up is Reason Tucker. His foot's been frostbit, needs doctorin' on it. Men, this is Miz Donner, George's wife."

The men nodded their heads in Tamsen's direction

"You've got another family here?" asked Mr. Rhodes.

"Yes, Jacob's family, my husband's brother." Tamsen pointed in the direction of the other camp. "Their camp is just over there."

"I take the men there," said Baptiste.

Mr. Rhodes instructed Mr. Moultrie and Mr. Tucker to proceed on to Betsey's camp to give her some of the food they had brought. Then he went with Tamsen inside the hut. George was depressed when he learned that the men hadn't been able to bring horses.

"We couldn't bring 'em up farther than the snow line, Mr. Donner. Sure wish we could've. It would have been easier."

Mr. Rhodes went on to explain that only those who were strong enough to walk could be taken back with them.

"There's several from the lake camps that aren't strong enough to go," he said. "We're gonna try to carry out some of the children. We haven't enough men to carry more, but another rescue party will be along in a short while. That is, if it quits storming. If it don't quit, well, it's gonna take longer. We'll leave what we can spare in the way of provisions."

Betsey stumbled over the log bridge and hurried to the other shelter, crying and wringing her hands. Tamsen was shocked at how bad she looked. Her face was gray and gaunt, her body nothing but angular bones.

"They're only goin' to take William and George, they ain't gonna take my Mary and my boys."

"They can't take our three little ones either, but Leanna and Elitha are strong enough, and Noah and Mrs. Wolfinger. We'll just have to wait for the next relief party."

"What have we done to deserve this?" cried Betsey. "If God loves us like the preachers say, why ain't he watchin' out fer us? How can God let this happen?"

"Elizabeth. Elizabeth, listen," said George. "There's always a picture that we, as mortals, can't see. Dyin's not that bad. We're all goin' to end that way anyway. We'll all be together again in the after-life."

"That's supposed to make me feel better, watching my children suffer an' starve? Nothin' to give but hide boilin's, their little hands beggin' for food? Oh, God, I just cain't bear no more."

Tamsen knelt next to Betsey on the floor. "We've got to get the children ready to go. The men are anxious to leave."

Betsey got up, wiped her eyes, blowing her nose on her apron. "Those men ain't leavin' enough food to keep us alive fer more'n a day or two."

Putting her hands over her face, she began sobbing again. "Did you talk to Juan Baptiste? He's wantin' to go, he tol' me. What're we gonna do if he leaves?"

"George promised him if he would stay that he would always have a home with us in California. He's reluctant, but he's agreed not to leave. I feel badly for him. He has no obligation to us, really."

Tamsen dressed Leana and Elitha in as many layers of clothing as they could wear. She sewed some money in the hems of their cloaks, cautioning them not to let people know they had money. "I don't know what kind of people you will encounter. Take out only a little at a time."

She tucked Leanna's hair under her hood, smiling at her through tears. Then she hugged Elitha. "Elitha, look out for Leanna, she's not nearly as strong as you are."

"I will, I promise."

Tamsen put a letter to Mr. Sutter inside Elitha's pocket. "All right, girls. Say good-bye to your father."

Leanna started to cry. "We want to wait until we can all go together. We don't want to go with strangers."

"Noah will be with you, and Mrs. Wolfinger, and your cousin William, and George. You'll be with people you know. Mrs. Reed and the children are going too."

Tamsen was hurting with grief, but didn't want to break down for the children to see. She'd been raised to keep a stiff upper lip, not show strong emotion. She'd been the rock in the flood, the glue that kept them from falling apart.

"Girls, come here, sit down," said George. They sat beside him on the bed, clutching their reticules, tears streaming down their faces. "You'll just be gettin' to California before the rest of us. There's more rescuers comin' an' spring will be here 'fore long. They'll bring mules to carry us out. It's just a temporary thing. You're old enough to be alone for a while, aren't you?"

They nodded their heads and rubbed the tears out of their eyes. "Yes, Father, we'll try."

"Come along, girls, the men are anxious to be off."

Mr. Rhodes stood up, bending over as he shifted his pack higher on his back. "Miz Donner, I tol' that Mex that he needs to stay 'cause you ain't got anybody to get yer wood an' such—he got some surly with me."

"He's agreed to stay, Mr. Rhodes. Please take care of our girls. Will you deliver them to Mr. Sutter?"

"Ma'am, I will do my best. Another relief should be here in a few days if the storms will hold off."

Tamsen, Baptiste, and the three little girls watched them move off, the strongest in the lead and each thereafter stretching to step in the footsteps of the one before. When the group disappeared they went inside, feeling sad and empty without the others.

"Now, little girls, be *ángelitas* an' I will tell you a story an' also I will teach you some more words in the *español, está bien?*

The girls clambered up on one of the beds and Baptiste sat at their feet. Eliza began to cry. "I don't want 'Litha an' Leanna to go."

Georgia started crying too.

"Little ones, you must not cry," said Baptiste. "They are

going to California where there is no snow an' the sun, it shines every day. There is food to eat. You miss them, but they are going to be happy! Now stop crying and I will tell my story."

Tamsen stooped as she entered the sleeping tent that she and George shared. She'd warmed some stones by the fire and now she placed them next to his body, pulling the blanket over him and tucking it in. She was deeply worried. The suppuration in his hand and arm had abated with the treatment of the stomach of the bear—Baptiste's idea—but the withering away of the flesh continued and the wound was very painful.

"Tamsen, do you have more of that willow bark?"

"Yes, I've made tea from it. If you can sit up a little—"

"Yeah, look, we've got to talk about you an' the girls goin' over to the other camp, ready for the next relief. I ain't gonna make it, Tamsen, we both know it."

"Hush about it, George. I'm not going."

Tamsen sat beside George until he fell asleep, then she went into the main room of the hut and sat down at the table. She looked at the little pile of food that the rescuers had left.

Baptiste was still telling his story to the children, but he stopped and came to the table. "The food the men leave, *no es mucho*."

Tamsen agreed. "I saw Mr. Rhodes measure it out. Six cups of flour, twelve biscuits, the beef—what he could hold between his thumb and forefinger, for each of us." She put her elbows on the table, held her head between her hands. Her voice was muffled. "He said there will be another party, but if it storms …"

"*Señora* Betsey, she ask me to dig up the dead bodies."

Tamsen looked up. "Oh, no. Not yet, Baptiste. We still have hides and this food the men left."

Baptiste looked at Tamsen, then his eyes shifted away.

• • •

The people from the Donner camps were taken to the lake cabins and the relief party started over the mountains with twenty-three people. They'd had to make hard decisions about who would be taken out.

From the Donner camps: Noah James; Mrs. Wolfinger; Leana and Elitha Donner; and Betsey's boys, William and George. From the lake camps: John Denton; Edward and Simon Breen; Margaret Reed, her four children; Eliza Williams; two of the Graves girls and William; Mrs. Keseberg and her little one, Ada; and Mary and William Murphy. Rescuer John Rhodes decided to carry the Pike baby, Naomi.

It was now more than two months since the snowshoe party had left the mountains. The rescuers knew their fate but kept it from the people in the camps. If they knew, they might lose their courage. Left in the Donner camps; George, Tamsen, and their three little girls; Juan Baptiste; Elizabeth and four of her children.

The Breen family still had some meat and hides, so they would be left, except for two of the boys. Mr. Keseberg still suffered from an injured foot and couldn't walk, Mrs. Murphy was left with nine-year-old Simon, two of her grandchildren and the Eddy boy. At the Graves' cabin, Mrs. Graves was left with four of her children and the baby.

A rescuer on snowshoes went ahead, and the others followed, stepping in his tracks. The small children could not reach from one depression to the next and had to scramble over the hill between the footprints. This wore them out. Within two or three miles Mr. Glover decided that little Tommy and Patty would have to go back.

Mrs. Reed was devastated by the prospect, didn't know what to do. Go back with them, leave her other children?

"Oh, God. No. I can't …"

"Miz Reed, on my honor, I swear I will come back with the

next relief and take the children out," said Mr. Glover.

"Mr. Glover, are you a Mason?"

"Yes ma'am, I surely am."

"Will you promise me, upon the word of a Mason, that you will return and bring out my children?"

"Yes ma'am, I will—I do."

Margaret took the children into her arms, hugging them for what could possibly be the last time. Could they survive until the next relief should meet them?

"Well, Mother," said Patty, "if you never see me again, do the best you can."

"Oh, Patty, don't say that. Mr. Glover has promised me he'll come back for you. The men have told me that your father is coming in the next rescue party, he's almost here."

Mr. Glover and Mr. Moultrie took Patty and Tommy back to the Breen cabins, where they met with a very disappointed Mr. and Mrs. Breen.

"Oh, and now you're bringin' them here? Mr. Glover, we can not take them in again," cried Mr. Breen. "We have barely the strength an' food to care for our own."

"We agreed not to go out with the relief if you would take Mrs. Reed an' the children off our hands." said Mrs. Breen.

"There's nothin' else for it. If you don't take them in, where will they go?" asked Glover.

"We've got nothing to feed them, man!" Breen shouted.

Patty was frantic, wondering what she and Tommy would do without the shelter of the Breen cabin, the security of their fire. She ran to Mrs. Breen, hugging her waist, crying.

"Mrs. Breen, please, we still have some hides here—I'll fix them for Tommy and me, we won't be trouble."

"Miz Breen, Mr. Reed surely will be here in a few days," said Mr. Moultrie. He put down his pack, taking out a small bag.

"This here's some provisions, it'll keep the children for a few days, the other expeditions will be along shortly. We got to get goin', we lost time here bringing the young'ins back."

Margaret looked over Patty's head to Patrick. "What else can we do?"

Tuesd. 23rd Froze hard last night to day fine & thawey has the appearance of spring all but the deep snow wind S: S.E shot Towser today and dressed his flesh Mrs. Graves came here this morning to borrow meat dog or ox they think I have meat to spare but I know to the contrary they have plenty hides I live principally on the same.

• • •

Mrs. Murphy struggled through the snow to the Breen cabin. It was a fine morning and they were all outside warming themselves in the sun. Mrs. Breen had just made a cup of tea for herself, but offered it to Mrs. Murphy.

Levinah shook her head, collapsing on a chair that had been brought outside. She was breathing in short gasps. She looked at the children, first one, then another, her eyes rheumy, red-rimmed, caked up. She looked at Mrs. Breen.

"My grandbabies died."

Margaret made a sympathetic sound.

Levinah went on. "The wolves are 'bout to dig up the dead bodies, they were all aroun' last night, howlin'. I tol' Mr. Keseberg he should go out there an' shoot them—he's 'bout as useless as tits on a boar—he cain't hardly move. Simon has to get what wood we got, we done used up all the wood those men cut for us."

"We'll get some wood for you," said Patrick.

Lavinah eased off the chair, shakily pushing herself up by

holding on to the seat. She looked at Margaret. "That little amount of food those men left didn't last no time at all. Do you have anythin' at all you can give us?"

"No."

Levinah nodded sadly, dropped her head and put her hands over her face. Her words were muffled. "I think I'll commence on Milt, we ain't got nothin' else."

Horror twisted Margaret's face. "Do you not have hides left, Mrs. Murphy?"

"I just as soon die as eat any more of that glue."

Patrick put his pipe down, stood up and waved his hand at his boys. "Pat, you an' Simon help Mrs. Murphy back to her shanty. I'll bring some wood and we'll bury the wee ones."

Frid 26th   Froze hard last night   today clear & warm Wind S:E: blowing briskly   Martha's jaw swelled with the toothache; hungry times in camp, plenty hides but the folks will not eat them   we eat them with a tolerable good apetite. Thanks be to Almighty God.   Amen   Mrs Murphy said here yesterday that [she] thought she would commence on Milt. and eat him   I don't that she has done so yet, it is distressing   The Donnos told the California folks that they commence to eat the dead people 4 days ago, if they did not succeed that day or next in finding their cattle then under ten or twelve feet of snow & did not know the spot or near it, I suppose they have done so ere this time.

Sund. 28   Froze hard last night   today fair & sunshine wind S.E. 1 solitary Indian passed by yesterday   come from the lake   had a heavy pack on his back   gave me 5 or 6 roots resembleing onions in shape   taste some like a sweet potatoe, all full of little tough fibres.

On the summit of the mountain the rescuers and the rescued stopped to rest. They looked down into the deep valley they'd just left. The air was clear and still. They saw the long white expanse of the frozen lake, the dark green of the forest marching up the mountain ridges on each side. In the far distance, three tiny, ghostly wisps of smoke showed just above the forest.

The rescuers hunched their heavy packs up on their backs. "Let's get movin', we want to make that summit valley 'fore dark. Rhodes an' Moultrie should be able to catch up with us tonight."

Margaret Reed was prostrate on the snow sobbing. Virginia knelt beside her. "Mother, we have to go."

It had been six miles from the lake camps to the summit of the pass. It would be twenty-four miles, more or less, to where a camp had been set up to support the rescue efforts. Most of the food that had been carried into the mountains had been left in caches. The first they would come to would be at the head of the Yuba.

On the second day they found that the cache had been devoured by animals. Two men were sent ahead to bring back food from the second cache and the party struggled ahead.

John Denton had been lagging behind and now he could not continue. He asked that if it was possible, they send someone back to help him. They left him with a blanket, food and a fire. John Rhoads carried baby Naomi, Tucker and Sels helped the other children along.

The days were sunny, the nights freezing hard. They had no problem finding their way, the charred trees the rescuers had left behind on their way to the camps marked the path.

Mrs. Keseberg's little girl died. Reluctant to leave her child in the snow, she continued walking with Ada in her arms.

"Lady," said Mr. Tucker, "you go on, let me take the little one, I'll bury her." Mrs. Keseberg handed over the child. She felt that part of her heart was being torn from her. She stumbled on, too numb to weep.

The next day the forward men returned with some provisions. The following day they left camp, walking on a hard crust. They'd made four miles when the leaders cried out that men were coming. It was the second relief party, led by James Reed. Mrs. Reed collapsed, overcome when she heard that her husband was coming. Virginia ran ahead into her father's arms.

"Your mother—the children—where are they?"

Virginia pointed. "Back there, she's all right. James is with her, but we had to leave Tommy and Patty. They were just too weak, the men sent them back. I think they're all right."

James hurried to Margaret. Jimmy clung to her cloak, looking at his father as if at a stranger. James picked him up, tears coursing down his cheeks. "It's your Pa, James, it's Papa."

The men opened their packs, taking out the biscuits and sweet cakes that James had made the evening before. They divided the food amongst the hungry people. Then the second relief, still led by James Reed, proceeded on up the mountain.

The first relief group continued down. At Mule Springs they found supplies and horses waiting for them, and farther on, the relay camp. Now at last the poor starved people had food, and the problem was not to allow them to eat more than their systems could handle.

William Hook, Betsey Donner's second oldest boy, ate too much and fell deathly ill. They gave him tobacco juice to make him vomit and he felt better. But that night, still ravenous, he climbed the tree where the provisions were stored and gorged himself. When found in the morning he was too far gone for tobacco juice. They buried him in the ground where the fire had melted the snow.

After resting for a night they were supplied with horses and sent on. Now, all around, they were greeted by green grass and budding trees. They were finally out of the mountains. The refugees were distributed to various places; Mrs. Reed and her children were taken in by Alcalde Sinclair.

Then the long-deferred storm broke at last. Margaret could not leave the doorway, watching the rain and weeping. She knew that heavy rain in the valley meant heavy snow and storms in the mountains. She was sick with worry that James would be delayed by the storm, would not get to the mountain camp in time to save Patty and Tommy.

• • •

In the mountain camps the food the rescuers had left was gone in a day or two. Tamsen was desperate, wondering what more she could do to keep her family alive until rescue should come again. She tried to maintain a positive attitude, at least outwardly. She would not permit herself to doubt that they might not live.

They prayed, asking to be released from the deadly grip of the mountains.

George was fatalistic. He knew that he would die and he tried to accept it. He believed that the earthly life was temporary; there was another life beyond that was fuller. But when he thought of the possibility of his children dying he couldn't come to terms with it. So he prayed and pleaded with God to spare his wife and children.

The weather had been pleasant, the snow had receded away from the huts. Spring was on the way—but the snow had been a barrier preventing the wind from whipping through the ragged materials that covered the hut.

Tamsen was sitting beside the fire, hacking and scraping on a hide. George was propped up on the bed closest to the fire, staring into the flames, the girls huddled under blankets in their bed. They heard the crunching footsteps of Baptiste and looked up when he entered the hut.

"How is Betsey?" asked Tamsen.

"Sick, the little ones too."

Baptiste laid something wrapped in cloth on the table.

"What is this?"

"It is food. The *niñas*, they must have more than the boilings you make of hide or they will sicken soon. And me, it no keep me strong to do the work, so I eat this. Betsey, she eat it too."

Baptiste was very nervous, anxious that Tamsen understand what he'd had to do. His face twisted from grief and his words came all in a rush.

"One day, I climb the tree to look for the rescuers, an' I see the wolves. They are digging the men from the snow an' already a leg of ... *Por Dios*!" He covered his face with his hands. Now his voice was low, muffled, but still they heard the terrible words.

"I think that we have no food an' meat is meat. The soul

that was there, it is gone, only the dead body is left. Like the deer, the buffalo. Is there a difference?"

"I don't know," Tamsen murmured.

"I have to fight the wolves. I am much afraid, but I hit at them with a heavy stick an' they move away, but not far. I dig out one of the men an' I take him to the old hut. There is no one there, anyway. There is no other way to stay alive."

"The next relief should be here today, it is past time. Baptiste, you can get more of the pine bark."

"Only a little can I get this way. I have taken from all the trees around here. It is much work an' I am getting weak. It is all my strength to get the wood for the fires."

George struggled to sit up. "Look, Baptiste, it's all right. There's no other way."

• • •

After Reed's group left the people in the first relief, they pressed on toward the mountain summit. He urged his men to hurry. The storm that had been holding off now seemed at hand.

They numbered ten in all: Reed; Hiram Miller; William McCutchen: John Turner; Joseph Gendreau; Matthew Dofar; Brit Greenwood; Nicholas Clark; Charles Cady; and Charles Stone. These were the hardy men that would struggle over the mountain.

They traveled a distance, then one of the men climbed a tree, taking up a cache of food. That eased their heavy packs a little, but only in measure to their decreasing energies.

They made camp, but pressed on about midnight, halting at a patch of soft snow, moving on about four in the morning. They made a second cache. The next night Cady, Clark and Stone set out to push ahead as an advance party. Clark, in the lead, was startled to see a dark shape on the snow ahead; the body of John Denton, still beside the remains of his fire.

As they crossed the pass and came within two miles of the cabins, they observed several Indians in the area. Becoming alarmed, they ducked down into some cover from the pine trees, spending the rest of the night without a fire.

The next morning they proceeded cautiously. In about two miles, they saw the top of a cabin sticking out of the snow.

The three men stayed just long enough at the lake cabins to distribute some food and then headed for the Donner camps. Reed and the rest of the rescuers came up in a few hours. Breen noted the arrival in his diary.

> *Mond. March the 1st To day fine and pleasant froze hard last night there has   10 men arrived this morning from Bear Valley with provisions   we are to start in two or three days & cash [cache] our goods here   there is amongst them some old [mountaineers] they say the snow will be here until June.*

· · ·

It had been ten days since the first rescue party had left the Donner camps. They were outside when they saw the men of the second rescue approaching.

Tamsen struggled through the snow to greet them. "Are there more men coming?"

"Yes'm, Mr. Reed and some others'll be comin' on shortly. I'm Cady, this here's Stone. The man comin' up is Clark. He seen some bear sign. Soon's he leaves his pack he's goin' after the bear."

"You have food for us?"

The men shrugged off their packs. Mr. Cady took out a package and handed it to Tamsen.

"This is all that you have brought?"

"Yes'm, we done cached most up on the mountain to use on the way out."

"Please take part of this to Jacob's family." Tamsen pointed in the direction of Betsey's hut. Only a wisp of smoke showed above the snow.

Juan Baptiste had been gathering wood when he'd heard the men's voices. He rushed back to camp as the men were making their way to Betsey's hut.

"Only three men? How they carry the children?"

"They say more men are coming."

Later that day, James Reed, with several other men, approached the hut. Tamsen went out to meet them. "James. How good it is to see you."

"How are you? How is George?"

"Not well. Please, come in."

James followed Tamsen inside, pausing while his eyes adjusted to the gloom.

"George, James is here." Tamsen helped George sit up. He put out his good hand to James.

"James, so good to see you. Have you brought mules?"

"No, we couldn't get through with horses or mules. The snow on top is twenty to thirty feet deep. I apologize for the lateness of my arrival here in the mountains."

"Do you have news of my daughters?" George asked James. "They went out with the first party."

"Yes, yes, they are safe. I met that party as we were coming up. My wife and children also. They are all on their way to Mr. Sutter's now."

"Your family? Are they all right?"

"Yes, thank God, my family is safe. Mrs. Reed and two of the children are now on their way out and the other two, Patty and Thomas, they're still at the lake but all right. I cannot tell you how distressed I am for what has happened. It is a most terrible situation."

Tamsen brought a chair for James and he sat down.

"George, it was difficult to move over the snow and fight the constant storms. Even now we are worried whether or not we will be able to get the people out. It is a good distance to an elevation where there is no snow. My group is too small to take children that cannot walk. It is extremely arduous—"

"James," exclaimed Tamsen, "the other men promised us the next party would take our children out! The men who came this morning brought little food. We cannot survive much longer."

"'There is another much larger party following me. They will be able to take them. I will leave as much food as I can. Hopefully it will be enough to last you until they arrive."

"Only a few days?"

"A week perhaps. Of course, that depends on the weather. Sutter told me that this has been an unusual course of storms."

James got up from his chair. "I can't express how sorry I am about Jacob. I'll come again before we leave, but we must make haste. I'm leaving men here to care for you until the next relief arrives."

James went outside, Tamsen and the girls following, squinting against the glare.

"We're all suffering greatly from the effects of this brightness on our eyes," said James. "Tamsen, I want you to know that as soon as I arrived in California—" James stopped, his voice breaking, a pleading expression on his face. "It was a hellacious journey. I worked diligently to form up a relief party. I could not obtain men as the rebellions and wars took most of the able men away from the area. Mr. McCutchen and I made an attempt in November, but the deep snow prevented us from ascending and we had to turn back. You know, we figured there would be enough livestock to keep the people ..." James touched Tamsen's arm. "As God is my witness, I've done everything I could possibly do."

They started over to Betsey's camp, meeting Hiram Miller coming towards them. He looked upset, and started talking to James before noticing that Tamsen and the girls were behind him.

"Reed, things are bad over at the other camp. They's been eatin' the dead. Did you go in that teepee-like hut? God have mercy—"

James raised his hand. "Yes, I did. Go ahead, get started on resetting the tents."

Hiram turned around and everyone followed him.

Betsey began crying when she saw Tamsen.

"They're taking Mary, Isaac, and Solly, but they won't take my little ones. Oh, God, what am I goin' to do?" She collapsed on the bed, moaning pitifully.

"James says another relief party will be here in a few days. It's a larger party, they'll be able to carry them out. We need to keep on until they get here."

"Tamsen, I ain't got no strength to keep on. I'm gonna join Jacob in the hereafter. But what will happen to my little boys?"

"Betsey, the men are going to reset your tents to make you more comfortable. James will be responsible for the children until you can go out but they'll need some money. Give James what you have, he'll see that it is properly used for the children."

Betsey went to a box and took out a bag. The coins inside made a clinking sound. "It's all I have, with seven kids to raise without Jacob—"

"Betsey, we'll help you."

"Oh, I ain't gonna make it anyways. I know you'll make it, you're strong an' you kept your girls strong. I should'a listened to you, but I just got so down with Jacob gone—" Betsey put her hands to her face. "How can I bear this?"

Hiram Miller conducted the selling of Jacob's store of goods to some of the rescuers. Hiram made a list, giving it to James. "It's about a hundred dollars, Mr. Reed."

Betsey became agitated as the men began bundling up the goods in packs. "Do they mean to carry goods and not a child?"

She grabbed some of the goods, throwing them away from the man packing them up. "You can take goods, but not my babies?"

"Ma'am, there'll be another company along. Yer kids'll be taken out."

"James, this is not right. The children weigh less than those packs," said Tamsen.

"I have no authority over these men. They do as they wish. But I can tell you they have suffered great hardship to get here."

"How has that helped relieve us?" Betsey screeched.

"All of the men have carried in heavy packs of food, most was cached along the way to feed the people as we go out. The labor was extremely hard. I have arranged for Mr. Cady and Mr. Stone to stay to help you. It should be but a short time before the next group arrives."

Betsey twisted her apron in her hands, walking aimlessly between the men and the packs of goods. "My babies're dyin', they cain't last more'n a few days."

James looked at her and frowned in sympathy. He turned to the men who were now ready to go. "These children need to be taken out. Will any of you carry them?"

"Mr. Reed, they ain't a'gonna make it anyways," said Hiram. "No point in even tryin'. The men've been counting on gettin' some goods. We're takin' three of the kids an' we got to help those people back at the other camp that're expectin' to go, that got a chance of makin' it."

James sighed. "Yes. There's just too much …"

He looked at Tamsen, made a helpless gesture.

Tamsen put her arm around Betsey's shoulders. "Betsey, we need to get the children ready to go."

Cady and Stone went out to find wood for the fires. Tamsen and Baptiste stood on a bank of snow and watched the group of rescuers and the three children until they disappeared.

"Those men, *Señora,* I no like them. Reed, he say I must stay. I do it because you need me, because the *niñas* they need me, not because of what Reed say."

The three girls sat on a bed, feet dangling, watching as Tamsen fed Samuel and Lewis soup she'd made from the jerked beef the men had given her. Betsey slumped on a bed.

"Tamsen, promise me, take care of my babies."

"Betsey, hush such talk. I will do everything I can to help you, you know that."

Tamsen stroked little Samuel's head. "You feel better, Sammy?" *Oh, how painful this is. This child is going to die.*

She tucked the blankets around both boys and put one over Betsey. "I need to go back, Betsey. Mr. Cady will keep your fire."

"Reed tol' those men they had to stay an' and see to us, but I heard them talking. They said they was goin' to leave."

• • •

James Reed led the group of rescuers and rescued back over the path that had been tromped out by the men on the way in. He felt badly about leaving the Donner families in such a state of despair. *Well, Tamsen seemed hale and the three girls, they'll make it. The next group is probably here already, over at the lake camps. Thank God my family is safe.* James squared his shoulders, lifted his chin. *I did everything I possibly could.*

He looked back at the line of people. Mary and Isaac were struggling. Solomon was lagging, barely able to keep up, mumbling to himself. James signaled the men to help them.

When they reached the lake camps preparations were made to leave. The rescuers helped some of the people cache goods and get ready for the departure. There were a few that wouldn't be able to go out. Mr. Keseberg was still too crippled to walk any distance. He and Mrs. Murphy would be left with Mrs. Murphy's nine-year-old, Simon, two of her small grand-children and little George Eddy.

Mr. McCutchen went to help Mrs. Graves get ready. He was puzzled when she asked him to take a thick board off her wagon. She'd been working at prying it off with an axe.

"Miz Graves, we're leaving shortly, what would you want with that piece of wood?"

Exasperated, she threw the axe down. "Help me get this damned thing off a' there." She looked around. "I need somethin' to get under it. I got to get that wood off. That's where all my money's been hid."

Mr. McCutchen picked up the axe and in his strong hands the board came away, revealing auger holes filled with coins. Mrs. Graves extracted the coins, putting them into a bag that she looped and tied on a belt around her waist. "An' this ain't none of yer look out, Mr. McCutchen!"

Mr. McCutchen thought the whole affair rather funny, but his next thought was sobering. The rescuers had felt it would be better not to tell Mrs. Graves about the death of her husband and son-in-law during the ordeal of the snowshoe party. They'd tell her later, when they were safe in California.

The next morning, seventeen emaciated, weak, starved people were led out of the mountain camps. Now there was hope, even laughter. They would live! But first they had to overcome the challenge of the snow-locked mountains. There was a stirring of wind that had a hint of moisture. The people, now attuned to the vagaries and habits of the weather, looked up with apprehension.

Margaret Breen, carrying her baby, Isabella, scanned the sky. "Oh, God … Blessed Mother … don't let it storm."

Patrick looked up. He could feel the change of the atmosphere too. "If it holds off a little, we should be all right."

They started across the frozen lake, strung out in knots of rescuers and rescued. They'd gotten a late start, and it was difficult for them to move along as fast as James thought prudent. He scanned the mountain and the sky. *The next rescue party should be coming in. Surely we'll meet them shortly.*

He went back along the line, urging the rescuers to help the children along. He noticed that Mrs. Graves had wrapped baby Elizabeth in a blanket and was carrying the baby on her back, a violin sticking out on one side of the bundle.

Elizabeth waved at him. "Mr. Reed, can one of the men carry this baby for awhile? I'm about to give out."

By evening, they were only half-way across the lake. The men cut down a tree, putting the green logs down for a base for the fire and pine boughs on the snow for the people to lie on. The mood was joyful for death had been stayed. Patrick Breen picked up Mrs. Graves's fiddle and squeaked out an Irish ditty.

In the morning, most of them were ready before the call to move out, anxious to get on the way. California! Warmth, food, loved ones. Before they had gone very far, Mrs. Graves began to worry that her bag of money would get too heavy for her to carry. Lagging behind, she secreted the money in a place she thought she would be able to remember.

The next day they continued on across the lake, but made only the foot of the pass by evening. The refugees crept close to the fire, ate the slim rations, wishing they had more. There was only a day and a half of food remaining, and fifteen miles or so to go to the cache of food the men had left coming in. Clouds were building up over the pass, the wind whistled through the swaying trees.

James expected that Midshipman Woodworth would be leading in another rescue party, and was exasperated that he hadn't come on. He told Turner, Dofar, and Gendreau, good mountaineers, to go ahead to the next cache and send one man back with food. The other two should go on to the next cache.

"You should reach the first one today—there'll be food—I can't let you take any of what we have," said James.

"An' what if we find that the cache's been eaten by the animals, what then?"

"Go on to the next."

"I'm thinking we're gonna need food, just in case."

"I can't give you any," said James. "It's highly unlikely that the cache will be completely gone."

The men went ahead, not too happy.

Now, Reed's group must scale the pass. They would have to make the full distance, an excruciating climb, before night. The towering wall of granite was treeless, windswept slippery rock, a few twisted trees sticking out here and there. There was nothing they could hold to pull themselves up. Painfully, slowly, they moved up the face of the mountain.

By mid-afternoon, they'd made it to a valley at the summit and made camp. The wind swept across the open valley, sharp edged, stinging. It seemed that the dark clouds were only inches above their heads. A coyote loped across the valley, sat and stared at them, then loped again. James picked up his rifle.

"Naw, Mr. Reed, too far," growled one of the men.

James put the rifle down. He shivered, pulling his coat

tighter around his body. "I sure don't like the looks of those clouds, it's likely to storm."

Most of the rescued people had stomach aches, their guts growling and knotting, protesting against the food that had started through their systems. Their limbs, feet, and hands were numb with cold, stiff from the exposure they'd endured for months.

That night the storm struck. First came a fierce wind, then snow blasted them, wet, heavy. The mothers put blankets over their backs and drew the little children underneath, trying to protect them from the terrible wind. The able-bodied men labored continuously to find wood to build up the fire and make a windbreak of sorts out of limbs.

James divided up the last of the very meager provisions, then sat down with his back to one of the logs, pulling his coat over his head. Holding his notebook tightly to keep it from flying away in the wind, he wrote in his diary.

Mar 6 I dread the coming night. Night closing fast, and with it the hurricane increases.

The fury of the storm pounded them. James had the first watch, but he'd become exhausted from the labor of keeping the fire and so chilled from the fierce freezing wind that he'd lapsed into something like a coma. The untended fire gradually became less and less, and then a final hissing as the coals sank into the melted slush beneath. The people began to awaken as the terrible cold gnawed at them.

"Mother, the fire's gone," whimpered a child.

Mrs. Breen aroused herself and shook Patrick out of his slumber. "Patrick, Patrick! There's no fire."

McCutchen struggled to uncover the wood. Miller sifted through the wet remains of the fire and found some coals. With strenuous efforts, they managed to get the fire going again. Then the two men worked on James, rubbing his hands, feet and frozen face, finally bringing him to consciousness again.

The storm continued throughout the next day and into the night. Without food, they grew weaker. On the morning after the third night, they found that Isaac Donner had died. His sister, Mary, suffered a burned foot; she'd lain too close to the fire.

Finally, about noon of the third day, the storm ceased. The rescuers decided they must press on with those who were still strong enough, those who were not would have to stay put and await rescue.

Reed muttered to McCutchen. "What else can we do? We can't rely on Woodworth, he's a broken stick. Let's get the people up and moving, see who's strong enough to go on."

"Miz Graves an' her children's in bad shape, Mr. Reed," said Miller. James went to the Breen family, huddled together under blankets. "Mr. Breen, we're ready to move out."

"We'll stay here, await relief," said Patrick. "I'd rather die here where we have a good fire than somewhere out in the snow."

"Breen, if we stay together, we'll make it through."

"No, we'll stay here. We'll look after Mrs. Graves and her children, she won't be able to keep a fire. You said that more men were on the way."

"I don't know what has happened—we should have met them. If I were you I would not take the chance. If any of you die here, it is on your soul. I will not take responsibility. My men are witness."

The men piled up enough wood to last perhaps three days, but they had no food to leave. Mary Donner got up, limping painfully, insisting that she not be left behind. Soon after they started off she floundered helplessly in the snow and was taken back.

Reed, the six men of the relief and the three children, Patty and Thomas Reed and Solomon Hook, continued on. It was terribly cold. Patty failed. James put her on his back and struggled on.

Towards evening the exhausted group made camp. There was no food. When Patty had failed and become delirious earlier in the day, James had given her his last meager supply of food, some crumbs he'd scraped out of a pack and stuffed into the thumb of his glove.

James took out his diary, jotted down his daily report, and silently cursed Woodworth.

Where the hell were they? Where are the men I sent for food? They should have been back by now. We're going to die if aid doesn't come soon.

Nobody came. The next day they struggled on, finding a cache that the three mountain men who'd been sent ahead had left where they could find it. As they made camp that night they heard hallooing in the distance. Someone went ahead and found Woodworth and two of his men loaded with provisions.

A few more people had been snatched from the jaws of the snowy mountains. But there were still those people they'd left behind.

Woodworth asked for volunteers, but his men held back, and he himself made no offer to lead them. Finally, he offered his men three dollars a day and fifty dollars for each child they brought out. Five men agreed to go; John Stark, Howard Oakley, Miller, Stone, and Thompson. Going too were William Eddy and William Foster. They'd given out during the first relief, but now they were ready to go back, worried sick about their children left with Mrs. Murphy. Reed had told them the children were still alive, so the fathers still had hope. This was the third relief party to climb the mountain.

• • •

Back in the summit valley, those that had been left there by Reed were in a bad way. Patrick was dispirited, morose, ready or willing, to die. He'd decided that it was God's will, after all.

Mrs. Breen pled with God, with the Virgin Mary, with Saint Jude—the saint that was called on for the impossible—to save her family. It just could not be God's will that her whole family should die! It seemed that she alone had the strength—the iron will—to go from one to another, chafing hands and feet, getting them to move around to keep the blood flowing.

Margaret had come away from the cabin with a small bag of seeds, some coffee and tea, and a small loaf of sugar, saving it for the last extremity. Now she doled it out—a little sugar-water, a few of the precious seeds, and a spoonful of coffee or tea to stimulate the nerves. The first night Mrs. Graves and five-year-old Franklin died. Nine-year-old Nancy Graves was left with the care of baby Elizabeth.

The fire was sinking deeper and deeper into the snow, melting it away. John Breen carved steps into the side of the pit and they descended down to the bottom where the fire had exposed bare ground. It was warmer in the pit with the fire reflecting off the snow walls, the wind not as fierce, but that was of little concern in the face of starvation. Patrick, knife in hand, climbed the snow steps. He stood for a moment, the wind whipping his hair and beard. Shuddering and gagging, he went about his task. There was no choice but to use the dead for food.

• • •

The wind moved down the mountain and into the valley of entrapment. It was like a stormy ocean swell, bending trees and blowing the snow into eddies and whirlwinds, pausing before gathering itself and rushing against the cabins and huts that sheltered those left in the camps. Betsey had been right. Cady and Stone seemed to get more and more nervous and started gathering up their packs. Tamsen heard them tromping around outside the hut. They met her with sullen countenances.

"Miz Donner, we gotta leave. We need to catch up with Mr. Reed's party. Our provisions is near gone an' we're a'feared'a bein' trapped here for days, mebbe weeks before another party kin get o'er the mountain."

"You were charged with our care."

"We ain't bein' paid to risk our lives becomin' trapped our ownselves. There be a storm a'comin'."

"Then take our girls out with you. Please."

"We'd have to carry 'em and we cain't."

"I believe they can walk. If you break the snow for them they'll walk in your tracks."

"No. We'll need to move fast to catch up with Reed."

Tamsen turned to Mr. Cady, who seemed to her the better man. "Would you do it if I paid you? For five hundred dollars?"

Thought moved across his face. It was a fortune. Five years of wages, if you could find anyone willing to pay wages. An army man might earn ten dollars a month. He turned to Stone, his eyebrows asking the question.

"Five hundred for each of us, missus." said Stone. "But we ain't a'carryin' them, they'll have to walk. We'll leave as soon as they're ready. Best you hurry, ma'am."

"And Mr. Clark?"

"We cain't wait fer Clark to git back. Ma'am, you should go with us. Your husband and the other woman and kids, they ain't gonna last more'n a few days."

Tamsen hurried inside to talk to George. He agreed that it was a good thing to get the children out. He begged Tamsen to go too.

She shook her head. "Girls, quickly, we must get you ready to go. The men are going to take you to California."

All three girls began to cry. Georgia and Eliza clung to Tamsen. Frances ran to George, burying her head in his blankets.

"We don't want to go with the men, we don't want to."

Tamsen was in agony. "I don't want you to either. But it is for the best. These men will take you to Elitha and Leanna. They'll watch over you until Father and I can come."

"What if you die and we'll never see you again? What if the men never come back for you?" cried Frances.

Tamsen went to her knees, gathering in the girls. "Oh, God, give me strength."

George pleaded with her. "Mother, go with them, they need you. It's best." His voice was weak, but Tamsen heard him, shook her head. "No."

Frances slipped off the bed to the floor, sobbing. George reached down and stroked her hair. What sorrow, what pain.

Mr. Cady came into the hut. "Ma'am, if the children's goin', we got to leave now, it's fixin' to storm."

Tamsen got to her feet, began gathering their things. She dressed them in layers of clothes and their cloaks. "Frances, where are your shoes?"

"Mother, don't you remember? The dog ate them."

Frantically Tamsen searched for shoes and finally put a pair of her own on Frances. She made a bundle of a few things and asked Mr. Cady to carry it. They went up the steps of packed snow, sniffling, noses running.

Baptiste had just returned from his daily hunt for wood and was surprised to see that the girls would be leaving with the men.

"The men, they leave? The *niñas* go with them? Clark, he no come back yet. Why they leave? I go too, they need me."

"No, no, Baptiste, these men are stronger than you. They

have promised to take good care of them. Baptiste, if Mr. Clark leaves I will have no one to help me."

Baptiste knelt down in the snow and took the girls in his arms. "*Vaya con Dios, mis ánjelitos.* I make the promise, you I will find in California. I will be leaving too."

Tamsen took each one in turn and hugged and kissed her, wiping away tears.

"We will come as soon as we can. Do not be afraid, God will take care of you."

The girls struggled to walk in the steps of the men, their little legs not able to stretch that far. Frances had a harder time because the shoes Tamsen had given her were too big, coming off whenever she would pull her foot out of the snow to take another step.

They struggled on and on. The wind began to blow, chapping their faces and hands with sharp edges. After what seemed an eternity, numb with cold and utterly miserable, they realized they'd stopped at the door to a cabin. There was a man standing in the doorway.

"These are the Donner children," Mr. Cady said to him.

"Why are you bringing them here?" asked the man. "You cannot leave them, there is no one to care for them. The lady here, she can not move from her bed. Take them with you."

Mr. Cady pushed the girls forward, past the man into the cabin. "Keseberg, they stay here."

Cady left the cabin, hurrying to catch up with Stone. It was very dark inside and the girls held on to each other. A quavering voice came from somewhere.

"Who is it?"

"It's the three Donner children. Some men came and left them here," answered Mr. Keseberg.

"Bring them over here," said the voice.

A form came towards them and led them to the back of the cabin, where they could see a fire glowing and the dim outline of a woman sitting on a bed.

"Which Donner children are you?" she asked.

Frances answered. "The children of Mr. and Mrs. George Donner."

"Yes, I see. The three little ones, aren't you?"

"Yes, ma'am."

Georgia nudged Frances. "It's Mrs. Murphy, and Simon."

The girls edged closer to the fire.

"Sit yourselves down," whispered Simon. "Mr. Keseberg is wrathy. Best you stay quiet."

"Simon, help the girls take off their cloaks. Give them one of my blankets to wrap up in," said Mrs. Murphy.

They huddled together, falling into an exhausted sleep. When they awakened, daylight showed through the cracks in the walls of the cabin. They stirred, and Simon edged over.

"Simon," whispered Frances, "do you have a necessary place? Where can we pee?"

"We use that corner. And there's a box for sittin'." Simon pointed to a dark corner.

"Simon," said Mrs. Murphy from her bed, "stir up the ashes and see if you can get some fire."

"We don't have any more wood. Mr. Keseberg gets mad when I ask for it."

"Where's the wood? I'll get it," said Frances.

Simon pointed to a faint glow reflecting off the big rock on the far side of the cabin.

"That's his fire over there. He's asleep. I can hear him snoring."

Frances crept towards the light of the fire. Finding some small sticks of wood, she pulled a few with her, a little at a time.

She handed the sticks to Simon and went back for more.

Simon stirred the ashes and found a tiny coal. He blew on it, feeding it slivers of wood until curls of gray smoke began showing and then smoky yellow flames started the wood crackling. They held their hands out to the warmth, glad for its cheery presence.

The misery there, in that dark cabin, went on for several days. They slept and woke, hardly aware of anything. Mrs. Murphy treated them kindly, but could do little.

They were frightened of Mr. Keseberg, who did not want to be bothered with three wet, cold, whimpering children who cried constantly for their mother. To them, he seemed like a ghoulish giant, looming over them when the crying annoyed him.

"Stop your sniveling! There's nothing that can be done for you!" he would yell.

One morning, as they huddled together, they were startled awake by someone close, touching and murmuring to them. They began to whimper, crawling away from the touch, not realizing it was their mother.

Tamsen gathered them into her arms. "Hush, hush, it's all right."

"Who is there?" croaked Mrs. Murphy. "Is it men from California?"

Tamsen had trouble getting to her feet with the children clinging to her, but managed to move closer to Mrs. Murphy.

"It's Tamsen Donner, Mrs. Murphy."

"Oh, Tamsen, thank the Lord you're here. I cain't do anythin' for the little ones. I cain't move about."

Mr. Keseberg limped toward them, bending to peer at Tamsen. "Ahh, Mrs. Donner. The men they leave the *kinder* here."

"Mr. Keseberg, we will go to the other cabin."

"That cabin is empty. The Breen family has gone."

"Yes. Do you have something I can carry some coals in? I need to build a fire."

"*Ja*. I think so."

Mrs. Murphy held out a trembling hand to Tamsen. "Don't go away."

"I will be close by, at the other cabin."

They made their way over a path through the mounds of snow. Tamsen had a hard time pulling the door of the cabin open as snow had drifted against it. It was dim and cold inside. There was a pile of firewood near the fireplace and Tamsen made a fire with the coals Mr. Keseberg had given her.

"Girls, let's get those wet clothes off. Mr. Clark killed a bear cub and I've brought some of the meat for you."

Tamsen bundled them up in a quilt that had been left in the cabin and they sat in front of the fire, eating the meat and drinking tea from Mrs. Breen's china cups they'd found on a shelf in the cabin. They asked about their father, Aunt Betsey, and the little cousins.

"Father is very weak. Juan Baptiste and Mr. Clark are to stay with him. I grieve to tell you, but Aunt Betsey and the little ones have died."

At daylight Tamsen made tea. "We're going back to our camp, but I need to get your clothes dry."

"I'm hungry," cried Eliza.

"I don't have any more food, but we'll be back to camp in a few hours. We have more bear meat."

"Can you go to the other cabin and get some?" Georgia asked. "Simon gets meat from the dead bodies and cooks it."

"I do not want to go there again. I feel very sorry for Mrs. Murphy but I can do nothing for her. I would feel compelled to stay with her. I must get back to Father."

They were preparing to leave when shouts were heard.

"Halloo, the cabin!"

They pushed open the door and were surprised to see a group of men, with them Juan Baptiste.

"Baptiste!" cried Tamsen, "you were to stay with Mr. Donner. Is he—?"

"*Señora* Tamsen, he was the same. I am afraid to stay in these mountains longer, so I leave with Clark. We go to the other side of this lake to the foot of the mountain pass. Clark is very tired because of the pack of things he carry. We camp there last night."

Baptiste waved in the direction of the four men with him. "This morning I see Eddy an' Foster, an' the others, I come with them. I have much worry about the *niñas*."

Tamsen looked past Baptiste to the other men, nodded at Eddy and Foster, and saw Hiram Miller. "Oh, Hiram, you didn't go out?"

"No ma'am, we met these men as they were coming up an' I decided to come back to help. This here's Thompson." He pointed to the last man.

"Mrs. Donner," said William Eddy, "we must hurry on. My son, and Will's son, were left in the care of Mrs. Murphy. We were told they were still alive."

"They've not survived, Mr. Eddy, I'm so sorry."

Mr. Eddy turned away, stricken.

"Did you say my son is dead?" asked Foster.

Tamsen nodded. "Yes."

The men hurried off toward the Murphy cabin. Shortly they came back with Simon, helping him through the snow.

"We can do nothing for Mrs. Murphy," said Eddy. "Mr. Keseberg is too weak and lame to walk. We will have to leave them here. I've left what food we can spare. We will take you and your girls and Simon. We must leave soon."

He took some biscuits and dried beef from his pack and

Simon and the girls sat down on a log to eat.

"Mrs. Donner, it does not seem reasonable for you to return to your camp. We were told that Mr. Donner would not live."

Tamsen put her finger to her lips, worried that the girls might hear. "Can you delay long enough for me to return to my husband and see—"

"We cannot. We fear another storm will come before we can reach the lower elevations."

Tamsen looked away, standing very still for a few moments. Then she turned to the girls.

"Mr. Eddy and the other men are going to take you over the mountains. Be good girls and do what they tell you."

"Mother, we want to stay with you."

"Everything will be all right. Think about how nice it will be in the new country. It will be green and warm and there'll be plenty of good food. Father and I will come soon."

It took every fiber of strength and the utmost of her will to send her children with Eddy and Foster. Tamsen knew that George was dying. She knew that he might not be alive when she returned to their camp, but if he lived still, she would not leave him to die alone.

"Mrs. Donner, I implore you to leave with us."

"Mr. Eddy, promise me that you will watch over my little ones and get them safely to Mr. Sutter. I will give you money."

"I will do my best. All that is within my power, but I will take no money." He looked away as tears began running down his face. "I tried to save my children. We could have gotten help earlier if only we hadn't become lost in the mountains."

"You went out with the group that left in December?"

Eddy sighed dejectedly as he tied up his pack. "We were dogged by misfortune and bad luck. Only seven of the fifteen survived. It was a month we struggled in the snow."

"Is there another party coming soon?"

"I can't say. It will be June before the snow melts enough so horses can get over the mountains. Some of the others will be coming back to get the things they have cached." He stood up, hefted his pack onto his back and signaled to the other men that it was time to go.

Tears streamed down Baptiste's face. *"Adios, Señora. Te espero ver otra vez. Vaya con Dios."*

Tamsen hugged the three girls again, then hurried away. Frances and Simon were helped along by Mr. Foster, Mr. Eddy took Georgia, and Mr. Miller put Eliza in a blanket and swung her onto his back. Juan Baptiste helped as best he could, but he was weak and straggled behind at times. When the group reached the head of the lake, they stopped for the night.

Mr. Thompson had noticed the trouble Frances was having with her shoes. "Lassie, we need to do somethin' about your shoes," he said.

He tried filling the back of the shoes with some leather he cut off his jacket, but they still slipped off her feet. Then he took a pair of gloves and fashioned some moccasins, filling the inside with wool cloth he cut off a blanket.

They started again at first light. It was a steep climb, treacherous with slippery rock and snow-covered crevices. Near the end of the day Mr. Miller told Eliza he was tired from carrying her, and enticed her to walk with a promise of a treat of a lump of sugar.

"Little girl, do you see that burned tree up there?" He pointed to a black speck way up on a ridge. "You'll only have to walk to there."

Eliza was glad to be put down because her arms and legs were sore from thumping against Mr. Miller's back. She stumbled and sank to her knees time after time, but pressed doggedly on, thinking of her reward.

After the evening ration of food, Eliza asked Mr. Thompson for the sugar.

"Little girl, we don't have any sugar. I just tol' you that story so's you'd walk. Now hush about it."

The disappointment was bitter. Huddled together with her sisters, Eliza cried until falling asleep exhausted. The next day, when Mr. Miller told her that she must walk again, she refused to go forward and cried to go back.

"Look, little girl, you're gonna haf' to walk. If'n you don't want to, you can stay here on the snow an' cry. I saw a big bear snufflin' around the camp last night. He might come an' eat you."

Eliza cried even more, sitting down in the snow. Mr. Miller pulled her up, but she refused to stand. Leaving her crying pathetically, he started off, saying he was going to leave her.

Frances and Georgia tried to get her up.

"We can't go back. Come on, we'll help you."

"I don't like that man. He's mean," cried Eliza.

Frances and Georgia began to cry too, fearing that Eliza

would be left behind. Then the other men came back and spoke heatedly with Mr. Miller and once again he put Eliza on his back and the trek continued.

At one point the men picked up a bundle lying on the snow, and Frances recognized it as the bag of keepsakes and clothing that Tamsen had entrusted to Mr. Cady and Mr. Stone.

As the Eddy group proceeded, they came across other people, rescuers and rescued, moving down the mountain. They passed the Breen family and Jonathan and Nancy Graves, being helped along by a rescuer, John Stark. Stark would carry one or two of the children, along with their bundles, then set them down, go back for another one or two and bring them forward.

They passed Stone and Oakley, carrying the Graves baby and helping Mary Donner along. Slowly, painfully, they reached the base camp, where food and the wonderful green spring of California awaited them.

Midshipman Woodworth was preoccupied making arrangements to carry the rescued to the settlements. The men of the rescue parties were exhausted, some suffering frost-bite and damaged toes and fingers. They were not going back in the snow-country, it didn't matter what they might be paid to do so. Rescue for the four people left in the mountain camps was stalled.

● ● ●

Tamsen hurried away from the cabins, not daring to turn and look back for fear she would lose her resolve. She paused, looking up at some geese flying overhead. *Spring is coming.* Her throat tightened with the next thought. *Even if the men brought in horses, it wouldn't be for three months. George isn't going to last more than a few days ... if he's still alive.*

As she approached the hut, she saw the leg of an ox sticking out of the snow. Leaving the bright sunlight she entered the hut. *Oh, how miserable it is inside.* Kneeling beside the bed where George lay, she put her hand to his throat. *He's still alive.*

"George, honey, I'm back."

He stirred and opened his eyes, only little slits, his voice a faltering whisper. "The girls … all right?

"Yes. Another relief party came while I was there. Everyone has been taken out except for Mrs. Murphy and Mr. Keseberg. He's too feeble to walk."

"Tamsen, you shouldn't have come back."

"I'll get a fire going. George, the snow is melting. It will be spring soon. I saw one of our ox showing in the snow. I'll make you some soup, it will make you feel better. And I'm going to get you warmed up. I just need to get this fire going."

Tamsen warmed a blanket and the stones at the fire, putting them around George, giving him a few spoonfuls of soup when it was ready. Then she pulled her rocking chair close beside him, holding his hand, going over and over in her mind what she should do—what she could do—about her situation.

Night came. Coyotes yipped up on the ridge behind the camp. She didn't mind the voices of the coyotes, but hated the howling of the wolves. The wolves were constantly prowling about the camp and loping across the meadow. They didn't come close to the hut since Baptiste had killed two of them, nailing their carcasses to trees on each side of the hut. They hung there, heads moving in the wind, mouths frozen in fanged snarls.

I need to get the guns out and make sure they're loaded. The Indians will know I'm all alone. She thought of the girls, of Baptiste. *Oh, how I wish Baptiste were here, I'm frightened to be so alone.*

Tamsen looked under the beds and in every corner of the hut for George's guns. *They just aren't here.* She thought about it for several days. Finally, steeling herself, she crossed the stream to Betsey's camp to look for Jacob's rifle. The water was high, crashing against the log bridge, overflowing the banks and flooding through the tents. She found Jacob's rifle but it was ruined from getting wet.

She heard noises from behind the camp. Curious, she walked around the tents. Several crows startled away and she saw with horror the scattered remains of Betsey and her boys. They'd been buried in the snow, but now it had melted and the wild creatures had gotten at the bodies.

Sickened, she turned on the crows that had settled down nearby. She hit at them with the stick she'd used to steady herself as she crossed on the log over the creek.

"Are you here for another funeral?" she screamed. "Yes, join me. We'll have services. You can be the mourners."

The crows flapped away. Tamsen watched them circle into the sky. Then she crumpled on the ground, the control that she'd had for so long leaving her. She wept until she was spent and could weep no more. She gazed for awhile at the mountain ridge. the sun warm on her head and face. When she felt calm, she got up and went back to her hut.

She set about organizing their things. She counted the money they had left, almost six hundred dollars. She took from a trunk the quilt that she'd made before they'd left home, stitching several thousand dollars in paper money inside the squares.

George's pain seemed to leave him and most of the time he drifted in and out of a deep sleep. One morning she awoke to find that he had passed on. Tamsen sat in her chair for several hours, not moving, not seeing, numb with grief and cold.

She'd known that George was going to die, but now the actuality left her adrift. Gradually, reason returned to her mind. *My girls! I must go to my girls.*

She wrapped George's body tightly in a sheet, resolving that she would come back and take him to California. The bag of coins was too heavy to carry, but she put the quilt that had the paper money sewn inside over her shoulders. Then she began walking to the other camps.

There'd been another storm since the last time Tamsen had gone to the lake camps and new snow covered the ground. Part of the way to the cabins she stepped onto a thin covering of ice and snow over a creek channel and fell into the icy water. Thrashing about, gulping and gasping, the weight of her wet clothing and the quilt heavy on her body, she struggled to crawl out of the creek. Finally she pulled herself up the bank by holding on to willow bushes. Frozen to her core, she struggled on.

The only cabin with a small twist of smoke above it was the Breen cabin, and she went there, too weak and frozen to do anything but hit on the door with a stick. The feeble scratching was no more than might be a branch moving in the wind, but Mr. Keseberg heard it and came to the door to investigate.

"My *Gott*, woman, you are frozen."

He helped Tamsen inside. She crept to the fireplace, getting as close as she could to the fire.

"Here, I have coffee."

Tamsen took the cup with a shaking hand. He offered her food, but she shook her head.

"Mrs. Donner, would you deny yourself the sustenance which you need to survive? Put the source from your mind and look at it as food, food you must have if you want to live. The rescuers left only a day or so of provisions for me. It was a long time before I could bring myself to—"

Tamsen's lips were so stiff it was difficult to speak. "I will rest. I will go at first light. Can you make more fire?"

"You must remove your wet clothes. I will find a blanket."

He rose from his seat by the fire and brought a blanket. Taking the soggy quilt off her shoulders, he threw it into a corner. Stooping at the fire, Keseberg took a few sticks of wood off a pile and put them on the fire, blowing on the embers. The flames flared, sparks shooting up into the dimness. Tamsen leaned toward the warmth, sipping on the coffee.

Keseberg fidgeted with a stick of wood, poking at the fire.

"I moved to this cabin a few days ago. It has a better fireplace, but it is not easy for me to gather wood. It takes me three or four hours to find a day's supply."

His voice trailed off and then he spoke again. "Mrs. Donner, you are not strong enough to withstand the travel. You must not attempt it."

He stared at her with wild, haunted eyes. "Yes, I want to see my child, my Ada. Ada's sister, her twin, is dead before we start this journey. My baby boy is dead. You are fortunate. Your children—" He stopped and gazed into the fire. "I know not whether Ada and my wife are alive or dead."

Tamsen shook her head numbly. "I'm sorry."

He put more wood on the fire, stirring the coals. Orange flames licked around the wood, the light flickering on his gaunt face. "Several times I have seen geese flying. If we could obtain some fresh meat we could restore our bodies and then we can walk over the mountain."

He removed one of his shoes. "You see the heel of my foot? It is so damaged from a slip of the axe it is difficult for me to walk. There should be another party coming to help us. It's likely we would meet them on the way."

He stared into the fire for a while, then spoke again. "The misfortune that has overtaken us was predestined. There is nothing we can do but finish our roles in this horrible tragedy. It began the moment we took that cut-off. If there is a God—many times I have wondered if there is—why would this suffering be allowed to happen? Perhaps God has kept me alive to make me suffer, to punish me. Many times I have put my gun to my head wanting to end my misery, but each time I thought of my wife and little daughter and I could not do it. I am conversant in several languages and I speak and write them with equal fluency, but I cannot find words that express the horror I have experienced."

Tamsen pulled the blankets more tightly around herself. She should have removed the wet frozen clothing, but did not want to disrobe in the presence of the man. She lay down close to the fire, quaking and shivering, hurting from the icy cold that had penetrated deep to the organs in her body. She gazed for a few moments at the fire licking against the wood, drawing comfort from the flames, but not warmth. Then her eyes closed. Sometime before the dawn, her soul passed from her body.

I wanted to follow those who survived but the energy to keep me with them was no more. I returned to the dimension that I had left. I cannot describe to you these dimensions in words that you would understand. They might be referred to as a heavenly abode; domains of existence; frames of reference; or other planes; you will experience what it is for yourself. What I can tell you is that there is no end to life, it is eternal.

• • •

Epilogue

The California Star, San Francisco, June 5, 1847

Mr. Fallon, better known as "Capt. Fallon" set out for the settlements in April last with six others, to extend relief to the remaining sufferers of the emigration, still within the mountains, and also to collect and secure the scattered property of both living and dead. He succeeded in reaching the cabins, and with the exception of Kesburg not a soul survived. They returned, bringing with them this man, and large packs of valuable property. Kesburg was found in truly a lamentable situation; a long subsistence upon the bodies of his deceased comrades had rendered him haggard and ferocious-looking.

The California Star, San Francisco, June, 1847

The following is part of a report from the mountain camps, by the hand of Edwin Bryant, who is a member of General Kearney's party returning to the East.

"The remains were, by an order of General Kearney, collected and buried under the superintendence of Major Swords. They were interred in a pit which had been dug in the center of one of the cabins for a cache. These meloncholoy duties to the dead being performed, the cabins, by order of Major Swords, were fired, and everything surrounding them connected with this horrid and melancholy tragedy were consumed. The body of George Donner was found at his camp wrapped in a sheet. He was buried by a party of men detailed for that purpose.

THE PEOPLE OF THE DONNER PARTY*

George Donner, 62

>Tamsen Eustis Donner, 45

>**Elitha Donner, 14, Leanna Donner, 12, Frances Donner, 6**

>**Georgeanna Donner, 4, Eliza Donner, 3**

Jacob Donner, 59

>Elizabeth Donner, 45

>**Solomon Hook, 14,** William Hook, 12, **George Donner Jr., 9**

>**Mary Donner, 7,** Isaac Donner, 5, Samuel Donner, 4, Lewis Donner, 3

>**Noah James, 20 Employee**

>Samuel Shoemaker, 25 Employee

>John Denton, 28 Employee

James Reed, 45

>**Margaret Reed, 32**

>**Virginia Backenstoe Reed, 13, Martha (Patty) Reed, 9**

>**James Reed Jr. 5, Thomas Reed, 3**

>Mrs. Keyes, 73, Margaret's mother

>**Eliza Williams, 31 Employee**

>Baylis Williams, 24 Employee

>Milford Elliott, 28 Employee

>**Walter Herron, 25 Employee**

>James Smith, 25 Employee

>Luke Halloran, 25

Charles Stanton, 35

Patrick Breen, 51

>**Margaret Breen, 40**

>**John Breen, 14, Edward Breen, 13, Patrick Breen Jr., 11**

>**Simon Breen, 9, Peter Breen, 7, James Breen, 5, Isabella Breen, infant**

>**Patrick Dolan, 30**

William Eddy, 28

Eleanor Eddy, 25

James Eddy, 3, Margaret Eddy, 1

Levinah Murphy, 36, Widow

Landrum Murphy, 16, **Mary Murphy, 14,** Lemuel Murphy, 12

William G. Murphy, 10, Simon P. Murphy, 8

Sarah Murphy Foster, 19, William M. Foster, 30, George Foster, 4

Harriet Murphy Pike, 18, Naomi Pike, 3, Catherine Pike, 1

William M. Pike, 25, Harriet's husband

Lewis Keseberg, 32

Philippine Keseberg, 23, Ada Keseberg, 3, Lewis Keseberg Jr., infant

Jacob Wolfinger, 26, **Doris Wolfinger, 19**

Karl Burger, 30

Augustus Spitzer, 30

Joseph Reinhardt, 30

Mr. Hardcoop, 60

William McCutcheon, 30

Amanda McCutcheon, 30, Harriet McCutcheon, infant

Franklin Ward Graves, 57

Elizabeth Cooper Graves, 45

Mary Ann Graves, 19, William C. Graves, 17, Eleanor Graves, 14

Lovina Graves, 12, Nancy Graves, 8, Jonathan B. Graves, 7

Franklin Ward Graves Jr., 5, Elizabeth Graves, infant

Sarah Fosdick Graves, 21, Jay Fosdick, 23, husband of Sarah

John Snyder, 25 Teamster

John Baptiste Trudeau, 16

Antoine, 23

Luis, 19, Miwok Indian

Salvador, 28, Miwok Indians

*Bold type signifies those who survived the ordeal.

List of Resources

Acuff, Marilyn. Keseberg family history.

Angier, Bradford. *Field Guide to Medicinal Wild Plants*. Stackpole Books

Bancroft, Hubert. *History of California, Vol. Five, 1846-1848*.

Bornali, Halder. Article: *Lakota Sioux Plant and Stone Symbolism*. LakotaArchives.com.

Breen, Patrick, *Diary.* Manuscript in Bancroft Library,

Brown, Dee. *The Gentle Tamers*. University of Nebraska Press, 1958.

Bryant, Edwin. *What I Saw in California*. University of Nebraska Press.

Clyman, James. *Journal of a Mountain Man*. Tamarack Books, Boise, ID

Curran, Harold. *Fearful Crossing*. The Central Overland Trail.

Davis, William C. *Frontier Skills, The Tactics and Weapons that Won the American West*. Lyons Press, Guilford, Conn. 2003.

Devoto, Bernard. *The Year of Decision 1846*. Little, Brown

Donner, Tamsen. *Letter, May 11, 1846*, Huntington Library.

Donner, Tamsen. *Letter, June 16, 1846.* Sangamo Journal, July, 1846.

Durham, Michael S. *Desert Between the Mountains*, Henry Holt & Co.

Egan, Ferol. *Fremont, Explorer For A Restless Nation*. University of Nevada Press. Orig. published by Doubleday, 1977.

Farnham, Eliza. *Narrative of the Emigration of the Donner Party to California in 1846*. California Indoors and Out. New York, 1856.

Graves, William C. *"Crossing the Plains in '46,"* The Russian River Flag (Healdsburg).

Graydon, Charles K. *Trail of the First Wagons Over the Sierra Nevada*. The Patrice Press, Tucson, Arizona, 1986.

Hardesty, Donald L. *The Archaeology of the Donner Party.* University of Nevada Press, Reno, Nevada, 1997.

Harlan, Jacob Wright. *California, '36 to '48*. The Bancroft Company.

Hassrick, Royal B. *The Sioux, Life and Customs of a Warrior Society.* University of Oklahoma Press, 1964.

Houghton, Eliza P. Donner. *The Expedition of the Donner Party and Its Tragic Fate*. A.C. McClurg & Co., 1911

Johnson, Kristin. *"Unfortunate Emigrants" Narratives of the Donner Party.* Utah State University Press, Logan, Utah, 1996.

Johnson, Kristin. *Article: Tamsen's Other Children.* Donner Party Bulletin, September/October 1997.

Kelly, Charles. *Salt Desert Trails*. Western Epics, Inc., Salt Lake City, Utah.

King, Joseph A. *A New Look at the Donner Party,* K & K Publications, 1992.

Korns, J. Roderic & Morgan, Dale, Ed. *West From For Bridger 1846-1850*. Utah State University Press, Logan, Utah,

Laycock, George. *The Mountain Men*. The Lyons Press, Guilford, Conn., 1988.

Lockley, Fred. *Conversations with Pioneer Women*. Rainy Day Press, Eugene, Oregon, 1981.

Lavender, David. *Bent's Fort*. University of Nebraska Press.

Luchetti, Cathy and Olwell, Carol. *Women of the West*. The Library of the American West. Orion Books.

Marcy, Randolph B. *The Prairie Traveler.* Applewood Books.

McGlashan, C.F. *History of the Donner Party*. A.L. Bancroft Company.

Morgan, Dale Ed. *Overland in 1846: Diaries and Letters of the California-Oregon Trail.* University of Nebraska Press.

Mullen, Frank Jr. *The Donner Party Chronicles*. Nevada Humanities Committee.

Murphy, Virginia Reed. *Across the Plains in the Donner Party.* Outbooks

Myres, Sandra L. *Westering Women and the Frontier Experience, 1800-1915.* University of New Mexico Press.

Peterson, Lee Allen. *A Field Guide to Edible Wild Plants.* Houghton Mifflin Company, New York, 1977.

Pringle, Lawrence. *Wild Foods,* Four Winds Press.

Reed, James Frazier. *"From a California Emigrant,* Sagamo Journal (Springfield), November 5, 1846.

Reed, James Frazier. *"Narrative of the Sufferings of a Company of Emigrants in the Mountains of California, in the Winter of '46 & '47."* Illinois Journal (Springfield).

Reed, James Frazier. *"The Snow-Bound, Starved Emigrants of 1846."* Pacific Rural Press.

Reed, James Frazier. *Letter, May 20, 1846.* Transcribed by Kristin Johnson, published by the Utah Crossroads Chapter of the Oregon-California Trails Association.

Schlissel, Lillian. *Women's Diaries of the Westward Journey.* Schoken Books, 1982.

Schmidt, JoAnne. Donner family genealogy.

Stewart, George. *Ordeal By Hunger.* Henry Holt & Co., 1936.

The Gaps Index, *Listing of Old Disease Names and their Modern Definitions.* Genetic Information and Patient Services.

Thornton, Jessie Quinn. *Camp of Death: The Donner Party Mountain Camp 1846-47.* Harper & Brothers, New York, 1849.

Tilford, Gregory L. *Edible and Medicinal Plants of the West.* Mountain Press Publishing Co., 1997.

Whitman, Narcissa Prentiss. *My Journal, 1836.* Ye Galleon Press, Fairfield, Washington

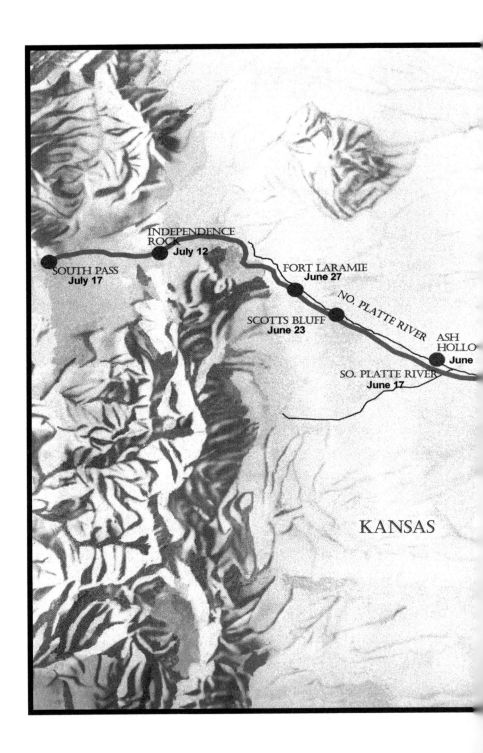

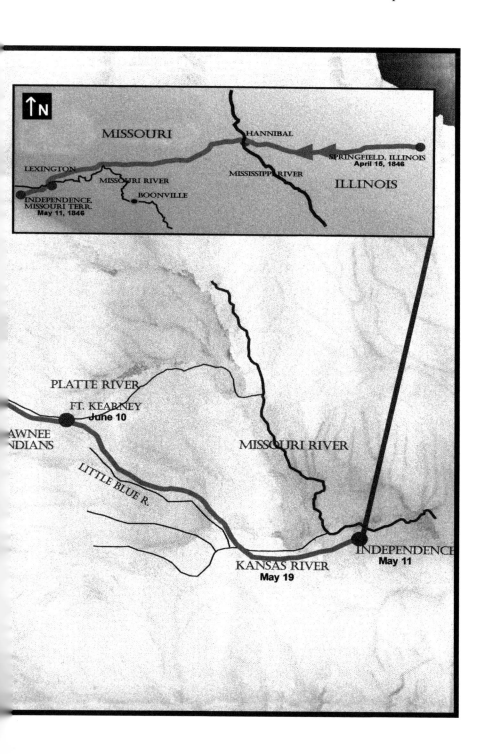

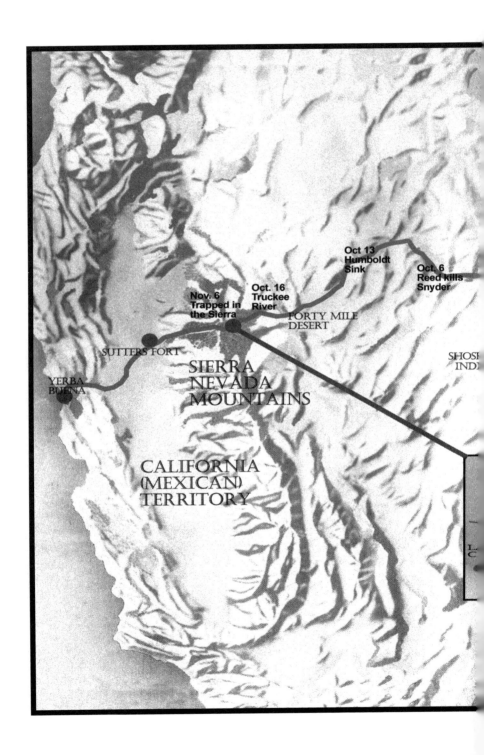

Oct 13
Humboldt
Sink

Oct. 6
Reed kills
Snyder

Oct. 16
Truckee
River

Nov. 6
Trapped in
the Sierra

FORTY MILE
DESERT

SUTTERS FORT

SIERRA
NEVADA
MOUNTAINS

SHOSI
IND)

YERBA
BUENA

CALIFORNIA
(MEXICAN)
TERRITORY

L.C

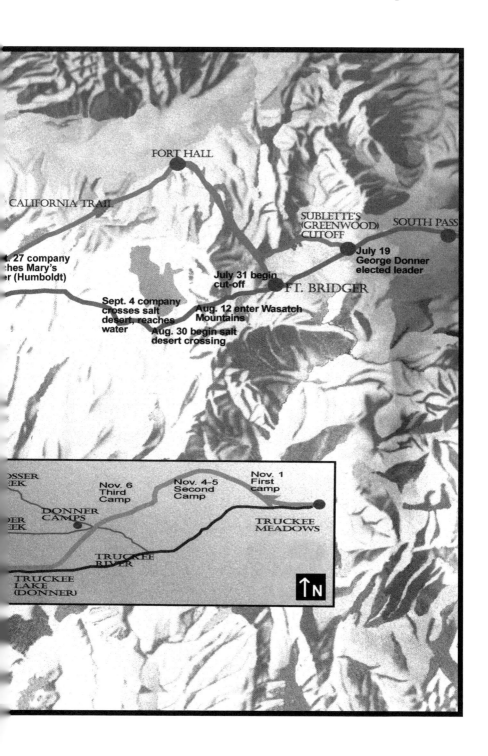

FORT HALL

CALIFORNIA TRAIL

SUBLETTE'S
(GREENWOOD)
CUTOFF

SOUTH PASS

. 27 company
:hes Mary's
:r (Humboldt)

July 19
George Donner
elected leader

July 31 begin
cut-off

FT. BRIDGER

Sept. 4 company
crosses salt
desert, reaches
water

Aug. 12 enter Wasatch
Mountains

Aug. 30 begin salt
desert crossing

)SSER
:EK

Nov. 6
Third
Camp

Nov. 4-5
Second
Camp

Nov. 1
First
camp

DONNER
CAMPS

)ER
:EK

TRUCKEE
MEADOWS

TRUCKEE
RIVER

TRUCKEE
LAKE
(DONNER)

N

Illustration Credits

Cover: Author's Collection

Pages 1V-11V: *Donner Lake,* Nevada Historical Society

Pages 1, 17, 31, 49: Roy Kerswill

Page 71: *Fort Laramie,* Joslyn Art Museum, Omaha, Nebraska

Page 84: *Scotts Bluff,* The Art of William Henry Jackson,
      Wyoming Division of Cultural Resources

Page 89: *Independence Rock,* The Art of William Henry
      Jackson, Wyoming Division of Cultural Resources

Page 103: *Fort Bridger,* Wyoming Division of Cultural Resources

Page 111, 151: Adaptation, Roy Kerswill

Page 167: Author; Portraits, Diana Monfalcone

Page 129: Roy Kerswill

Page 175: Adaptation, Roy Kerswill

Page 189, 193: From a painting by Robert LeBron, Emigrant
      Trail Museum

Page 195: Author; Portraits, Diana Monfalcone, Roy Kerswill

Page 213: Sutter's Fort, Sutters Fort Museum

Page 216: Bancroft Library

Page 218: Author; Portraits, Diana Monfalcone, Roy Kerswill

Page 227: *1879 Lithograph of Donner Lake,* Nevada Historical
      Society; Portraits, Roy Kerswill,

Page 244: Mrs. Breen in Tribulation, *Camp of Death,*
      J. Quinn Thornton

Page 246: Author; Tamsen portrait, Diana Monfalcone

Page 255: Author; Portraits, Diana Monfalcone

About the Author

Frankye Craig became interested in the Donner Party saga while developing a sesquicentennial event at Donner Memorial State Park, in Truckee, California, in 1996.

Since then she has become one of a number of people active in Donner Party history and has been interviewed several times for radio and television programs. She has also put together a series of Donner Party events, including several cross-country tours.

Frankye Craig's Other Donner Party books:

The Fateful Journey of Tamsen Donner

This book focuses on the Donner families. Tamsen Donner serves as the narrator in a personal story of the journey and entrapment.

Daughters of Destiny

Eliza Donner serves as the narrator. This book has 36 illustrations. Focusing on the Donner families, the story tells of the journey and entrapment and follows the daughters as they are taken out of the mountains to a new life in California.

Frankye's web site: www.donnerpartyhistory.com